Waves

and

Secrets

The Merworld Trilogy

Prequel

B. Kristin McMichael

ISBN-10: 1-941745-85-7
ISBN-13: 978-1-941745-85-4

Cover design: Jessica Allain
Editor: Kathie Middlemiss of Kat's Eye Editing
Melissa of There For You Editing
Ashton M. Brammer

CONTENTS

CHAPTER 1

Sam paced his arm strokes perfectly. Though it still felt strange to kick the water with his human feet, Sam was the picture of perfection while he swam by the students sitting on the edge of the pool. He glided across the water like a pro swimmer as he faked needing a breath partway across the pool. Stopping at the wall, Sam pulled himself up onto the edge in one fluid motion.

"And that's how you do a perfect freestyle," Mark said from the other end of the pool. The students who had been watching Sam now all turned to Sam's bleach-blond friend, Mark.

Sam was glad to have the eyes off him. He had been on land posing as a normal human high school student for a couple years, but it was still strange to hide who he really was. It was especially hard to be swimming and pretend his life wasn't better in the water. While the chlorine was a constant reminder that the ocean was far healthier, water was water and felt amazing to be in.

"Leo will show you how we float on our backs with an elementary backstroke," Mark continued addressing his attentive audience of freshmen. These were the few incoming students that had never had a swim lesson once in their lives. Since the school was by the ocean and swim classes were required of each student—due to some mind persuasion of the Siren attending the same school—all students had to take lessons.

Sam's other friend, Leo, laid on his back to flap his arms and easily made it across the pool in a couple strokes. Sam was glad Leo was doing that one. It was ridiculous to swim on their backs for the Siren who could breathe underwater, but it was the best way to teach students who feared the water. Sam almost laughed the first time he heard that people on land were afraid of the water. The water wasn't bad. It was what lived in the water. That's what they needed to fear.

Mark continued to talk to the students as Leo hopped out of the pool to sit on the edge beside Sam. They would both prefer to be in the ocean but duty called and that meant their lunch was spent sitting on the side of the pool. When Mark was done with his lecture, he would divide the students up into groups for each of them. Then one little song would render the new students into a dream world where Sam and his friends could have their fill of blood before sending them on their way.

"Looks like your girl is here," Leo commented under his breath as to not interrupt Mark's lecture.

Sam looked up at the open gate of the swim pool fence. His childhood friend, Amber, was standing there watching Sam and Leo and ignoring Mark. She had a crush on Mark at one point, and he turned her down. Now she pretended like he didn't exist. Sam was acutely aware Amber was turning her attention to him, but he was never going to see her as anything but the brat that followed him all over the island they grew up on. She was like a sister, and there was no way it was ever going further than that.

Standing up, Sam walked over to his waiting friend.

"New recruits?" she asked, eyeing the group of freshmen.

Amber easily found her food on the various beaches she visited after school. There was no shortage of young men who would follow her off into the ocean waters when she worked her charm. Sometimes Sam felt like the female Siren had it much easier. Men were suckers for a good-looking girl in a bikini. She could entice almost any one into the water with her. But the problem for the male Siren was that most girls would never venture off alone into the ocean with a guy they didn't know. There was a good reason why they shouldn't, but it made feeding more difficult for the males of his species. Hence the reason Sam and his friends became swim instructors.

"We have to rotate new ones in since the old ones can swim well enough to pass their gym classes now," Sam replied. Unfortunately, once his charges learned how to swim, they needed to find new ones.

"I don't see why you don't just tell them they can't swim and leave it at that," Amber answered, peering over at the girls sitting on the edge of the pool. Mark was in front of one, trying to coax her into the water for a demonstration. If Sam caught it right, there seemed to be a bit of jealousy seeping from his friend.

"Because if they never learn to swim, the school will grow suspicious," Sam replied.

"Then tell them not to," Amber replied, like it was that obvious.

While the Siren could persuade any normal human to do what they wanted, Sam was sure if they messed

3

around with too many people it would become dangerous. One slip up and the hunters would be called. Sam had already implemented the rule of no killing humans on land, which helped keep the Siren on shore safe, but he was extra cautious to avoid the one group of people who could kill them. The hunters would make easy work of most of the young Siren in the school, but not of Sam and his friends. Sam had been training, ever since he could walk, on how to protect himself. However, not all Siren had that training. Most relied heavily on their voice. Even though he was confident in his abilities, Sam didn't feel the need to test it.

"Amber, we've been over this before. We need to stay hidden," Sam replied.

Amber shrugged. "That's not what Tim says."

Tim was Sam's older brother, and everything that came out of that Siren's mouth was about getting higher on the food chain in the Siren world. Tim cared about no one and wasn't trying to keep anyone safe. He couldn't care less if the hunters were called to the city they currently called home. That was Sam's job. Tim only cared about Tim. There was no way that guy's advice should ever be followed, and Sam saying the opposite was the best thing ever.

"And how many people died while Tim was in charge? Come on, Amber, we both know Tim isn't the one to be giving orders. My father left me in charge for a reason."

Amber shrugged. He was pretty sure she wasn't convinced, but at least they were friends, and she would listen to him because of their friendship. She was like most Siren in that they didn't care about human life.

Humans were merely food. Sam really didn't care much either, but he understood how the game was played. Multiple deaths by draining blood brought hunters to the area. Hunters meant Sam had to keep everyone safe and he was happier teaching the young Siren to blend in instead.

"When do you head back for your last council meeting before being named heir?" Amber asked, her eyes twinkling with mischief.

Sam sighed. "I'm not going to be the heir," he replied. Amber had been bugging him for weeks since his father said Sam was to accompany him to the Council of Mer meeting. Normally the old man took one of Sam's various older brothers, but this year he insisted he return home to go with him.

"Sure, whatever you say," Amber replied. "You just happened to be the only one free to go with him."

That had been Sam's first excuse, but he knew it wasn't true. He had seven older brothers, and he was pretty sure Tim would drop everything to go if their father asked him to.

"I'm not picking a mate and thus can't be named heir," Sam reminded his blonde friend.

That was one of the main reasons he knew he would never be chosen as the heir. He had to be mated to carry on as the next king of the Siren, and so far Sam had no interest in tying his life to any Siren he had ever met ... and no mer for that matter. He didn't want to be caught in the Merworld. He needed to be free to leave and see the world, free to choose his own mate when he finally found one. He didn't want to be pressured into anything.

Sam wasn't about to play his father's games, no matter what the old man told him to do.

Amber shrugged. "You know as king he can order you to do anything. This really is just one more step to your place as the heir, even if you don't want to admit it."

Mark waved to Sam and thankfully saved him from further arguing with his friend. Sam had no wish to imagine letting his father decide his life for him, but what she said was completely true. His father, as king of the Siren, and leader of the whole world of mer, could command Sam to do just about anything, and Sam wouldn't have a choice. His father was the most powerful night human in the ocean. His orders were followed no matter what. Sam planned to stay as far away from it as he could. He didn't want to be forced into a mating, and actually, Sam was pretty determined that he was going to spend his whole life alone, at least if he could help it. After growing up in his family, Sam didn't want to have a mate or an offspring of his own. He didn't need the pain family caused. He would stay on land pretending to be a regular human as long as possible, and maybe his father would just forget about him.

Leo sat in the empty studio with his guitar. Slowly he picked through the complicated string of notes. A couple more times through and he could tell it was getting easier. It would take a few more hours before he considered it perfect, but what could he do? He wasn't born a prodigy like his best friend, Sam. Sam was the son of the king and second only to his father, which was saying a lot since his father was the king of the whole mer world. Everything Sam did came naturally, but not for Leo. He needed to practice. And since they were going to record a new album in a couple weeks, he spent his free time, when not teaching swim lessons, practicing.

Again, he ran through the string of notes. It was getting easier but still wasn't quick enough. Leo wanted to quit practice and run around chasing girls like their third bandmate, Mark, was likely doing, but Leo didn't have a choice. There was no way he was going to fake it like Mark; he didn't have the confidence to do that. Mark was in the same boat as Leo. He wasn't naturally gifted like Sam either, but he didn't care. Leo did. Even if the mer back home never heard a single song of theirs, Leo still cared enough to want to be good.

Stopping the song he was working on, he closed his eyes. Slowly he began a new tune; one he would never forget how to play. They had just finished their first album and actually had a real gig. It may have been more because of Sam's influence than anything else, but they had a legitimate place to perform. Playing in a recording studio was one thing, but live was completely different. Leo was concerned he was going to mess everything up, but Sam had been there to reassure him that he didn't need to worry. Sam put a little bit of his Siren power behind his voice when he sang and forced everyone to love them. It was part of a "little band takes over the world" scenario that Sam had been planning for years. He figured, why couldn't Siren make money singing? It made such logical sense. He only forgot that most, if not all the Siren, weren't as good as him at controlling their songs. It was easy to get distracted while using Siren power and put your prey into a dream instead of leaving them awake.

The notes strung together seamlessly, and Leo was still lost in his memories of that earlier concert. Which was the main reason he could never forget that particular song. He could remember the feeling of being relieved that Sam was going to make it simple. However, the concert ended up being anything but. Sam didn't even get the first word out before he noticed that there was a hunter in the audience. Leo knew about hunters, but that was the first one he had ever seen. Toward the middle of the crowd was a blonde who couldn't be any older than eighteen. It was strange to see the innocent-looking girl smiling away with her friends and knowing that she spent her nights hunting and killing off night humans. It was especially a problem for the mer as they were outlawed night humans. The order was to kill them on sight. When he looked into her eyes, that was when Leo saw the truth—she would kill them if she knew what they were.

Leo could remember every little detail of that gig and probably would for the rest of his life. That night he played like his life depended on it. He only made two mistakes the whole set and was thankful to run from the stage afterward. That was the first hunter he had seen and luckily the only one since he had come to land. He hoped to keep it that way as he had nightmares about the blonde for weeks.

"Still here?" Sam asked as he walked into the studio, interrupting Leo from his thoughts.

Leo shrugged. Sam could see that he was still there. It

was kind of obvious.

"You should head out and get some water and some rest," Sam commented. He always tended to be bossy, but Leo knew from years of growing up with Sam, it was a good sort of bossy. Sam was eternally worried about the Siren and their well-being.

"I want to practice for at least another hour," Leo explained as he glanced at the clock. It wasn't even midnight yet, and they needed only a few hours of sleep each night as it was. Besides, it was the weekend, and they didn't have to be at school early in the morning either.

"You'll probably want to rest because you're coming with me tomorrow," Sam replied.

Leo raised an eyebrow. Yep, typical Sam. He wasn't asking, he was telling.

Sam grinned at his friend like he knew exactly what the face Leo was making was for.

"My dad is making me attend the annual mer meeting and told me to bring another Siren with. I have a feeling the old man is up to something. He didn't tell me what, but I'll need someone I trust beside me. If I don't have someone with, I'm sure my dad would love to ask Tim to come instead, and we both know that doesn't work for any reason."

Sam's brother Tim was older by two years and definitely saw how much his father favored Sam. Tim was doing everything possible to discredit Sam and earn the place as his father's favorite, so yes, having to spend time with Tim wasn't beneficial to Sam.

"Why would he want you to bring a friend?" Leo was

pretty sure only the leader and their heir could actually attend the meeting part of it.

"I have no idea, but if he told me to bring someone, I want someone I trust with me. You know how he likes to play his games. I need you as my wingman."

Sam was just trying to butter him up. Leo could see that much. He'd known Sam his whole life. He wasn't the kind for deception and playing games. If Sam said he didn't know what was up, then it was likely that he really had no idea.

"What about Mark? I'm sure he has tons of free time," Leo suggested. "Or Amber." Leo wiggled his eyebrows at that.

Sam shook his head. "There's no way I'm taking Amber with me anywhere formal. She already thinks she has a lock on being my mate; I won't encourage that any further. Did you know she actually told Beth that she had to keep at least five feet away from me because she was standing too close the other day? No way is Amber a choice ... and Mark? Really? You think I should take Mark anywhere where the clans meet?"

Okay. Leo didn't actually believe Sam should take either of them. Amber for the obvious possessive reasons, not to mention the fact that it would completely go to her head if Sam took her; and Mark because he was Mark. The last time there was a meeting between the Siren and the Undine, Mark had hit on a girl who happened to be the daughter of one of their generals. He didn't take to kindly to it, and there was a lot that had to be smoothed over—which was surprising as the Undine were the most passive of the mer clans. If Mark could upset them, he could destroy a meeting with all the clans.

"Amber and Mark aren't bad people," Sam quickly added. He was loyal to his friends, which was probably the main reason why everyone loved Sam over his older brothers. "They just can't be trusted around the opposite sex. I need someone who will be beside me and stay focused. My father doesn't send me off to do easy things. If he has something brewing, then I need someone I can trust to not go chasing after the girls there or chasing girls away from me for just glancing."

"Fine," Leo replied as he set his guitar back into its case at his feet. "Let's go party with the clans and hope your father just wants your pretty face. Then we can get back here, and I can finish perfecting the lineup for the next album."

Grinning at Leo, Sam slapped him on the back. "Just what I like to hear. I knew there was a reason you're my best friend."

Leo fought the urge to roll his eyes at Sam. He was one of his only friends. While Sam was well loved, Sam didn't trust the Siren in general and he kept them at a distance. He did trust his few friends, Leo included. And Leo completely understood. The night human world was all about power and being aligned with the victor. Sam was a chess piece everyone wanted their hands on, and he knew it. He was used to people trying to earn his favor. The problem was that Sam didn't want to play the game. Which was why Sam and Leo made a perfect friendship. They both detested and wanted out of the mer world they were stuck in.

The water broke on the shore as Leo stood waiting for his friend. It was going to be a long day, but he didn't mind. The ocean was calling to him, and Leo was very happy to be going off on a long swim. The rhythmic sway of the waves on the shore created a constant beat that the music of the water sung with. He could always hear the melody, even from their school farther inland, but close to the ocean made him miss it like he hadn't heard it in forever. Being a mer meant being drawn to the water and for Siren that meant the song of the ocean was the greatest calling they would ever feel.

Leo had been taught that with the power of their voice, which could make an ordinary human do anything, Siren were more attuned to music than any of the mer clans. He hadn't met all the clans, but Leo was entranced with the music playing for him from the waves.

"Ready for a fun filled swim?" Sam joked.

The swim would be fun, but joining up with the various mer factions wasn't. As bad as the Siren were alone, the mer clans were always trying to get more power. Leo didn't worry about the Siren—they would always be on top as their voices could control even the strongest mer from the various clans—but he did worry about playing the games. It was easy to forget all that when they were on shore pretending to be normal humans. The only abnormality in their life was feeding on the students they were teaching to swim, and they had to do that to keep living. Leo could live with that. Sometimes Leo wished he could have been born a naïve, normal human.

Sam led the way to the dilapidated pier that they used as a launching ground when going back into the water. If you climbed under the pier, people couldn't see you from either side as you entered the water. You could just disappear and not draw any attention to yourself. Even better was that the Siren weren't the only ones climbing around the pier; they never looked too suspicious. Leo followed Sam as they entered the cool sea water. He much preferred the salt water ocean to the chlorine-filled swimming pool any day.

Sam neared the end of the pier, hidden from the world. Glancing back at Leo, he motioned for him to go ahead and get under the water. Leo didn't need to be told twice, and he sunk down in the chest-high waves that were calling to him. Once submerged, he finally felt at peace. The water encased him like a warm hug. That was the whole scary part about wanting to leave the mer. Nothing felt more at home than being in the ocean.

Sam dove down into the water next to Leo and easily swam past him without a backwards glance. He just assumed Leo would keep up with his lead, and he would. Leo didn't mind his aggressive leader friend, and followed behind as Sam led the way through the shallow water and into the ocean deep.

Fish, dolphins, and even whales as they got deeper, swam past. Besides the humans they fed on on land, landside always seemed devoid of the assortment of life under the water. Up above there were a few smaller animals that Leo would see, but it was mostly just humans. Below the water, there was everything from small fish to great big whales and sharks. Animals came in all shape and sizes, and none of them hid from the mer. It was strange to go from the land to the sea and back again. Most of the mer just tended to stay in the ocean, but the Siren were one of the few who lived on an island out of the water. It didn't matter that Leo grew up going between them; it was still hard to adjust for the first ten minutes.

Sam kept the pace going faster than Leo would prefer, but he followed behind dutifully. He knew where they were going and when they needed to be there. Leo didn't have the slightest clue as he didn't think to ask him. Knowing Leo wasn't the kind to just drift off, Sam never looked back once. Mark, on the other hand, was very easily distracted.

The swim would have been boring as there was no way to talk under the water, but because of the music, Leo didn't mind. Even under the waves crashing above them in the open ocean, the call of the sea was still there. As he hadn't been given exact details, Leo just listened to the water as she sang her tune and followed his blue-finned friend to wherever they were going.

After more than a few hours of swimming, the sky above was turning colors with the slowly setting sun. It probably seemed to descend even quicker than normal because they were swimming away from the sun, into the east. Leo had no clue where they were. While the Siren had built-in radar to find their home, Leo hadn't traveled far beyond going back and forth to land. All he knew was that they were somewhere in the Atlantic Ocean.

The only indication that they were nearing the

meeting place was the sudden emergence of other mer. By custom, the Siren only sent a few people to the meeting, but the other clans each brought close to a dozen apiece. Leo noticed a flash of yellow fin as a man passed them heading in the same direction. Slowing down, Sam pulled out of the current they were using to help propel them forward faster than normal. Leo followed his friend. The Undine continued on his way and didn't acknowledge that he had seen them.

Though Leo seldom interacted with the other mer clans, he knew who each one was. It was easy to tell. All the clans had a distinct fin color. The bright-yellow-haired man with his yellow fin could only be an Undine. Sam and Leo with their blue tails were Siren. And each clan was the like. Leo, like all Siren, was forced to memorize them as a child even without having met the various clans that were in the ocean. And if he hadn't been going to the meeting of the clans with Sam, he would have spent his whole life maybe only seeing one or two other clans. Each mer clan had their own distinct area in the ocean and very few traveled outside of it.

Sam led the way just outside the warm current. Leo was fine with the slower pace, especially once it became clear they were nearing their destination. More and more mer began to fill into the same current and made Leo thankful Sam had pulled out of it. Leo wasn't afraid something would happen, but he wasn't sure he wanted to be so close to the other clans. It seemed like Sam had the same train of thought.

Leo didn't notice until Sam was diving deeper into the water that something was going on. Above him, in the now almost dark water, several mer were coming out of the current, but they couldn't get out fast enough. They were drifting farther away. Leo turned to Sam and could only make him out by the glow of the swirls around his torso. He was pushing much energy into going somewhere quickly. Leo followed his friend, only to stop when he almost ran into him. Sam was holding a small mer—not a Siren, but from the looks of the brown, furry tail a Selkie—in his arms. The poor child was shocked but also not fighting the tight hold Sam had on it. Sam pointed up to Leo and began to climb back up to where the current was still pulling mer to their destination.

By the time they made it up to the current and followed it to where the frantic Selkie were searching the dark waters, the child leaned into Sam's arms and almost asleep. Leo had a feeling that was what lost the child in the first place, but unlike whoever dropped the sleeping child, Sam had a tight hold on it.

A very large Selkie came barreling toward Leo and Sam as soon as he noticed that Sam was holding the child. Leo moved in front of his friend, ready to take the first blow that seemed to be coming. Not being able to talk under water sometimes was very disadvantageous, especially for the Siren who could not only control humans with their voice but the other clans. Heck, had they been above water, a child falling asleep wouldn't be as deadly as one sinking down into the depths of the dark ocean.

Sam placed a hand on Leo's shoulder, and they both stopped. Sam didn't use Leo as a shield and moved over to stand next to his friend.

The angry-looking Selkie seemed relieved when Sam jostled the child, and its eyes popped open. Without a hesitation, Sam offered up the child to the man that was now eyeing Sam and Leo over. The man scooped the child into his arms and only nodded to Sam before turning and swimming back to the searching group. Leo wasn't surprised. That was about as much thanks as you could get from a mer.

Continuing on his way, Sam didn't look at the group of Selkie as they passed them and followed the current to a large stone-like structure that Leo could now see. When they finally broke the surface to climb up the entrance to where the meeting was being held, Leo could talk.

"Why did you go after that child?"

Shrugging, Sam stared back at the dark ocean before replying. "Instinct."

Leo studied his friend. He wanted more of an answer than that. Mer, in general, kept to themselves, and the Selkie's immediate reaction of attacking was the reaction most would give. Sam was lucky the man didn't keep attacking. Either Sam or Leo could have gotten hurt for what Sam did. Sam sighed, knowing that Leo would keep asking if he didn't give more to him.

"My dad is always going on about the Siren being the greatest clan, but what makes us so different? We're all mer. If a mer is in trouble, being the greatest mer means nothing if you don't use your power to help." And that was it. No more explanation. Sam pulled himself up on the ledge and walked away.

Leo followed and nodded to his friend's back. That was what made Sam perfect to be the next leader, even if he couldn't see it. No one cared more for the Siren and the mer in the ocean than his friend. When he turned eighteen and defected with Leo, the mer world was going to miss their best chance at the leader they always deserved. Part of Leo felt guilty for their plans to leave, but then again, there were more reasons to leave than stay.

CHAPTER 2

Sam nodded to his friend as he left Leo to climb the rock stairs to where his father waited. He would have gladly waited in the lower level of the structure with Leo, but he didn't get a choice. His father's booming command in his mind was still humming. Sam hated that his father could enter his head any time he wanted to look around or tell him what to do. And with his father being king, Sam didn't get the option to say no.

The meeting place of the mer was a magically made rock that for the time being was almost completely covered by the ocean water. The very top layer was above the water, and the layer below where Leo waited was getting clear as the tides lowered. Sam had been shown images from his father so that he would know his way around. Eight steps carried Sam to his waiting father.

Sam didn't know what to expect, but he kept his surprise hidden as he made it to the top of the rock. More than a dozen leaders and their seconds in command were seated around a rather large throne where Sam's father sat. He hadn't been allowed to see the meeting the last time. The king's eyes were fixed on Sam as he walked up the last step, and Sam didn't have to look down to know his father's proud blue fin was on display. Then again, everyone else that was a leader of their clan also had their fins out. At the bottom of each chair was a large enough indent that there was water collected for them to sit in. And that was a good thing. Mer tended, in general, to get testy out of water.

King Longray nodded to his son, and all the eyes of the people gathered turned to stare at Sam. The feeling of being on display got old after the first hundred times, so Sam didn't acknowledge the eyes on him. Striding across the rocky surface to his father, he moved to stand behind the man as the other seconds were already in their places behind their leader. Sam would play his part because he was being forced to, and he just kept counting down the days until he could get out of the mer world.

One chair remained empty, and as the leaders of the mer world sat around staring at each other silently, Sam wondered who was missing. Discreetly he looked from fin to fin, and tried to remember which clan should be there. It wasn't like Sam routinely left the Siren waters, so he didn't have time to interact with the other clans much, but he did know what colors meant which clans.

The second most powerful mer, the red-finned Lara clan was there. Their leader's beady green eyes never left King Longray. She openly stared at the king and Sam had a feeling her studious look was only hiding her real feelings of dislike. The yellow Undine clan was also there, but as much as Sam didn't want to be there, it was evident, neither did the Undine. The orange-finned Mavkas clan and the gray-haired Lobast leaders were also there, each gazing off to the ocean around them. He tried to remember which ones to check off the list. As he got to the last leader, he was sure there could be at least four different mer clans left, but not all of them got the invitation to sit on the council meeting each decade.

Sam turned to the last man to walk up the stairs. His face seemed familiar, but Sam was certain he had never spoken to him before. Obviously, the man recognized Sam, too. However, he said nothing as he took the last seat without a second behind him. His brown, furry tail appeared as he touched the water, and Sam finally knew who the man was. It was the mer he had handed over the child he'd saved from the ocean deep not even an hour ago. The last leader didn't say anything but nodded to Sam like he understood what Sam was thinking.

'I brought you here to study the leaders, but the Selkie is no concern for us,' Sam's father chided him in his mind.

Sam didn't reply. He tried his best not to ever talk to his father mentally. He didn't want to encourage the king to keep prying in his mind. Sam had secrets he was more than happy to keep from the old man. If the king knew Sam planned to leave the Siren after he turned eighteen, he would be in trouble. If the king knew Leo was going with him, Leo would be killed for insubordination. Those facts had to be locked deep in Sam's mind at all times.

'I'm concerned with the Lara and Mavkas. Keep your eyes on those two,' Longray ordered Sam.

It was going to be a long meeting, and Sam was sure he didn't want to be there. Too bad that was his life. He was always forced to be where he didn't want to be. Sam couldn't wait to leave the Siren. He would be free to live his own life and make his own choices. It wasn't going to be too hard to cut most of the ties to the Siren since Sam actually didn't like too many of them. They were a power-hungry group who told more falsehoods than truths. He would miss his mother, but her choice to bind herself to the king made it impossible for him to ask her to come with. Sam would rather take his chances with the rest of the night human world than stick around, listening to the mer argue about matters as they were now. Yes, Sam was ready to start a new life.

People milled about as they waited for the meeting to end. Leo kept to himself at the edge of the water lapping against the odd giant rock that was their meeting place. It really was just a rock in the ocean. He knew it was magic, but it was still strange. The water was now low enough that he couldn't touch it with his feet or his much longer fin, but he stayed there anyway.

Leo was bored waiting, but there was nothing he could do. No one would speak to him, even if he could get them to meet his eyes when he looked around. The rest of the clans feared the Siren so much that they only agreed to meet if there was less than five Siren attending, and it seemed like the king felt three was an even better number. With the king and Sam above, there were no other Siren for Leo to talk with. He was all alone as all the other clans huddled together, obviously scared of him.

After what seemed like forever, Leo felt his king coming down the stairs with Sam right behind him. Rising, Leo bowed to the older man that looked like he was only in his forties. Everyone around Leo did the same. King Longray was the king of all the mer, not just Leo's Siren clan, and everyone feared him. Longray had the power to make anyone who was there do what he wanted, which was more power than one person should have.

Leo kept his eyes down as the king looked at him. He really didn't need to spill his secret with Sam right about now. Quickly he did his best to think just about their swim to the rock. Yes, that would be boring enough if the king came searching through his mind.

Sam followed his father down the steps to the people silently staring at him now. Sam didn't look around, but focused on his father. Leo smirked as he watched his friend. Sam hated when everyone stared at him.

King Longray didn't even glance at the people around him as he walked over to another staircase. Leo wasn't sure how or who built the rock they were in, but he was positive it wasn't normal. What rocks had staircases? And he had no idea where this one led. The water had only just receded enough to see the staircase, let alone go down, but if the king was doing it, then so was everyone else.

Sam nodded to Leo to follow once he finally looked his way, and Leo was happy to oblige him. It had been dull sitting for hours as he waited; Leo was ready for some company.

Longray led all the mer down the stairs. Leo was close enough to see as he reached the bottom stair, Longray kind of hopped over the clear floor at the last step. From his angle, Leo couldn't see if it was actually a step or a hole in the stone. Leo was wondering if he would have to do the same as Sam deliberately stepped on it. If Sam said it was safe, Leo wasn't about to try the jump the king just made. The whole surface of the rock seemed to be slick. Following Sam's lead, Leo stepped on the clear area. It was surprisingly solid as he continued to trail behind his friend.

"Don't stray too far," the king warned his son.

Sam gave him a curt nod before walking ten feet away from his father. Leo joined Sam on the edge of the stone. The water that was slowly dropping was still up on all sides of the stone but not entering the cave-like place they were now standing. Sam turned to watch the people enter behind them.

"Care to explain?" Leo asked in hushed tones. Sam shook his head no and nodded with his chin to the staircase.

People filed into the cavernous space that was at least the size of their lunchroom at school. Leo wasn't sure what was going on, so he just stood silently beside his friend. One by one, people stepped on the clear space at the end of the stairs and continued into the room. As they stood and watched, Leo noticed that a string quartet appeared from what seemed like nowhere and was softly playing music. It was turning into a party with the guests arriving. King Longray had greeted someone and was now talking, but Sam continued to stare at the staircase. Leo was just going to look away when it happened.

A mer with unusually bright orange hair stepped on the same spot everyone else had, but instead of a solid surface, he was sucked right down into the water. Leo stared in shock. He had stepped there, and it was a solid surface.

"Anyone hostile to this meeting is removed," Sam said quietly. "It was obvious from all the fighting above, but no one would kick him out until he failed that step. That's mer politics for you."

Leo nodded. He wasn't too interested in politics and had no training like Sam. He was happy his job was to just sit around and wait, and was looking forward to getting back home. He needed more time to practice before they recorded. Hopefully, the one day and night would be all they needed to stay for and they could be on their way back to land and the recording studio.

By the time the last mer filed in from the staircase, they had lost no more attending mer, and the room was almost filled. People milled about as waitresses handed out drinks. Leo was sure the place was empty when they came down, but it was like a party had already been planned. Leo simply stood and watched everything in the same silence he had above, but this time at least he wasn't alone. Sam was silent as normal, and Leo was used to his serious friend. More than likely Sam was just biding his time to leave as much as Leo was.

"Friends, in honor of our fruitful gathering, a thought has just come to me," Longray said, and the room quieted immediately. All eyes turned to the king. "I think we need to grow this friendship of the clans. The only way we stay strong against the night humans and the hunters that wish to eradicate us is to be united and not just once every decade. I think today was a good step to cementing those friendships ... well, most of us at least."

The king chuckled at the mer who had been pulled

beneath to the ocean. Leo wasn't sure if it was deadly or not, but neither he nor Sam wanted to find out.

"I propose that we send our seconds to each other's homes to spend a week learning more about each other. They can, of course, bring a friend, so that they don't feel too alone."

And just like that, Leo found out quickly where he fit into the equation. He wanted to see if Sam knew what was going on, but Sam was still staring at his father. It wasn't a look of love.

"While we have a common cause, we still are different," the king continued. He was making a grand speech, and Leo was very surprised. King Longray was one of the most ruthless rulers the mer had ever known. He wasn't one for spreading peace. Leo's shock was mirrored in everyone's face except Sam's.

"Every leader should throw their family stone in to this shell. We will pull out a stone for each leader, so it's completely random." Longray held up a shell shaped like a bowl. A girl beside him took the shell and walked around the room. She collected a small stone that each leader had been wearing. She returned to Longray's side, and he motioned for her to take the first stone.

One by one, Longray divided up the people who had attended the meeting to go home with new leaders. Sam's face was tense the whole time his father was cheerfully talking and congratulating each person that got to see a new clan. Leo could read much more into his friend, but there was nowhere to go and have a quiet conversation about what was going on.

Sam stared at his father who was talking friendly with

the leader of the Mavkas clan. Both King Longray and the green-haired Mavkas leader were smiling and laughing at something King Longray said. Gritting his teeth, Sam turned from the two men.

"I take it there's more to this than he said?" Leo guessed. Sam appeared to be more than a little mad.

With a brief nod, Sam took off toward the staircase. Leo followed his friend up; not to the middle level, but all the way to the top where Leo hadn't been invited before. Sam turned around abruptly, and Leo almost ran into him.

"My father thinks there's something going on with several of the clans. He's always paranoid that the clans will disobey him. He wants us to investigate the Mavkas clan. He suspects they are planning something. And if we do what he wants, he'll forgive our plans of ditching the Siren."

Leo froze in shock. Sam and he had talked extensively about what it meant to defect from the Siren. They would be completely alone. Not only would they be outlaws in the night human world, but in the Siren world, too. The mer needed to stay a secret to stay hidden in the ocean. If the night humans knew how many were still alive, they would come for them all. The price for leaving the Merworld was death.

'How?' Leo wanted to ask, but he knew better. They only had less than a year to go and had been planning their escape for years. Of course, the king knew. The Siren king could enter anyone's head any time he wanted. One small moment of thinking about it was all it would take for him to latch onto the thought and know their intentions. Leo had done his best to never think about leaving when he was home on the Siren island. They had agreed that the only place safe to think and talk about their escape was on the mainland.

"So this isn't a discussion of what to do next. We only have one option," Leo finally said, knowing exactly now what was hanging on the line.

"We have to find out what they are planning, or we can be sure that there will be no planning our own futures."

Leo nodded to Sam's ominous words. *Why did things have to get complicated?* Leo was wishing Sam had chosen Mark to come with after all; at least then he wouldn't know that his life was hanging on the line.

Zia felt the Siren arrive before she could see them. Actually, since she had been told to stay out of sight until called upon, she wasn't really allowed to *see* them. She had been stuck in the Mavkas home for years and was used to the orange fins that swam around in the ocean waters, but to see a Siren was a wish come true.

Now she waited in the only room in the entire place that had real furniture. It was so much like living on land that Zia was sure the Mavkas leader had probably lived on the surface at some point, even though he refused to let the Mavkas do so. Zia had found it strange. Yes, over a hundred years ago—before the night human wars that banished the mer from existing—green hair would have been thought strange, but with all the changes in the world, they could easily go to land. In fact, there was the invention of hair dye that could make blending in easy, but the Mavkas mer people didn't question their leader on it. They were content to be on the bottom of the ocean forever.

"You're right," Min said as he entered his office where Zia was waiting. His oldest son was right behind him. Zia glared at the younger version of his father. She had nothing but disdain for him.

"If we could catch Sam, we'd be set. The Mavkas would never have to bow to the Siren again. Sure, he's beneath his father right now, but give him five or ten years, and Sam will be stronger than Longray," Lan told his father.

Zia changed her face back to neutral as he moved enough to see her.

They both seemed to ignore Zia as she waited there. That was typical. Zia couldn't remember how she fell for Lan in the first place. His beady, dark brown eyes were set too far back in his head, making him look like he was always scowling, and his dark green hair appeared almost black. Had she still been on land, Zia would have pictured him as a great bad guy to cast for a movie or a TV show.

Min shared those characteristics with his son, but his eyes were slightly large, making his appearance softer than Lan's. However, Zia had found out the hard way that even though he didn't look like the bad guy, Min was as dangerous as his son.

"We probably should work on a backup plan, too," Lan continued to talk. "I'm sure Cate won't mind chasing after Sam, but we need to try to capture his friend also."

Min grinned. "And that's just what Zia will be doing." When Min turned his dark eyes to her, Zia tried not to flinch or back down from his stare. She might have to follow his orders, but she didn't have to like it.

Zia held the older man's eyes and didn't blink. It was typical mer fashion to try to test the power and strength of another. While she couldn't openly defy him since she had the same orange tail as her leader, she could challenge him every step of the way.

"Dearest Zia," Min said with fake sweetness, "you are ordered to try to win over the Siren that comes with Sam. Make him want to bind to you however you must, and we will add another Siren to our army."

Zia let a glare slip out. She would do everything in her power to not do that. He could order her to behave a certain way, he could order her to sing and entertain the Mavkas as they had their dinner, but he didn't have enough power in him to make her fall in love with someone. And she wasn't going to bind herself to anyone she didn't love. She already knew where that got people.

Without saying anything more, Zia stood up and left Min's office. She wasn't about to stay any longer and give away where he made the mistake. He had told her to try to win over the Siren with King Longray's son. He never said she had to do it. Good enough for her. She would stay away from the poor Siren who had the bad luck to be sent to the Mavkas underwater world, and he would head home in a week when their visit was over.

Zia walked down into the main room of the Mavkas home. People were already setting up the feast they planned to use as a welcome to the Siren visiting.

Excitement laced all their faces. Zia didn't hate the Mavkas as she hated Min and Lan. They were all completely innocent. Not a single one knew the truth about her beyond the Mavkas leader, but she still didn't feel at home. The Mavkas world would never be home, and she wasn't about to condemn another mer to the same fate as herself.

After passing through the main room, Zia went to her favorite spot to get away. There was a little alcove right off the eating room that had one spot in the whole place that was quiet. Zia walked over and sat down in her spot. She'd sit there the whole week if she needed to and that was a plan enough for her.

It didn't take long before their guests arrived, but Zia still didn't move. She would find food later or go pick something from the gardens herself if she needed to. It was safer to stay away.

As cheers erupted around the room, Zia couldn't help her curiosity. Rising, she peeked around the corner to see the two Siren entering. At the lead was Sam. She knew who he was. His dark hair was close to being black, but his blue eyes looked like the ocean. He was just as handsome as everyone said. But it wasn't the cute heir to the Siren throne that had her attention. Zia couldn't help but stare at the Siren with him, the tall blond who seemed as out of place as she felt all the time.

The mystery Siren walked behind Sam and sat down beside his friend as they were greeted by Min. Zia's heart skipped a beat when the Siren looked up and toward her direction. Zia knew she was hidden enough in the shadows of the wall, but she still felt exposed, like he could see her. Zia pulled back around the corner into her spot. She needed the silence more than anything now, and she needed to stay away from that mer, or she would do just what Min asked of her.

For Leo, leaving to go to an underwater world sounded fun only in the movies. While Siren were fine in the water, they actually lived their lives on land on a private island. In fact, Leo was more than a little worried about this visit. Yes, he was a mer person and could breathe underwater, but he didn't like the idea of spending a week at the bottom of the ocean. At least he thought he'd be in the ocean. He didn't exactly know where the Mavkas lived. For that matter, he didn't know where any of the other clans lived.

It was hard to let go, and more than a little terrifying. Against the feelings inside of him, Leo allowed his guide to pull him along. It wasn't like he had a choice in the matter. His life literally depended on it. If King Longray knew Sam and Leo planned to leave the Siren in the coming year, it was very well possible he was already plotting some hideous torture method to use to kill Leo. Sam would likely get to live; he was the king's son after all. Unfortunately, Leo wasn't that lucky. He didn't have family that would be able to speak up for him, if any of them even cared. Siren life was all about allies and power. Leo wanting to leave would make him a disgrace to his family, and the little he had would turn on him.

After the uncomfortable blindfolded journey to the Mavkas, Leo was surprised to find that while they survived underwater, they actually lived kind of like how people did on land. The whole underwater Mavkas home was made up of giant bubbles that were pockets of air. The Mavkas all walked around on two feet and could talk and converse like normal humans. It wasn't what Leo had been expecting at all.

Leo and Sam had arrived at a party that was occurring in their honor. People sat on the ground and ate at low-standing tables. Food was passed around in dishes, and Leo had to decline much of it as he couldn't be positive what they were eating. Nothing about the place was how he had expected it, and reality was setting in that Leo knew very little of the other mer clans. While King Longray wanted them to spy on the Mavkas, it really did seem like learning about the other mer clans was a good idea.

It was well known that many of the mer clans such as the Mavkas didn't venture to land for anything more than blood and that they preferred to feed on people at sea. It was obvious why, with various shades of green for hair. There was very little way of fitting in with the normal humans without drawing attention to themselves. The world Leo now found himself in was a variation of acting human, just a little strange, especially all the green hair. Sam's dark locks and Leo's own blond stood out tremendously.

Sam seemed comfortable in their new setting. He chatted away with the people seated around them. Leo kind of recognized one of the males as he saw him more than once with Sam's brother, Tim. Beyond that, Leo knew no one. He tried to be polite, but he wasn't about to start any conversations.

Even if Sam didn't want to admit it, Leo was seeing a side of Sam that he was sure his friend's father knew about. Sam was a people person. He was a diplomat and so charismatic that everyone around him was eager to join in the conversation. Leo knew Sam well enough to know he was likely already gathering information. While the Siren, in general, weren't very trustworthy in terms of friendship, Sam wasn't like the rest of them. He was serious in insisting on doing exactly what his father asked and without getting into further trouble ... at least for now.

When the food was done, people around Leo began to stand. Sam took that as his cue and stood, too. Leo wasn't too far behind. Though he'd casually looked around during the meal, Leo remained confused by where they were.

There was a clear film that went up the sides and made up a ceiling for the large room they were in. On land, Leo would guess that the room was close to the size of a hotel ballroom. Plants swayed beyond the barrier and were certainly in water, but all it did was make an illusion that the room had walls. The sand under his feet told him that they were at the bottom of the ocean. For the most part, the room was just a giant bubble sitting at the bottom of the sea. Leo was confused and wondered if they lived outside the bubble when they weren't celebrating. There weren't distinct walls beyond the few places of plants, but off to one side, Leo could make out something that looked like coral blocking off a portion of the room.

As Sam continued to talk to the people around them, Leo began to drift away from the crowd. Luckily the meal had lasted long enough that most people were done staring at him. Or rather it was lucky that Sam commanded attention, and no one seemed to care about him. Leo wanted to see if there was anything beyond the coral-like partial wall, so he headed in that direction. No one noticed or tried to stop him.

Leo made it to the coral wall and walked through the one opening. The chatter of the bubble behind him seemed to quiet as he passed the porous wall. Leo didn't notice much around him as he stared in front of him. In the room behind him, there were plants just outside the barrier keeping the water out, but now there was nothing to block his view. As it was getting closer to day time, there were vibrant shades of color peeking through the water and lighting up the world he was standing there watching. It was like standing in front of a huge aquarium wall. Fish swam by, not even caring as he stood there. Walking closer, he reached up to touch the barrier.

The clear bubble making up the wall around the underwater mer home was soft and squishy. Leo pushed a little, and the space in front of him wiggled. If he pushed hard enough, his hand might go into it, but he wasn't sure he wanted to. It had to be magic, but at the same time, it was a little awe-inspiring. Leo stared a bit more at the clear magical wall. It was confusing but kind of fun to tap, causing ripples to turn out in every direction.

"I wouldn't push too hard," a voice said quietly from behind him. "There's been a few visitors who have found themselves swept into the ocean and land is quite a distance away."

Leo turned around to face a green-haired Mavkas that was watching him. She was partially hidden in the shadows of the coral wall, keeping Leo from being able to tell if she were a child or his own age. Her voice was high, so he knew she was female.

"If someone punches a hole in it, does water come flooding in?" Leo was curious about the underwater mer world he was now going to stay in for the week.

"No. If you go through it, it closes right back up. Not even a drop of water will come in," she replied, not leaving her spot.

Glancing around, Leo noticed that there were short chairs that looked a lot like low-standing beach chairs in the weird outside room where he was now. He moved over to one and began to turn the seat to face the girl.

"Don't," she whispered as she pulled back into the shadows and completely hid herself from view now.

Leo was confused until a mer at least a few years older than himself marched into the room.

"Zia ..." he grumbled before stopping in his tracks and staring at Leo. "I'm sorry. I thought someone else was out here."

The man turned and marched away as quickly as he'd entered. Leo was left scratching his head.

"I take it you're Zia?"

The girl stood up and moved from the shadow to look around the corner. She only peeked a tiny bit beyond the wall before hurrying back to her hiding spot. But that was enough. Leo had a perfect view of her and knew for sure. She wasn't a kid, and she was the most beautiful mer he had ever seen.

CHAPTER 3

Sam stood and listened to Chris drone on about his latest adventure somewhere Sam had never been nor planned to go. While the Siren were technically in control of the mer world, they still mainly stayed to their boundaries. Exploring wasn't a trait of mer in general, but it seemed Chris had a little adventurous spirit in him. Since Sam and Leo had arrived at the party, Chris had talked non-stop about all the places he had been.

Leo had wandered off, and Sam kept a discreet eye on his friend. He could tell the news that his father knew of their plan had upset him. Sam didn't blame him either as they both knew what the punishment was for leaving the Siren. Neither one would ever know how his father found out. The old man never shared his sources. Sam was going to have his work cut out for him when he got back to convince his father that since they hadn't actually left, there was no reason to punish Leo for thoughts alone.

King Longray was an expert at punishments. Sam actually thought his father enjoyed it a bit too much, but he could never tell him that or he'd be on the receiving end of his tortures. While it would be nice to think sending Leo and Sam off to another clan where they very well could be assassinated was punishment enough, Sam was pretty sure this wasn't the only thing that would be coming their way.

Sam watched Leo make his way to the spot Sam had been eyeing himself. It looked like a partition or something, and Sam was just as eager to look around the Mavkas underwater home. They had been blindfolded until they arrived in the Mavkas room they were in now. Unfortunately, Sam was left playing diplomat and listening to the Mavkas leader's son, Chris, talk more about his life.

"It really is too bad Tim couldn't have come with you," Chris commented as he broke from his latest tale. His hair was a deep green color—it was dark enough that people on land could almost mistake it for black. Sam had a feeling that was what made Chris confident in exploring the regular world. He could fit in. Not like his sister, who was next to him with her almost neon-green hair.

"Tim had a job to do," Sam replied with a shrug. There was no way possible he would ever ask to purposely spend time with his older brother, Tim.

Sam had seen a little girl try to sell her brother at a garage sale he had passed once. Tim was that sort of brother. One you'd sell if you got the chance. Though he was only two years older than Sam, there was not a single thing redeeming about his brother. Tim had done nothing while they were growing up to make Sam like him even the tiniest bit. While his older brothers were ruthless and mean, Tim took the top of the list. At least Sam could excuse everyone else for their behavior; Siren in general only respected strength, and until Sam was as strong as them, they didn't plan to give him the time of day.

Tim was completely different. Tim had spent his whole life going out of his way to make Sam's life difficult. If they weren't related, Sam would have put Tim at the top of his list of enemies. Okay, relation or not, Tim was at the top of his list. And that was what was scary about Tim. He didn't respect the fact that their father was king and would never allow one brother to hurt another. Longray might only value strength, but he respected the bonds of family. Tim did not.

As a mer approached where Leo was, Sam almost moved to follow, but thankfully didn't. The man seemed to only stay a second before walking away. It would have been nice if Sam had his father's power to talk to other mer in their mind. Then he could strategize with Leo a bit. They really needed to come up with a plan. One week wasn't long enough since they didn't know what they were looking for. Maybe that was the whole point. His father could punish them for failing and take whatever information they gathered and send Tim back to do the job easily. Actually, for that matter, maybe there was nothing to find. That wouldn't surprise Sam either. Games, trickery, and lies seemed to be the foundation of the Siren world he came from. This was the world he was desperate to leave.

Plastering on a smile, he nodded his head as Chris kept talking. He needed a plan, and Chris didn't seem to care as Sam studied the room around them. Nothing was coming to mind for the moment. It would have been nice to be able to get a Mavkas alone, and he could just force them to talk, but with the bubble-like walls, it wasn't an option. The shape of the walls made sound carry. He heard dozens of conversations and not everyone was seated near them. He would never be sure if he was talking to one person or more.

Time was going to go by quick, and sitting around talking wasn't solving anything. Unfortunately, Sam had to play his role, but as soon as he could, he was going to go exploring. They needed to figure out something; their lives depended on it.

Leo moved to sit beside the girl once he recovered from finally seeing her. However, she quickly scooted away in the shadows. Leo frowned at her. Did she want him to go away?

"Sorry to offend you," Leo told her before turning to leave.

"Please stay," she said quietly. "But pretend like I'm not here."

Okay. That's confusing. Leo wasn't sure what she meant.

"If you sit down and face away from me, we can talk," she added.

"As opposed to sitting and talking face-to-face like normal people? Is there a rule against Mavkas talking with Siren?" That had to be it. Leo was sure. Well, not completely sure. It didn't seem like anyone had a problem talking to Sam in the bigger room. But maybe a female and male couldn't talk in private. There was always mer politics even if Leo didn't understand them.

"No. We can talk to anyone. It's me. If they see me

talking to you, it'll be a problem. Just sit and pretend to be watching the ocean and we can talk. If you still want to stay," she added, sounding unsure.

Leo wished he could see her face better. The pain behind her words broke his heart. Something inside of him made him want to march into the other room a demand why that one Mavkas was scared. Leo had no idea where the feeling came from and dropped into the chair as she had asked. There wasn't any way he could just walk away from her.

Zia. At least he had a name to go with the pretty face, even if he didn't know anything else. And he wanted to know everything. Who was she? What did she like? What did she hate? He wanted to know it all.

Leo sat staring at the water while Zia remained in her shadowy hiding spot. He would have much rather been staring at the girl he had to picture in his mind instead, but he didn't have the slightest clue how to start a conversation with her. Leo turned to her spot, and she motioned for him to face forward again. He just wanted another glimpse of her. Her pale green hair seemed different from the other Mavkas, and her pale skin looked like it was missing some of the glow of the others. She was different; at least he had to keep telling himself that was why he was sitting there. He wanted a reason why that one Mavkas caught his attention when there was a room full just beyond the wall.

"It's dangerous for you and your friend to be here," Zia stated.

"We weren't exactly given an option," Leo replied, trying to focus on the school of fish swimming just outside the clear wall. They had bright yellow stripes that were almost green in tone, like Zia's hair. "And my friend happens to be the son of King Longray. I don't think anyone will try to do anything to him." At least that's what Leo kept telling himself.

"It doesn't matter whose son he is; the Mavkas can't be trusted."

Now if that wasn't a warning he didn't want to hear, then what was? Leo already didn't want to be there, but she was talking like there was a reason behind her words. Leo had no idea what he was supposed to find with Sam, but it seemed like maybe this mer knew something. Now if he could only get her to tell him more.

"Does that include you?" Leo teased, trying to ease the tension hanging in the air.

Zia didn't reply. Leo found a new fish to watch. He was larger and eating a few of the smaller fish. Not the nicest thing to watch, but that was life in the ocean. Fish ate fish, and the mer were no different. They pretended to be allies and get along, but everyone wanted to be on top. Luckily for Leo, he had been born a Siren. They were at the top of the mer world food chain. They were the only clan that could control all the others with their voice. A few of the other clans, but not the Mavkas, could also use their voice to control normal humans, but no one could control the Siren. That really was the only protection Leo had from anything in the Mavkas home.

"Why are you here?" Zia finally asked.

"All the clans sent two people to another clan. It's this bringing clans together thing King Longray came up with."

Zia went quiet again. Leo had to really fight the urge to turn around and watch her. He wanted to see her expression as he told; more than anything, he wanted to look at her again. There was something he couldn't put his finger on, but she was different. Obviously, she was different than the Siren—her green hair alone made her stand out—but it was more than that. There was something that made her different from all the other green-haired Mavkas mer people, too.

"How long will you stay?" she finally asked.

"One week," Leo replied. "And then home to face my punishment."

He had no idea why he added the last part, but it was true. It was quite possible that the king was going to kill him for just thinking of leaving the Siren. While Leo had yet to actually commit an offense, it was Leo who approached Sam about leaving. Leo had no idea what Longray knew, but if he knew that, then Leo was pretty much a dead man.

"What did you do?" Zia asked so quietly he could barely hear her.

"I didn't actually do anything, but I thought something that the king didn't like," Leo replied. She didn't need to know the specifics. It really didn't matter. Longray was emphasizing why Leo and Sam wanted out. You could be punished for thinking something in the Siren world if the king found out.

"That makes no sense. Why would you be punished for thinking something?"

"The Siren are bound to the king just like you are to your leader. He can go into our heads whenever he

44

wants. It is supposed to keep us all honest, but in reality, it's to keep everyone scared." Okay, that was probably a bit too much. Leo was glad to be watching the ocean— this way the beautiful girl behind him couldn't see that his face was going to be flaming red if he talked too much more.

"He holds you prisoner in your own mind."

She explained it perfectly.

"So, tell me more about this place. How is this possible?" Leo changed the subject as a bright yellow and orange fish swam by.

"This? As in how do we live in gigantic bubbles at the bottom of the sea?" Zia's voice held a bit of laughter in it. Leo was happy he had changed the subject and was able to actually hear happiness in her voice.

"I'd have to guess magic, but since none of the mer practice magic, I don't know how," Leo replied.

"Well, you're right on both counts. It's magic, and it isn't by the Mavkas. These homes are ancient. They were put down here hundreds of years ago before the night human wars, before the mer were cast off to sea and thought to be dead."

There they went again, going back to a dark subject. Zia's voice seemed to mimic the conversation and dipped slightly lower in tone as she talked.

Leo, like every other mer, was well educated on the night human wars. The world consisted of two different types of humans: day humans and night humans. The difference between them was that the night humans needed the blood of the day humans to live. All mer were night humans. But they were the only ones who resided in the ocean. The other night humans all lived on land. Hundreds of years ago the night humans began to fight over the way they lived. Most day humans were unaware of the night human world. Yes, there were the few who knew that things roamed the night searching for unsuspecting people to feed on, but for the most part, day humans thought that they were myths and legends. One group of night humans wanted to come out to the world, and one side did not. Really, the whole war that followed didn't matter except that the mer chose to be on the losing side. The winning side decided it wasn't safe to allow any of the losers to live, and banished them all to death. Luckily for the mer, the ocean is a huge place, and they could hide from the night humans hunting them.

"So are the walls made of Jell-O?" Leo asked, trying to get back to a brighter subject.

Zia giggled. "No, but it sure feels like it. But don't tell anyone else that. I don't think the Mavkas know what Jell-O is," Zia answered. "That's actually how thick the magic has to be to protect their underwater world here when it was built. The ocean can be very heavy."

"And they didn't want to just live on land like everyone else?" All the clans Leo knew of lived on some sort of land above the sea.

"No. The Mavkas want to be at the bottom of the ocean. Something about feeling the sand on the bottom of the sea connects them to water better. Really, I don't know the full reason. I wasn't taught that much. For me, it just is what it is."

"So why didn't they just live in the water if that was

the case?" Leo really was curious. Why build a whole underground world? Mer could breathe underwater, so they didn't need to go to the extreme of making a world of bubbles.

"Sure we can all breathe underwater, but would you want to live that way? You'd never hear words or voices. We'd have to find a whole new way to talk ... and don't get me started on eating under water."

No, Leo wouldn't want to spend his whole life in the water. Voices he could do without, but he couldn't imagine a world without music.

"We're all still human, you know."

And that was the truth. Even though they could turn their legs into fins and breathe through gills, the mer were all still human. That was what got to Leo the most. Mer were hunted like animals in the night human world, but no one seemed to stop and think about the fact that the mer were humans, too. In the hundreds of years that had passed, the original mer who chose the wrong side weren't even around. All that were left were innocent mer.

"So what is it like living down here?" Leo asked. Zia seemed to be happy talking about the Mavkas even if they kept diverging onto the same dark subjects that followed the mer everywhere.

"The same as living anywhere I'd assume," Zia replied with a chuckle.

Leo smiled at the sound. She was laughing at him, but he deserved it.

"So you've never left here?"

"Since the day I arrived in this world, I've been inside

these bubbles and the water that surrounds them only. That's what life is like for the Mavkas. The majority of us never leave. We are born here and will die here."

"Which is why Chris has quite the audience with his stories," Leo guessed.

"Oh, yes, Chris is always the entertainment. Yet I never know if he's entertaining the mer around him or himself."

Now that did make Leo laugh. From the little he had seen of the Mavkas leader's youngest son, he was the most talkative mer he had met. All Leo hoped was that Sam was getting something out of his excessive talking. Leo knew he should take the opportunity to ask questions of Zia, but he felt like that was betraying her. They'd just met, but he didn't want to get her in trouble.

"Can you tell me more about the homes down here?" That was a great way to get information without feeling like he would get her in trouble.

"It's not homes like you find in other places. Here it's like four big apartment complexes," Zia replied.

"Wait a second. All seven hundred Mavkas live in four of these bubbles?"

"Yes, and these bubbles aren't just what you've seen. This is the meeting and eating room. We come here for gatherings of our pod and for three meals a day. They are hard to see, but each meeting room has five hallways that go off it. Off each hallway are dozens of more rooms for sleeping."

Now Leo wanted to go exploring. And he wasn't going to have fun telling Sam that there were three more of these they might have to search. Then again, they didn't really know what they were looking for, so it could be easy. Probably not, but a guy could dream.

"So every family has their own apartment?" Leo replied, understanding her comparison to a complex.

"Not exactly. We have a room to sleep. That's it. Everything else is more—" Zia stopped talking. "Shoot." Standing, she peeked around the corner again.

Leo moved beside her to see what she was looking at. He was close enough to tell she smelled like a flower he couldn't remember the name of, yet reminded him of home on the Siren's island. It was the perfect tropical island with hundreds of different kinds of flowers. Zia's light green hair whipped him in the face as she turned around. He hadn't meant to be standing so close to her, but she was practically in his arms. It wouldn't have taken much at all to lean down and kiss her.

Zia's eyes went wide as she ducked under his arm and behind him to give him a push toward the open entryway.

"You need to leave. Like I said before, it isn't safe here for you, and you shouldn't be talking to me."

Leo froze in his spot.

"I don't see anyone around looking this way. No one knows we were talking, and I did as you asked, so if anyone came in, no one would know." Leo wanted to spend more time with her.

"I can feel my family searching for me. It wouldn't be good for them to find me with you," she added.

Pushing him farther forward, she stayed behind the barrier, hidden from the party. He understood. Each clan in the mer world fought with the others. There was never peace, and no one agreed unless forced to by the king. But one thing they all did the same, though they would never admit they agreed, was that they shunned relationships between the different mer clans. He knew what Zia was saying, and basically, her family would take offense to him talking with her because he wasn't a Mavkas.

Leo turned off the hurt he felt at the mer policies and put on his best happy-to-be-there face as he walked back to Sam. It didn't matter what he felt, or that she was the most captivating mer he had ever met, Zia was a Mavkas and Leo was a Siren.

Zia watched the Siren walk back to the crowd at the party. She regretted that she hadn't asked his name, but that was fine. She wasn't supposed to be speaking with him. She didn't want to fall for him, and she didn't want him to be stuck in the Mavkas world. And no way was she going to let him kiss her. That would make it impossible to let him go. No matter how much her heart beat when he was near, she wasn't condemning him to a lifetime at the bottom of the ocean.

It took only moments before Cate arrived. Zia pretended to be surprised when Lan's younger sister walked into the alcove. Lan had connected Zia to the Mavkas, but none of them knew that her connection went two ways. It wasn't just useful for them to find her, but for her to keep track of them, also. It was the same type of bond families had, even though she certainly wasn't family.

"Father says to get dressed and ready to perform," Cate told her as she glared at her.

Zia nodded and slipped past her adoptive sibling who pretty much hated her. Zia kept her thoughts to herself, but she also hated Cate. There was nothing she found redeeming in the girl since she had met her, and she was pretty much convinced there never would be. Cate was pretty much as evil as her older brother, Lan.

Walking away, Zia knew she wasn't alone. Cate followed behind her as Zia made her way back to her own sleeping room. Zia walked past the barrier into the room, and Cate stood outside of it. At least Min allowed her that much privacy. Only Lan could access the room because she was technically blood bonded to him.

Zia took her time deciding between the three outfits she owned. She really didn't need to, but it was driving Cate nuts to stand there waiting. She could take her time *and* bug Cate. It was a win-win. Zia made a show of being indecisive, and she felt the emotions of Cate through their connection.

"We're going to miss the first song if you don't hurry up," Cate complained, flipping her neon green hair over her shoulder.

That was the hardest part of being a Mavkas to get used to. Zia was in awe of all the shades of green hair could come, but she didn't like her own pale green hair. She would have much preferred a light blonde. But then again, she would prefer her life not bonded to a jerk like Lan. She could feel he was just down the hallway, also waiting. He was harder to annoy than Cate.

Finally, Zia couldn't put off her command any longer.

She randomly chose the short purple dress, which made her hair look more yellow than green. She wasn't about to let the tiny spark of hope show through to Cate and Lan that she hoped the new Siren would like how it looked on her. Those thoughts she had to banish from her mind. She didn't want him stuck, and she was going to save him from her if that's what he needed.

Zia walked out of her room to find Cate getting red in the face with anger. Zia kept her own expression neutral as she tried to hide her joy from the bond.

"About time," Cate complained as she turned and marched back to the main room.

As they entered the meeting room from the hallway, Zia stayed just inside the doorway. Without looking directly at the hallway, their visitors wouldn't be able to see her. She didn't want to enter yet since Lan was standing right beside the doorway, probably observing every little fact about her. She didn't want him to know that the Siren boy she didn't know the name of had captured her attention quite easily. She didn't need Lan to see she cared. And she didn't need Lan to know she wasn't going to do what his father ordered, since he wasn't completely clear on his order.

"Chris plans to ask Sam to sing as we agreed," Lan said quietly to Zia. "You'll join in."

Again with the bossing around. Zia was pretty sure if she had more time with Lan she would have realized what a jerk he was, and that there was nothing between them, but the stupid magic spell had fooled her. Maybe it was hindsight, but she couldn't believe that even magic could make someone like Lan appealing. He was nothing but a power hungry brute, just like his father who was across the room laughing at something Chris had said.

"Do you remember your orders?" Lan asked as he continued to study Zia.

She glanced around the room before coming back to him. She rolled her eyes, knowing that was the one thing that would irritate him.

"I heard them all right," she replied.

Grabbing her arm, Lan pulled her back farther into the hallway. "Don't think this changes anything," he growled at her, pushing her against the magical wall. "You're still mine, and binding a stranger to our family won't change that. Your second one will be only to trick that stupid Siren who came here to parade around how great they are. Siren are nothing. Just you wait and see ... all of them will be dead by the time we get done with them. Just remember, night human bindings are forever and you'll never get away from me."

Lan had pushed her right into the magical wall. Just a little more and she would be pulled out to sea. Zia didn't budge as she knew it was dangerous to exist anywhere but the end of two of the hallways. She was pretty positive Lan wouldn't let her get away, but she didn't want to bank her life on someone she never could trust.

Lan stared at Zia, his face only inches from her. Zia wasn't stupid enough to fight back directly. Lan was twice her size. She was never going to best him physically. She was good at annoying him and his family, but she rarely did more than that. Now she wanted to fight back, but she was smart enough to know head on wasn't the way to do it with him.

"You'll be the perfect hostess to the Siren with Sam. You'll be friendly and do whatever he asks," Lan told her. "Do you understand?" Lan pushed harder on her hand. If she went into the wall, then there was no coming back; she would be pulled out to sea.

Zia nodded her head.

"Good. Now follow the plan, and we might even feed you this week."

Releasing Zia, Lan strolled back to the main room. He didn't wait around to see if she was with him because he knew she didn't have a choice otherwise. Zia was trapped in the horrible Mavkas world, and Lan was the reason why. He didn't really care for her at all like he had promised. The Mavkas were all full of lies, and he wanted her to be the same. She hated every last bit of him.

After leaving Zia in the outer room, Leo joined the group but didn't really pay attention. Sam was busy nodding along with Chris as the mer kept talking. Leo had already missed most of his tales already, so he didn't feel the pressure to nod along. The fake smile on his friend alone made Leo's smile genuine. Sam wasn't one for sitting around listening to stories. He had seen more of the ocean than most of the other mer. Chris used his stories to gloat, and Sam would never be like that.

When a Siren teen came of age, it was tradition that their family arranged for them to secretly be taken to a different location, and they would have to find their way back to the island. Siren were born with a sense of the ocean and where home was. It was a tradition of survival of the fittest. If you couldn't find your way home, you didn't deserve to be there. They didn't mourn the few who never made it home, and celebrated those that did return by giving them their own place.

Leo's parents waited until he was sixteen to take him to an uninhabited island. It took him less than a few hours to make it home. He encountered no trouble and didn't have to fend for himself or talk to any regular humans. It was easy and the way most parents did it. Sam's parents sent him off at thirteen and put him in another ocean. It took him over a week of constant swimming to get home. He had to go ashore to figure out the way to go and not get caught. In that one adventure, Sam had seen more than anyone Leo had ever met. And even so, it was hard to get Sam to talk about it. Chris was nothing compared to Sam.

Leo took the opportunity to look around as Chris kept yammering on about some great island he had been to. Leo wanted to see the doorways that Zia mentioned, but there were too many people standing around. And unless someone walked through one, Leo wasn't sure he would see an open tunnel next to a clear wall.

"I hear from Tim that you have a band," Chris said the one thing that would bring Leo back to the conversation.

"Figured I could use my voice for something to make money. You wouldn't believe how much land stuff costs," Sam replied. The mer clans knew that the Siren went ashore often, but they didn't tell others that they lived on shore for years as teens. Many of the clans couldn't pass as a regular human like the Siren, so Sam left those details out. It also kept the teens safe from being targeted.

Looking around, Leo was pretty sure they had no idea how much things cost since everything in the room seemed to be handmade from items found around the ocean. He was curious what the beds would look like, but he was going to find that out firsthand when they finally went off to sleep.

"We'd love to hear a song from you," Chris said, and the people around him cheered. Chris leaned in closer and added, "I might have swiped your brother's copy of your album and played it more than once around here."

The people that had been standing around in other clusters talking at the same time now were getting the message from everyone else. An aisle opened up between the groups of people, and of course to the far side of the room, where Leo couldn't see before, was a small raised stage.

Leo looked at Sam. He wasn't against playing a concert. Normally they prepared for days, and Sam could always use a little Siren charm to make the audience love them. Leo had a good feeling Sam wouldn't be able to do that without upsetting the Mavkas. Sam smiled back at him as he turned to Chris.

"Sounds like fun. Got a guitar for Leo?"

Leo rolled his eyes. Why did Sam have to rope him in, too?

Chris nodded, smiling as he led the way to the stage. Another mer was already there with a guitar in hand.

"Thanks," Leo told the man before sitting on the edge of the three-foot-tall stage.

Sam sat down beside Leo.

"Really? Let's perform?" Leo whispered to his friend.

"Spreading good will," Sam replied with a smile.

Yes, that was Sam. He was never unconfident. Sam was one of those friends that you could easily be jealous of. He was the kind of person that could do everything perfect on the first try. Leo had never seen him once flustered. Heck, he hadn't really seen him get excited. Life was easy for Sam, and it didn't help that he looked good doing everything. There was already a gaggle of girls hanging off to the side of the stage, watching his every move. If Sam noticed, it didn't make him nervous at all.

Like any Siren, Leo loved music, but he didn't love the spotlight. He had agreed to be in Sam's band, but only if he could be off to the side and far enough back to not draw attention. As a solo guitar accompanying Sam, there was no way he was hidden. He could feel his palms start to sweat.

"Come on. It's like a hundred people. Nothing like the Crystal Center. You did that one, and it was over six thousand people," Sam commented.

Leo would have replied, but he could feel everyone watching them. Six thousand was actually easier because you couldn't see the faces beyond the first few rows in the crowd. Leo could see every face now, and they were all staring at him.

"We'll just do *Sink or Swim,* and that's it. If they ask for more, I'll tell them no," Sam promised Leo, offering to do one of the easier songs on their last album.

It wasn't like Leo could say no. He glanced down at

the borrowed guitar in his hands. He didn't have a choice. Leo nodded to Sam. Quickly he picked over a scale to check the tone of the guitar. Everything seemed fine, and he was ready to get it over with.

Taking a deep breath, Leo tried to block out the staring people. The room was already quiet; it was beyond nerve-racking. He closed his eyes and felt the strings under his fingers. *Sink or Swim* was a song he had played hundreds of times. He didn't have a reason to be anxious beyond the faces staring at him. With one more deep breath, Leo began to play the song. The song reverberated around the room, almost like it was amplified without using any sort of equipment. If he made a mistake, everyone would hear it well. Sam began to sing before Leo could worry more.

With Sam singing and drawing the attention from him, Leo was able to relax a bit, but not enough to look up. He really didn't want to mess up in front of everyone. Sam finished the first verse and began the chorus. A second voice joined him.

Leo glanced up at the female who walked onto the stage and offered a hand to Sam to have him stand. Her face was blocked as she looked down, but the yellow-green hair seemed very similar to the same shy girl Leo had just met. She was now hidden from view by Sam's body as she sang the next verse. Leo was tempted to look around Sam.

It wasn't often Sam sung with anyone else. There were very few Siren who could sing and have the control that Sam did to not affect the audience. Bringing a non-Siren into their world would be a disaster, so they never looked for anyone else. The girl singing was perfectly in tune, and Leo found himself wanting to stand and see who she was.

Sam moved slightly, and Leo got the view he wanted. While now wearing makeup and a much smaller skirt, he realized the singer was definitely Zia. She didn't have the same glow as the Mavkas watching the song, but she had a different aura around her that he hadn't seen before. Leo was entranced by Zia as she sang. She looked ecstatic. While she'd hid in the shadows before, she was confident on the stage, and Leo didn't blame her. Her voice was perfect. She was perfect.

Leo finished up the song and couldn't keep his eyes off her. It wasn't until she was bowing and the guy who had given him the guitar was taking it back that Leo realized everything was over. The moment Zia walked out on the stage, all his nervousness at performing was gone. What in the world did that mean?

CHAPTER 4

Sleeping in the Mavkas underground world was an experience Sam could do without. The sand-floor bed wasn't comfortable, and the rooms having no doors was another weird experience. Sam didn't feel safe, and neither did his friend. They took turns sleeping; luckily the Siren didn't need as much sleep as most humans. When Sam woke and found his friend watching the ocean, he had the feeling Leo had as much fun in the weird Mavkas world as Sam had the hours before. They might be mer, but they weren't used to life on the bottom of the ocean.

"So a witch makes this world for them but doesn't happen to add anything like furniture to it?" Leo commented when Sam finally got up.

"Sleeping on sand isn't your thing either?"

"Your dad is just pure evil," Leo added. "Not only does he send us off on what will probably be my last week alive, but then he sends us to a place without any internet or cell phones and no beds to sleep in. 'Here you go, Leo. Your last week alive will be spent roughing it in a place where someone could kill you in your sleep since there are no doors'."

Sam would have laughed if it wasn't close to being true.

"I won't let him kill you. It was my idea to leave

60

before we turn eighteen."

"And it was my suggestion to leave at all," Leo replied a bit glumly.

Sam was certain his father didn't know that. He had never mentioned a thing before to Sam, so Sam was going with he only caught a small glimpse of their plan. Sam had to believe that, otherwise the king wouldn't have offered Leo a chance to redeem himself. Longray would have killed Leo outright if he knew the truth of how much they already had ready.

"So what is the plan today, boss?" Leo asked.

Sam rolled his eyes at his friend but didn't answer. Putting his thumb in his mouth, Sam used his abnormally sharp night human teeth to break the surface of his skin. Leo understood and did the same before offering Sam his hand. As their thumbs touched, Sam made contact silently with his friend.

'We only have a second before anyone passing will know what we're up to. We can't afford to be suspicious,' Sam said as he remained seated on the ground. *'Did you get find out anything yesterday?'*

Sam hated people in his own mind, but this was the only way their conversation could be truly silent. It was one of the good benefits of being a night human. As long as fresh blood was connecting them, night humans could talk to each other in their minds. Especially helpful for times when you were in a bubble, and the acoustics could broadcast your private conversation anywhere.

'I don't have a clue what's going on here, but I spoke to that singer girl before she performed with you. She told me it was dangerous to be here and that this is only one of four places

down here in the ocean.'

'Okay, then we go for a swim.'

'But she said not to just push through the magic barrier because there are strong currents around this place that will sweep you out to sea,' Leo added as he gave a good yank and pulled Sam to his feet.

Someone was standing in the doorway to the room watching them. Sam dropped his friend's hand, and the connection was gone.

"I see you've both slept well," Chris said as he stood there.

"It was an experience," Sam replied, not agreeing or disagreeing. It was diplomatic to not tell him it was strange, but probable he'd overheard the conversation between Sam and Leo already. Sam had felt someone near, and it was likely the Mavkas leader's son was sent to keep tabs on them.

Chris led Sam and Leo back to the large, open room from the night before. There was food set up along the stage area, and it seemed like a buffet was going on. Not as many people as the night before were seated in the room, and a few people were going through the line to get food. Chris seemed to be tired from the night before and wasn't in his usual talkative spirits. That worked for Sam who was busy looking around. Leo hadn't found out much, but it was more than Sam had.

They only had six more days to find out what their king was looking for, and he had no clue where to search. Everything about the Mavkas was odd, but it wasn't odd in a suspicious way. They were just different. Their plant-based meals—Sam was ready to be back on land eating a greasy hamburger after only one day—didn't mean they were plotting against the king, and neither did their communal living. They were different, but just that. Sam wasn't sure what they were looking for, but he hoped that something would pop up soon, or Leo would need to find a way to hide for the rest of his life. And that was a hard thing to do when the king could enter any Siren's head to find you.

Leo sat and poked at his green slime for breakfast. He understood that living at the bottom of the sea did have limits, but it was still gross. No one around him seemed to think otherwise as they had no problem shoveling their food in, but he had a feeling none of them had ever had a real breakfast of pancakes and syrup, either. His stomach clenched at the thought.

He tried his best to nonchalantly look around the room for Zia. Her pale green hair wasn't there. Dark green, light green, lime green, blue green, all different shades, but no green that was almost blond. Leo was beginning to see a pattern. It seemed like the groups who sat together had similar shades of green hair. To the far right was a group with almost blue-green hair. The shade only varied a little between the five people talking together. To the left was a group that had a more lime green color to the hair. It was strange because he had yet to see someone with the same yellow-green color as Zia.

"Are you guys up for a tour?" Chris asked.

"Of course," Sam replied as he stood with Chris. "But first could you show us how to go back into the ocean? I need to check in with my father, and don't want to be a bother every day to have you escort us around."

"Yes. I'm sure your father keeps tabs on you as much as my father does." Laughing, Chris patted Sam on the back like they were old friends.

Leo just shook his head as he followed behind the two of them. To any outsider, they would see Sam's laid-back smile and attitude as friendly, but Leo knew better. Leo had known Sam his whole life. He understood the guy better than strangers. Sam trusted very few people, and he was never laid-back. If he did get one thing from his father, it was a great mind. The king was very seldom bested by anyone, and Sam was the same way.

Leading the way, Chris walked toward what appeared to be another wall. Leo followed directly in his footsteps because it was all still very confusing. Again, as Leo had noted the night before, it was impossible to see a hallway unless someone was in it. It was best to stick close to Chris for now. They were headed down a hall to wherever Chris was taking them. Leo was interested to see how the Mavkas could come and go safely.

"It will be good to take you guys up a little. Maybe it will give you a better idea of what each pod looks like. It's confusing unless you grow up here, and I really don't want either one of you accidentally being sucked away into the ocean if you walk into one of the walls thinking it was a hallway. That wouldn't look good for us," Chris explained. "I think we might get on your father's bad side." Chris was joking, and Sam laughed, but they all knew the Mavkas already were on King Longray's bad side since he had sent Sam to investigate.

His words were nice, but not convincing to Leo. Chris had a friendly attitude and personality to match Sam's, but Leo knew that anyone who was truly friends with Tim couldn't be trusted. Leo had grown up on the Siren island with Sam and had seen firsthand what Tim was like to his younger brother. Everyone knew it was jealousy, but even so, Tim was as two-faced as you could get. If you counted him as a friend, you had to be either really dense or on the same wavelength as him. Leo had the distinct feeling that Chris wasn't dense.

"So we come and go into each pod via the outside hallways," Chris continued to talk.

There was something about five hallways, tons of rooms in each hallway, and something else. Leo hoped Sam was having a better time paying attention. Leo was a bit distracted as he peered into each room they passed. Every now and then he would see someone in a space that must be a room. But he wasn't seeing the light-green-haired girl he was looking for.

Chris stopped at the end of a hallway, the familiar sea in front of them. Leo was getting better at seeing through the walls, but he was a bit concerned that it meant he could find himself walking right through one if he accidentally thought the wall was an open doorway.

"The space between our pod and the next one right at this hallway is calm. If you push forward and just transform, the magic will pull you out to the ocean," Chris explained. "It works with the mer transformation. If you accidentally push into the wall and don't transform, you can pull yourself back. Well, sometimes you can pull yourself back. But once you transform, these walls push you one way."

It sounded easy enough, but Leo still worried. Zia made it sound dangerous to go through the walls. Was Chris telling the truth? It would be an easy way to get rid of Sam and Leo, letting them be thrown out to sea. But then again, it was Sam he was with, which gave Leo a lot more confidence. Sam wasn't someone who'd get lost in the ocean.

"Once we get out, just swim up a few yards with me, and you'll be able to see the whole place," Christ explained, proud to show it off. Chris walked up to the wall and pushed an arm through. His whole body was pulled through also. It wasn't as fast as Leo expected, but it also wasn't like Chris had a chance to stop and come back.

Chris was now outside the space, or at least Leo thought he was. There in front of them in the sea was a green-haired orange-finned mer. After waving for them to follow, he swam toward the surface of the ocean.

"Looks like fun," Leo muttered sarcastically as Sam stepped forward.

"Meet you on the other side," Sam replied with a wink before pushing his hand into the gel-like wall.

Sam was pulled through just as gracefully and was on the other side, his blue fin shimmering in the ocean water. Leo wasn't excited to follow, but it wasn't like he could say no. One of the main parts of being a Siren, or any mer for that matter, was that they needed the water. At least once a day, Leo had to be transformed in the water to rehydrate his fin. If he chickened out and stayed behind, he might lose his chance, and he had no idea how he would get his much-needed rehydration time.

Stepping up to the wall, he pushed his hand through before he could change his mind. What looked like a slow, graceful process for Chris and Sam wasn't that way for Leo. He felt a jerk, and his body was pulled quicker than he expected through the magic barrier. Luckily for him, transforming in water was instinctual, and before he could orientate himself, Leo was in his night human form with a blue fin that matched Sam's. Looking up, Leo darted to where Sam and Chris were waiting.

Chris waved his hands around, gesturing at the world below them. Maybe the water wasn't too bad after all, as it kept their guide silent for more than ten seconds.

Leo glanced down. There were the four pods the merpeople with orange tails called home. Each pod had a large area, which was the meeting place that Leo had seen more than once now, with several hallways jetting off from it. Each hallway had bubble-like rooms. Actually, from their viewpoint, Leo had to imagine it was what an airport looked like from above. It wasn't that Leo had ever flown—Siren, like all mer, weren't keen on being trapped in a metal box with limited water—but he had been to one to pick up people with their band.

Interestingly there were mer outside in the ocean water swimming around, but they were all in one spot. Where the four pods exited created a small square-shaped space between the buildings. That internal area was filled with swimming mer people, young and old. Leo turned around and still didn't find the head of green hair he was looking for. The strange thing to see was that even though the pods were surrounded by water, no one was outside in that area. In fact, where Leo and Sam floated now was just above the exit. Leo looked toward the ocean, away from the Mavkas home area. A hand clamped down on his arm before he could move that direction.

Leo turned to find Chris holding onto him. He shook his head and pointed to go back down to the pod. Luckily, they were right above the one they had left, or Leo would have had no clue which one they came from. All four looked exactly the same.

Entering was just like leaving. Chris motioned for Sam to go first. Placing his hands on the jelly-like wall, Sam pushed. It was now blurry to look through the barrier from the water, but Sam melted through and just walked away. Chris then motioned for Leo to do the same. Leo followed, pushing his way much more gracefully into the inside part of the place. This time the pulling sensation was calmer, and he had time to transform into his human legs to walk without flopping on the ground first. Chris followed right behind him.

"I guess one thing I forgot to mention," Chris began talking the moment his head was free. "Don't go beyond the barrier of the pods. There are strong currents to pull you out to sea, but we also have a lot of predators circling the area, searching for a stray easy meal. They will all follow you, no matter how far you are pulled, to eat you."

"Good to know," Leo replied, and truly it was good to know. Siren were powerful and didn't fear much in the ocean, but one Siren against many predators was never a good combination.

"Were you able to contact your father?" Chris asked, turning back to Sam and returning to ignoring Leo.

"Yes. He was happy to know that everything was going good here."

Chris nodded and began talking again and leading them back toward the main room. Leo was ready to disappear. Chris talked way too much for him. There was never a moment that Sam could even reply as the guy just kept talking and talking. Leo didn't know how Sam had the patience to keep listening.

Zia had spent the morning hiding from their Siren guests. At least by spying from her various hiding spots she learned the name of the guy, but she didn't want to go near him. She would have to be nice and make him want to stay even though she wanted him to leave. She hated when Lan or Min gave her orders. Over time it faded, but there hadn't been enough time yet. She'd be exactly the mer Lan thought Leo would fall for.

Watching as Leo ate breakfast, Zia almost laughed to herself. He didn't seem to like the food, and she couldn't blame him. It was horrible. That's why Lan's threat of taking food away from her was kind of ridiculous. Forcing her to eat the really bad stuff would be way more of a punishment. The only bad thing about going without meals was it made her weak. The Mavkas didn't have access to blood like the Siren, so once she got weak from not eating, there wasn't an easy solution to feel better. She'd have to eat the gross mush to gain energy back.

When Leo had gone outside, Zia took the opportunity to move to a new room and watch them. It had been a long time since she had seen a Siren tail and the bright blue tails swimming outside. It really was a sight to see. It wasn't just Zia that was draw to the two guys; everyone below was watching them, too.

When they returned inside, Zia hurried back to spy on them. She knew exactly where to stand to hear every detail from the strange acoustics of the bubble home of the Mavkas. It took weeks, but Zia knew where every voice in the pod transferred to. Because of the shape of the ceiling and walls and how they reflected sound, there was always a place or two where your conversation could be perfectly overheard. Her room had been chosen for her because Lan could hear anything from her room back in his own.

Zia was never going to forgive herself for stupidly falling for Lan. Yes, he was the first mer who had caught her interest, but she could see now that was because of her situation and not because he liked her. He had shown her nothing but contempt since she had moved in with his family. Even now he was waiting where he could hear her and follow her movements. It didn't take long to realize that Lan saw her as a prize and tool to do his bidding. He didn't love her, just like she didn't love him.

Life was never free for Zia. She didn't want Leo, or Sam for that matter, to get caught in the Mavkas world. She had bonded herself to Lan; there was no way for her to get out. But they were both still free, and she wanted to keep it that way. She hated the control he had over her, and she just needed to keep avoiding Leo to keep him from getting caught up in everything.

As Chris talked about his life and adventures that were likely fake—Zia knew more about the outside world than he did—she sat and listened, waiting for Leo to say something.

"Still not doing what we ask of you?" Lan asked as he came up beside Zia.

She ignored him as best she could and kept listening while pretending to just be relaxing in the chair she was sitting in instead.

"Why do you keep following me around?" she asked, finally opening her eyes. "It's not like you actually like me, and yet every time I turn around, there you are."

"Ah, poor Zia is having a sad moment," Lan taunted her. "I follow you around because it seems like you're having trouble following our instructions. And I don't get why. Why don't you want more Siren around? Why wouldn't you like to have someone here who understands you? You've been asking forever for us to let you go. Isn't this the next best thing?"

Was he serious? There was no way Zia would condemn another Siren to the fate of the Mavkas. She knew that Siren belonged free in the sea. They needed sunlight and song to stay happy. There was nothing but darkness and dread in the Mavkas world. Sure, the Mavkas didn't seem to care, but a Siren would.

"You need to be smart about this. You do as we command, and you stay safe and fed. Don't, and there will be consequences."

It wasn't like this was the first time she'd heard that one. In fact, the first time he threatened consequences was after she mistakenly bonded herself to him. He seemed to think it was a real bond, or think he could trick her into it, but Zia knew otherwise. She had read about real bonds. What he had done to her was magic, and strong magic at that. She wasn't getting out. Not now, not ever. And she sure wasn't going to bind someone else to the same fate. Leo and Sam were going to stay free.

Zia stood up. She'd rather sit alone in her room than listen to Lan talk. He was a sorry excuse for a human being.

"Zia," Lan grumbled as she pushed past him and back to the hallway where her room was. Lan hurried to block her entry into her room. "You might not agree with my father or me, but you're a Mavkas now. You have to do what I say. You bonded yourself to me. You're mine to command."

"And I regret it every day," she replied as she ducked under his arms and into her room. Lan could follow her, but she didn't care. She was going to take a nap. She knew her statement was only going to make him mad, but that was life. When it got to be too much, she did lash out occasionally, and words were her only weapon. She couldn't do anything else.

Leo sat impatiently in the waiting room by the Mavkas leader's office. It seemed that while they lacked chairs, tables, and beds in the Mavkas mer world, they didn't lack desks, Looking through several hold-the-water-away walls, Leo could see that the Mavkas leader,

Min, had an actual desk in his office. Leo and Sam sat on the low chair-like benches in the waiting room while Chris stood before his father. Min motioned with his arms, and Chris replied, but the clear magic walls weren't clear enough to see what Chris was saying or to hear for that matter. The only noise they heard was from them in the room alone.

"Your father have anything more to say?" Leo asked. If they couldn't hear Chris and Min, Leo doubted anyone could hear them.

"Nothing to add to what he said before we left." Sam seemed tense. Leo didn't need to know the actual words of the king to understand it hadn't been good news.

"So we're still at step one," Leo said under his breath, knowing perfectly well that Sam heard him. Leo was already making a mental list of who he'd want to say good-bye to before he was executed for treason.

The Mavkas so far had been nothing but hospitable. While Leo wanted to find some great big secret, he was getting less and less sure it was possible. From the whole open life within the pods, Leo was pretty sure if there was a secret, everyone would know about it. Thus far it seemed like either everyone was good at keeping their mouths shut, or there was nothing to hide. He was beginning to wonder if it was the second option. King Longray had grown a little paranoid over the years.

Leo looked up as someone entered the room.

"Chris is being a bad host, I see," Chris' sister commented as she sat down beside Sam, a little closer than it seemed Sam would like, but Sam didn't move.

"I understand how fathers can be," Sam replied,

letting Chris' sister lean on him a little bit. Her intentions were quite obvious. Leo instantly felt like a third wheel.

"I think I'll try to make my way back to the room," Leo said as he stood.

He didn't need to sit around and watch a girl throw herself at Sam. It wasn't like Leo wasn't used to it, though. The whole rock band thing meant girls were constantly throwing themselves at Sam at each performance. Leo knew Sam's stance on girls. He didn't plan to get attached to anyone in case his father could use that to make him stay on the Siren island. Sam, like Leo, didn't want a single reason to keep them there on the island.

Glancing up at him, Sam nodded. He didn't seem happy to be left behind with Chris' sister, but he would manage. He always did.

Leo nodded back to his friend and left the way they came. It was hard to see the walls at times, so Leo took his time walking down the almost straight hallway back to the main room, sometimes nudging with his foot first to be sure that there wasn't a wall the way he was walking. Leo just wanted to get away from the Mavkas for now, and the only place he was certain to be alone was the room he was sharing with Sam. It seemed that the rooms, while having no doors, were still protected. The magic that made the place made it possible to assign rooms, and no one could enter without permission. It wasn't like Leo knew who had permission to enter their room, but he felt confident enough that it would be a safe, quiet place to contemplate his last week alive.

Chris had explained in detail how to make their way around the pod. After taking a swim above it made more sense now. The hallways were hard to see because they all curved a bit, causing the magic walls to blur where the pathway would go.

Leo took one glance around the open meeting room before walking toward where the room he was staying should be. He stopped to look at the floor. Five giant stepping stones marked the hallways, and Leo was standing just by a stone with a large single starfish carved into it. They were in the starfish corridor. The other stones had other sea life carved on them, and Leo was sure he was heading in the right direction.

Taking his time to stop and check each room, Leo had to be certain which was his before he tried to enter. Chris also explained that if you tried to go into a room that wasn't yours, you would get a sting like you touched a jellyfish. Leo had touched a few jellyfish in his time in the sea, and he knew how bad it felt. He didn't need a repeat. He would find his way back carefully. He was in the room with two starfish marking the doorway. While he was searching for the right one, he also couldn't help but glance at the people he passed. Zia still was a no show, and Leo couldn't help wondering where she'd gone.

He had only met the other mer the night before, but he wasn't able to stop thinking of her. There was something different about her, and he wanted to know more. It wasn't like he hadn't had a crush before, but he couldn't explain it to himself or Sam who was bound to notice soon.

Luck was on his side as Leo made the soft turn toward the end of the hallway. Someone was walking toward him, and from the green hair, he had a good idea who it was. Leo paused where he stood and waited to watch her pass. As she was right next to him, the girl finally looked up.

Zia stared in shock at him with her beautiful ocean blue eyes. Leo could say nothing as any thought left his mind when their eyes connected. Zia shook her head and began to walk again, away from Leo. That brought him quickly back to reality.

"Wait." Leo walked back a few steps, and she turned to face him. "I was looking for you all morning while we had our tour."

"You're one of those Siren guys that are visiting, right?" she asked innocently, like they had never spoken before. She knew perfectly well he was "one of those Siren guys."

"Yes." Leo stared at her, trying to read her face.

She looked perfectly innocent.

"You must have liked my singing," she added. "Most of us don't get to go up to land because of the whole green hair thing, but the ones who do always bring back items. Your album was one of the newer items brought back, and I love all the songs. It's got to be great singing about water all the time. Sam is such a good singer, too."

Now she sounded like the groupies they had at their concerts. The girl Leo had met the night before was gone. Leo looked her over again from head to toe. She was the same girl, but her personality was different.

"You don't happen to have a twin sister, do you?" Leo

asked. Really it was confusing. She was acting like they had never spoken before.

Zia laughed, but her smile was fake. "Isn't that, like, some cheesy pick-up line?"

"It's just you're ..."

Leo didn't know what to say as he tried to hide his disappointment. It was his own fault. He'd been thinking of her non-stop since the night before, and the whole take turns sleeping thing meant he had plenty of time to imagine the perfect girl he'd met. In reality, they'd spoken once, and he was ready to ask her to leave the Mavkas and join the Siren. But he knew the truth. The clans didn't mix. It was very rare for one to leave their clan, and harder to get them accepted in a new clan. He had just been wishfully thinking.

Leo looked at the waiting mer. Her eyes were watching him, and that made his heart pound. He wasn't one for embarrassing himself, but what did he have to lose? Only the week left alive was a bit of motivation for him to be brave about the girl standing in front of him.

"I thought there was something more," he finally finished his thought, embarrassing as it was.

"Aw, that's sweet. I seem to have that effect on people. Sorry if you thought my singing was for you."

That made little sense. It wasn't the singing Leo was talking about, but he was done getting his ego bruised for the day. All his brave energy was gone.

"Sorry about that," Leo added and turned to walk away.

"Well, just so you know, I don't have a twin sister, and I'm the only Zia in the Mavkas colony."

Leo turned back around, but she was already walking away. Leo watched her go. That added to the confusion. It was like she was speaking in riddles. One minute she was cute and innocent, and the next somber and foreboding. What she was saying didn't make sense. Unless it was what she wasn't saying that was important.

Leo thought back to the night before and the scared girl who hid in the shadows, not the confident singer that was a perfect match with Sam when singing. Maybe it was wishful thinking, but Leo had a gut feeling that there was more to Zia. Then again, maybe she just didn't feel the connection he thought was there. That was more likely it. Leo had a countdown to the rest of his life. Five more days to go and they'd return to the Siren. He was grasping at straws and wanting one last connection before his certain death. That had to be it.

CHAPTER 5

Sam sat in the common room with his arm around Cate. She snuggled into him and laid her head on his chest. It was late, and all the other mer had already gone to bed. Cate was obviously tired, too. She sighed, content in his arms. Sam had no interest in the girl, but he played like he did. She was a source of information.

He was getting more and more worried every day they spent in the Mavkas world without any clue what to be looking for. Sam knew his friend's life hung in the balance, and it made everything more urgent. Sam had talked with his father briefly when they went for their swim earlier, and the old man was very certain there was something going on, but of course, he didn't elaborate. All he would emphasize was that if Sam and Leo didn't find the secret, then they would be punished.

"I suppose it's time I get you back to your room," Sam said to the almost asleep Cate.

"Are you sure you don't just want me to crash with you?" she replied with a yawn as she sat up.

"I'm sure Leo wouldn't appreciate it. And don't ask me to stay with you," Sam added. Meeting fathers wasn't part of his game. He had absolutely no interest in Cate, and he'd hate to anger the leader of the Mavkas by pretending he was more serious than he really was.

"I wouldn't do that."

Rising, Sam pulled Cate up before she could finish.

"I still sleep at my parent's place; I'm sure my father would kill me if you stayed the night." Cate stumbled a bit as they started walking and giggled at her sleepy feet.

Sam scooped the neon-green-haired mer into his arms. Cate giggled again as Sam began to carry her back to her place. Sam made it to the doorway to her place, and she was already asleep in his arms. He waited just long enough. He stood at the doorway as Chris came up to them.

"Just tell me where to put her," Sam said. "It seems that Siren can go longer without sleep." A fact he already knew.

Chris nodded as he rubbed his eyes. He must have been sleeping also. Chris reached down the sea urchin just inside the doorway.

"I need your hand," Chris told Sam.

Sam held out a hand. He remembered from the night before how this worked. His blood on the key to the room would allow him in. It seemed his planning was paying off. Chris poked the creature into Sam's outstretched hand, and Sam's blood dripped down the spine that had poked him. After placing it back into the wall of magic, he motioned for Sam to follow.

Chris sleepily led the way to a room that had a bed already waiting for Cate. It was nice that Chris was silent for once. His everlasting chatter had been pushing Sam's limit all day. At least Cate was a bit easier to listen to. She wasn't all about boasting, but instead wanted to know everything about Sam. Okay, it wasn't much easier, but it seemed like it was worth it. He was now free to snoop around their place and had earned his entry.

Sam placed the sleeping Cate gently onto her bed. She didn't stir a bit, and he was thankful it was easy to manipulate her with his voice. She wasn't going to remember a single answer he gave to her questions the day before and now had access to the room she shared with her parents. Now Sam only had to find the key to get into the office, and he would be able to snoop more. And, hopefully, no one else would forget the answers they heard today when he ordered Cate to with a joke that might have been overheard by the acoustics.

Sam wasn't one for betraying people or running around behind people's backs—in fact, the whole operation at the Mavkas wasn't sitting well with him— but his friend's life was on the line. Sam would do anything to protect those he cared about, and Leo was one of the few people that he didn't want to see dead. His plan seemed to work, but it took longer than he had hoped. Only five more days to go to find a secret hidden in the Mavkas world, and Sam was going to do his best to keep Leo alive.

Leo woke to find Sam leaving already. They had only talked briefly the night before, but Sam was working on a plan. Leo hoped it was something good as he didn't have anything. But that wasn't completely his fault. With the king being vague, it was close to impossible for Leo to know where to start looking. And the fact that he couldn't stop thinking about Zia didn't help the matter.

Zia had made it clear that she didn't feel anything between them as Leo had. She acted like she hadn't spoken to him at all, but he knew that his mind wasn't playing tricks. He was certain they had a conversation that she was now pretending never happened. Leo hated how confusing girls could be.

Leo made his way out to the common room when he could no longer stand his rumbling stomach. He wasn't looking forward to any more green goo, but it was better than nothing. He hoped when they left he would get one more meal before King Longray killed him. He'd plead for a last meal with a juicy burger and greasy fries and pie. Yes, he would ask for pie. And nothing green. He'd seen enough green food to last him years.

The room was almost empty, but the buffet was still set up. Leo walked over and viewed the choices. Green goo and some round ball things. Neither one seemed like breakfast or a good choice, but since he already knew the green slime was pretty bad, he opted to try the cream-colored ball-shaped things.

"Use a fork for those or they crumble," Zia advised from beside him.

Leo nodded and used tongs to pick up the food and place it on his plate. He continued down the row to the waiting two piles of slop. Even those weren't distinguishable—a deep orange color or a bright red color slop. What Leo wouldn't give to be back home on land.

"The red one isn't bad. Tastes a bit like strawberry jam," Zia added from his side. She was keeping pace with him and not passing him as the other two mer who had gotten their food had done.

Leo took a scoop of the red one and walked to the end of the line to grab a fork and spoon. He wasn't looking forward to the meal, but it was better than nothing. He tried not to notice as Zia stayed behind him and followed as he made his way to an empty seat. Zia plopped down beside him.

"So, we have never been formally introduced," she said. "I'm Zia. I was taken in by Min and his family when mine was taken away from me."

She held her hand out to Leo with a big smile on her face. Yes, girls were beyond confusing. Yesterday she was crushing his heart and every ounce of bravery he had, and today she was being his friend. He would have given anything to have seen that same smile the day before. He'd have to take the little bit he got now and hope it was going to stay.

"I'm Leo," he replied, taking her smaller hand in his.

Leo felt a shock zing from his fingers up his arm as their hands touched, followed by a warmness that trailed the zap, but he pretended not to notice. The momentary expression on Zia's face showed him that she felt it also, but she was back to her smiley self without missing a beat.

"Well, it's great to finally meet and talk with you, Leo the visiting Siren. It isn't often we get visitors here, so we're all excited to learn more from you."

She was back to being confusing again. If she had been any other girl, Leo would have walked away, but there was something about her that kept him in his seat, even with all the weird talk.

"Would you like a tour of the place when you're finished eating?"

Leo already had one tour, but a second couldn't hurt, and maybe if they were alone he could finally ask her what was going on. Then again, they'd been alone in the hallway the night before, and she was acting strange then, too. He really wanted to believe that he imagined meeting her the first night, but he was certain he hadn't.

"Sounds good," Leo replied and began to eat his strange food.

The round off-white balls really did crumble when he pressed too hard. Zia just smiled at him and motioned for him to eat it as daintily as she was. He wasn't sure he liked food that had to be held carefully, but he was hungry enough to try. It took several tries and piles of crumbs before he successfully got one into his mouth without crushing it. Zia laughed when he smiled at his success. He had heard that sound before and was just as entranced by the girl as he had been a few days ago.

"You know food is meant to be enjoyed. Why do guys feel the need to eat things as fast as they can?"

Shrugging, he concentrated on getting the next one to his mouth. Two in a row and he decided it was enough concentrating as he reached for his spoon to try the red slime. With the first bite, he completely understood the description of strawberries. It was sweet and almost like them. The only difference was a sour aftertaste. Leo used the sticky strawberry slime to catch the crumbs from the white balls to finish everything on his plate. It was the first meal he didn't want to throw up; a success in his book.

"It's not that guys want to eat fast, we just have bigger mouths and can fit more in," Leo finally replied as he finished off his plate of food. Day two was much better than day one for breakfast, but there were still two more meals to go; Leo wasn't holding his breath on being well-fed.

"Sure," Zia replied as she finished off her own food. She had taken less than Leo and took longer to eat than him. She did have a point of guys eating fast.

Leo followed as Zia stood and dropped off her plate at the table next to the buffet. Leo did the same. After dropping off his plate, he turned back to find her waiting, closer than he expected. When he accidentally knocked into her, he reached out to steady her. The zap he'd felt when he shook her hand didn't happen, but the warm, fuzzy feeling that had followed was still there.

"Sorry," she mumbled as she stared up at him.

Leo just stood and held onto her. He was speechless, having her so close after thinking about her non-stop pretty much since he'd arrived in the Mavkas world. For a second time, they were so close it would take nothing to lean down and finally kiss her. It was like fate was trying to put them together.

Zia broke the stare between them as she backed up. She was as dazed by their contact as he was, and he was certain she felt what he was feeling, even if she was strange. She glanced behind her quickly and then back to Leo. Her face went from the awe that he was feeling to a fake smile quickly plastered across her face. She was one confusing girl.

"So, did Chris show you guys how to find the hallways?" Zia asked as she motioned to the corridors jutting off the main room.

Leo shook his head. A little white lie couldn't hurt, and he was ready to listen to her speak more. She was such a mystery to him, and unlike the quest he was on with Sam, she was a mystery he didn't mind spending time figuring out. Another tour of the place wasn't going to hurt anything, and it was the perfect opportunity to study her more. Sure, he was supposed to be looking for clues, but that could wait a little bit.

Zia smiled at him and began explaining the Mavkas underground world. While listening to Chris was annoying, Leo was pretty sure he could listen to Zia all day. If she wasn't from a different clan, Leo would have thought he found his mate. His mother had always told him that when he finally found the right girl, he would know, but he never understood. That was part of the reason Leo wanted to leave the Siren. He was positive there wasn't a single girl there for him like his mother described. He understood now, even if it was impossible. He only had five more days to live anyway. Leo would pretend it wasn't impossible and dream of a future he'd never have.

Zia smiled at Leo as he followed behind her. She knew that he already had a tour, but that didn't stop him from wanting one with her. He didn't need a second one as the place wasn't that big, but it was the only excuse she could make to get him alone with her. She was pretty sure she would do a better job anyway. The Mavkas, in general, had no imagination. She did.

Starting with the first hallway, she slowly led Leo away from Lan, who was intently watching them eat. Lan had been excessively creepy and clingy since Leo arrived. She hoped that he didn't suspect there was something more between them.

"We begin with what I refer to as hallway one," Zia began her tour.

Leo watched her intently as she led the way. She tried not to think of the feelings she got when she touched him. The zing of their hands first meeting had been unexpected. She had better control of her emotions the second time, but Lan was already there in the room watching them. She wasn't giving him anything more to go on. She wanted him to think she was detached and just doing her commanded job. If he got any inkling that she really was starting to develop feelings for the Siren she had just met, she would be doomed to trick him into staying.

Zia walked them to the very end of the hallway. It was a quiet spot that only reached to one of the adjacent rooms.

"From here you can enter and leave." She pointed to the wall. Leo had used hallway five to leave the day before. "Straight across there is pod S. Well, I call it pod S, but don't ask anyone else where pod S is."

"S?"

"For south. It took me a while to orientate myself. The sunlight is a little strange under the water, but I mapped out which direction these pods are all seated.

This is the most western pod, and that's the southern one. Hence pod S."

Leo nodded with her description, and she was glad she didn't have to go further into her adventures of trying to leave the Mavkas to get those directions. It still didn't help much. She wasn't sure where she was or even what ocean they were in. Directions only helped when you knew where you were going.

"Sam would like to hear that," Leo commented, and Zia raised an eyebrow. "Sam likes to know which way is what, even if we don't know where we are," he quickly added.

Zia had seen that they were blindfolded upon arrival, but from what she heard Sam wouldn't let that hinder him. Even if he didn't tell tales like Chris, everyone knew the sons of the Siren King were well traveled.

"I heard he's been all over," Zia added casually, trying not to give away that she knew more than that.

"Yeah. Sam is like a perfect traveling companion. He never loses where home is and can find it no matter where it is. The best part is that since he was younger he could always go ashore and talk to humans and force them to answer him without hurting them."

"He never gets lost?"

"Never," Leo added.

Zia nodded. Then if all else failed, she could just push them through the wall, and they could find their way home. At least now she didn't have to worry about that part.

"So that guy that keeps following you around ..." Leo didn't finish asking.

"He's Min's oldest son. He's responsible for me; he likes to creep around making sure I stay safe. It's all brotherly like." Okay, that was making it sound nice which it was far from, but she was certain Lan was hanging around and possibly eavesdropping.

"If you look closely, you can see the other pod." Zia took the conversation back to her tour of the place. It was strange to have to lie about Lan and Min. In fact, it was hard to think up excuses. Most of the time, no one spoke to Zia. She wasn't used to lying. And a big part of her didn't want to lie to Leo. She wanted him to know the truth.

"I actually can," Leo replied as he walked up right to the wall. Zia placed a hand on his chest to stop him from going farther and out of the pod, which made Leo grin more. She had a feeling he was being that way on purpose. She grinned back at him as she pushed him away from being sucked into the ocean.

Leading the way, she left hallway number one and took him down the second one. There wasn't really much to see, but she wanted to keep going long enough to bore Lan. Maybe he would give up. Probably not, but she could wish.

Zia answered Leo's questions as he thought of them, and for once she felt at home in the Mavkas place. She was lying if she said she didn't want to keep Leo around, but wanting company didn't outweigh the fact that he would be a prisoner like her and the rest of the Mavkas. She couldn't do that to him, no matter how much he made her heart beat faster.

Leo was disappointed when Zia finished her tour. She didn't offer to take him outside the pod, but Leo didn't care. He was happy to simply follow her around. It was nice that he could get a few questions in and she was being friendly enough to answer.

So far Leo knew her family was gone, and she was placed with Chris' family for protection. Leo was completely right in that the families all had similar hair color, but it wasn't just the hair. Families were the basis of their whole clan. Family dictated everything, and without one, she had no one to boss her around yet no one to protect her either. That was why she had to accept the offer of Min to let her join his family.

Zia had also explained that every mer living there had certain chores and jobs. She had been lucky since she could sing so well, her job was entertainment when they had their large get-togethers. And that actually happened a lot more than the Siren. According to Zia, it was almost once a week that they were celebrating something.

As the tour ended, bringing them back into the meeting room, Leo was disappointed. It was past lunch time but nowhere near bedtime. Sam was still missing in action, yet Leo was far from caring. After seeing the whole place a second time, he was convinced that King Longray was just torturing him on his last days alive. There was nothing that stood out at all. They had been over the whole place and heard dozens of people talking. Resolving himself to his fate, Leo decided to make the best of his last days alive.

"So we have this cool room off to the side that I haven't shown you yet," Zia said, bringing Leo back to her finished tour. "I think it will probably be at least another thirty minutes to an hour before food is set out. We can just go and sit and watch the ocean. It has probably the best view of the water around here."

If she was talking about the room to the side, Leo was certain that was true but was back to being confused. He had met her in that room, but if she was playing a game of forgetting that, he was just going to go along with it. What was the use trying to figure out the confusing meaning behind her words? He was just going to enjoy spending time with the most beautiful girl he had ever met.

Zia led the way back into the alcove off the main room. With the midday light, Leo could see farther than just the schools of fish swimming outside of the barrier.

"I told you it was the best view," Zia said as she stood beside him.

Leo looked back down at her as she talked and smiled to find she was watching him. She quickly turned from him, but he had caught it. She could pretend she just met him, she could pretend she didn't like him, she could pretend a lot, but that didn't change what he really saw.

"Have a seat." She offered one of the same low-sitting chairs that he had sat in before. She pulled up a second right next to the first but didn't sit down. Leo moved to follow.

"No, stay there," she told him in a playful tone.

Yet again she was playing a game he didn't understand, but he was willing to trust her, confusing as she was. Leo sat in the chair.

"I've searched this whole place, and this is the only dead zone I've found," Zia continued. All playfulness left her voice.

"What do you mean?" Leo asked, sitting up a little bit to turn around and see where she had gone.

"No. Just stay there," she directed him again, "and don't reply back. You are still in a spot where if anyone wanted to hear you, they could."

Leo thought about that for a second. Sam had been sure that the shape of the magic that held the water off also made it easy to overhear things, but Leo hadn't been eavesdropping since he had arrived. It sounded normal to him wherever he went.

"Acoustically this place is perfect. When someone wants to keep tabs on someone, there's always somewhere to go to overhear a conversation. I've tested every little corner in this pod, and this is the only place I found where I can speak and not be overheard by anyone but the person sitting in front of me."

Well, that explained where she was now. She had to be hiding in the same spot as the first night. Now Leo really wanted to turn around and ask her questions.

Leo began to turn when she slipped into the seat beside him. Reaching over, she took his hand as she lay back against the seat, keeping her head from the top of the chair. Leo took that as a cue to do the same and slid down a little to be hidden, also. Smiling, Zia looked straight ahead at the water in front of them. Leo was confused but did the same. The girl was puzzling and full of secrets, but he trusted her. Someone he had just met, and he had complete faith in her. That much he couldn't explain.

Within moments, Leo heard someone approach. He didn't turn around, but he knew that they were close enough to see him with Zia. Not dropping his hand, she continued to stare off at the ocean. It took all of his self-control to not turn and look at the intruding silent person. It was only a few moments and then the person left without a word.

Leo sat there waiting for whatever they were doing when Zia tugged on his hand. Leo turned to her, and she smiled, putting her free hand to her mouth to signal to him to be quiet. Leo nodded as she then motioned for him to follow her. Dropping his hand, she crawled off the chair to the other side that couldn't be seen from the open doorway. Leo followed, keeping low to the ground as Zia led him back to her corner.

The silence washed over him, which made Leo finally realize why he hadn't noticed the conversations around him. There had been a constant buzz since he had entered the place that he just had been ignoring. Now he remembered what it was like to not hear all the additional noise.

"I come here often. He won't check on us again," Zia told Leo.

"Who is he?"

"Chris' older brother, Lan. His job is to follow me around today, and probably the rest of the time you're here."

That wasn't what Leo was expecting, and she went back to cryptic talk.

"Why?"

"I can't answer that," Zia replied sadly.

And that was enough for Leo to realize that there might just be something going on after all. There was something Zia wasn't explaining, and Leo could feel it was big. Unfortunately, it included Zia. Leo would have much rather that Sam found it with Chris' sister instead of Leo with Zia, but it was something and something that was giving him hope. Leo didn't want to have hope, but being next to Zia made him desire a future he was trying to convince himself he didn't need.

"You and Sam need to leave this place as soon as you can," Zia told him in a foreboding tone.

Turning, Leo gazed into her eyes. She was pleading with him, but he was hooked. He couldn't just walk away from her.

CHAPTER 6

Cate was beyond clingy. Sam wasn't the least bit afraid to use that to his advantage, and now that he had access into Min's home, he wanted to go snoop. The only problem was that she was still clingy and now that was stopping Sam from getting any clues. Sam didn't make any moves toward her, but she didn't seem to notice.

"Tell me again about the concerts. They sound like so much fun," Cate begged, stroking Sam's arm as she stared at him. Sam had a feeling that she wasn't as much into him as she pretended, either. He had seen it a couple times, but there was something behind her words.

Sam had already told her about life on land, including the concerts he performed at. He was pretty sure she wouldn't appreciate the girls in the audience throwing themselves at the band, so he left that detail out. Getting frustrated by her constant need for his attention, Sam leaned down lower to her ear.

"We stayed out way too late last night. I think it's time that you take a nap," he suggested, putting Siren power behind it and making it a command. It was dangerous to use his Siren voice where people might overhear him, but he was beyond done with her.

He had spent all morning listening to her and answering her questions and still hadn't gotten a chance to slip away. And it had been perfect timing. Her father and brothers, in fact, her whole family, seemed to be off doing something else. He had a feeling that was Cate's whole intention when she invited him back to her place, but he wasn't going to go for what she intended. He had his own agenda.

Cate stretched her arms. "I'm feeling really tired all of a sudden."

Grabbing his arm, she pulled him farther into the sleeping rooms and off to her own room. Had he not just suggested her sleeping, he would have refused. But he knew that she would have no choice but to follow his command.

"Just a short nap would be good for both of us," she suggested as she pulled Sam to the floor. He nodded as her eyes drooped, and she leaned against him. It wasn't even that forceful of a suggestion, but that was the key to using small amounts of Siren power. Just a little bit of a suggestion of something that was partially true could go a long way.

Sam gently untangled himself from her and placed her on the ground covered up. If she woke, he could always use the excuse that he wasn't tired. Cate didn't flinch as he positioned her. She wasn't going to wake soon, hopefully.

Walking back to the main room, Sam paused to listen around him. Where Min's office was, he could tell no one was around. He was getting better at seeing through the magic walls of the place, but he still wanted to be sure. Sam heard Cate sleeping and people down the hallway. It was still pretty clear in the area. He had a slight idea that most people didn't frequent the area where Min lived, but Sam had to be safe.

Once he was completely sure no one was around, Sam silently made his way into the Mavkas leader's office. After three days of being in the underwater world, it was strange to see the table on one side of the room and the desk on the other. They seemed out of place.

Keeping tabs on the clear wall, Sam ducked down and made his way over to the desk. That way if someone did pass close enough, he'd be hidden well enough that they wouldn't notice him unless they came into the room. He hoped for his safety and Leo's that no one came into the room.

Kneeling by the desk, Sam lifted the few papers that were messily thrown around. He only had to glance at each one to know it wasn't what he was searching for. His father had no need for the knowledge of what animals the Mavkas were hunting or what agreements they had with their neighbors. Each mer clan butted up against another's territories, and agreements were made and broken all the time. Longray stopped caring years ago since they changed often.

Sam ducked down and went over to the table. No one had passed the room yet, and he had a little time to find something that might help him figure out what was going on. Sam sifted through the papers on the table and was still drawing a blank. There were maps of the oceans but nothing that said they had some great big, evil in the plans. All the clans kept track of the ocean and knew the general area where each clan called home. This was nothing incriminating, and Sam was certain he was out of time.

Hurrying out of the room, Sam made it back to Cate's in time for someone to enter their sleeping area. Sam lay down beside Cate and tucked her into his arm as he closed his eyes. Cate snuggled closer and whoever had entered stopped in the open doorway to the room. They paused only briefly before walking away.

Sam wasn't sure who had checked on them, but it didn't matter. There was nothing in Min's office, and he wasn't sure where else to look. They were running out of time to find whatever his father was searching for, and that wasn't good news.

Leo stared at the ocean wall in front of him. Zia had asked him to leave, but he couldn't. Unfortunately, he also couldn't get answers out of her. Leo needed something to go on. If the Mavkas were up to something, he wanted to know what. It was possible it could save his life, but then again, it was possible it wouldn't. Either way, Zia needed to know the truth.

"If I go back to the Siren, I will be killed," Leo finally told her. Zia sucked in her breath. "Sam and I've been talking about leaving the Siren when we turn eighteen rather than joining the clan. Neither one of us want to be forced to mate against our will, and more often now that's what Longray is doing. We want to be free of the Siren and live a normal life on land. King Longray found out and told us that if we didn't come back with something we will be punished. For me that means death."

"He can't do that," Zia exclaimed, reaching out and

taking Leo's hand in her own. "He can't kill you for something you haven't done." Her touch was distracting, and Leo had to concentrate to understand what she was saying.

"He can for trying to take away his son," Leo replied. He knew all along it was dangerous to include Sam in his plans, but they both agreed. They didn't want to live the Siren life forced on them.

"But—" Zia tried to disagree.

Leo reached up, placing a finger on her lips to keep her from talking further.

"My fate was sealed the moment I was sent here. I know what waits for me at home, and I've made peace with that."

Okay, he hadn't made peace with it, but he was sure there was no reason to dwell on it any longer. The girl of his dreams was sitting here, her side pressed against him. She was scared for some reason, and he wanted nothing more than protect her. If he only had a few days left, then that was what he would do with them.

"So don't worry about me. There's nothing the Mavkas can do that will be worse than Longray's plans for me."

Zia didn't seem to have an argument for that.

"But it isn't safe for you here either," she finally said, still not elaborating.

Leo laughed. "It isn't safe for me anywhere."

She smiled at that, and it warmed his heart. Her smile was much better than the fear he saw in her eyes.

"So you can't tell me why it isn't safe?" Leo continued to prod.

"Yes. I've been forbidden from telling you the truth."
Zia went back to pouting.

"But have you been forbidden from talking to me?"

"No. They want me to talk with you, but they're listening to everything we say as we walk around this place."

Leo looked at the back of the chairs they had been sitting in. "Hence the reason we're sitting here now."

"Yes."

"So someone is out there waiting for us to talk again. What do they think we're doing now?"

Zia blushed in their dark corner, and it just made Leo want to embarrass her more. In reality, it made him want to see every side of her. Only days wasn't going to be long enough for him. Zia opened her mouth and then shut it again.

"That bad?" Leo asked when she didn't answer.

"No. Well, yeah, but no. I can't seem to get the words out. Guess it's another thing I'm not supposed to tell you." Zia shrugged, but her cheeks remained red.

"So they didn't specifically tell you what you can and can't say?" Leo needed to figure it all out. She had a secret that she wanted to tell him but couldn't. How else could he figure it out, because he was pretty sure there wasn't anything that would scare him away.

"No. Basically when I want to tell you something, sometimes I can't get the words out. That's how I know I can't say it."

Getting information would be hard if she just couldn't answer. Whatever power they were using on her was good if she didn't know what she could and couldn't say.

When Leo used his Siren powers on people, he had to be specific. It was like her order was more non-specific, more magical.

"Was this done by mer magic?" Leo really couldn't figure it out. He drew a blank at every type of way he could command someone.

Zia opened her mouth and stopped. "No," she replied quickly before Leo could ask something else, and then smiled. "It seems I can say no. I wonder if I could say yes."

That was at least something. It would be hard to know what to even ask, but Leo was happy with something over nothing.

"Then let me ask you an easy yes question," Leo suggested. Zia smiled at that.

"Is your real name Zia?"

Zia scrunched up her face like she had eaten something sour. "No."

Leo couldn't help the smile fading from his face. Whatever type of spell she was under it wasn't going to do any good if all she could answer was no.

Zia touched Leo's arm to bring his attention back to her. Her mouth was open again with no sound coming out. She blew out a breath in frustration.

"Ask me again," she told him.

"Is your name Zia?"

"Yes," she replied, but then shook her head. "No. Ask me the question you just asked me."

How did that make any sense? She could answer yes it seemed, but she didn't like that answer. He had asked her the same question.

"You forgot a word in your question," she prompted him as he stared at her still in confusion.

Leo finally remembered exactly what he had asked. "Is your real name Zia?"

"No," she replied, and then smiled at him as he made the connection.

Her name was Zia, but it wasn't her real name. Leo had no idea what that meant, but the game of question and answer was going to take a long time.

"We have to move back now," Zia told Leo as she took his hand and pulled him back to the seats.

They were barely there a moment when someone entered the room. Leo tried to pretend he was just looking at the fish, but when Zia curled under his arm and laid her head on his chest, Leo forgot the ocean in front of him. At least now he had a better idea what they thought he was doing with her and why she had red cheeks. She cuddled into his arms, and he was content to simply sit with her. The question session would just have to wait.

Zia was happy to be in Leo's arms. It was as perfect as she thought it would be, but the reason why kind of stunk. She wanted to be sitting with him and holding his hand because he wanted to, not because she was forcing him to pretend to like her.

Not being able to say what was on her mind was frustrating. She stared at the fish in the sea as she listened to Leo's heart beat erratically. Either he was scared or excited. She was going to go with excited, because that's what she felt.

Lan only checked on them before leaving. He was doing his job, and she could feel his suspicions across the bond she shared with his family. As she snuggled into Leo's arms, she was sorry she had ever bonded herself to Lan and his family in the first place. The magic keeping her bonded to them was regretful, and she was sad she would never be able to undo what she stupidly did.

After the Mavkas left the room, Zia was surprised that there was no jealousy from Lan. He acted like their bond was an actual mating bond and he often referred to it that way, but either he didn't want to see, or was too dense to realize, it wasn't. Zia had always felt that it wasn't a real bond, but it wasn't until Leo showed up that her thoughts were confirmed. What she felt the moment she saw Leo wouldn't be possible if she was truly bonded to Lan.

"Don't you have anywhere you need to be?" Leo asked, not letting go of her.

"Not me. My only job in this place is singing. If they don't need a performance, then I'm free to do anything," she replied. Well, anything but leave. That was still very much part of the magical bond on her. Lan knew perfectly well where she was at all times.

Zia felt Lan right outside the door. He wasn't taking any chances; they weren't going to get another moment alone until he backed off.

Leo bobbed his head directionally behind them, and she nodded at what he was asking.

Zia searched for a safe subject. "How long have you been friends with Sam?"

"Pretty much my whole life," Leo replied, easing back into his chair. He didn't seem to like being listened to either as he didn't elaborate.

Zia decided it was best to just sit tucked into his arms. There was nothing she could do to make Lan leave them alone. And they needed time alone. She wanted to help Leo guess what was going on. She needed him to. He had to know how much danger he was in.

Sighing, Leo pulled Zia closer. It made her heart beat fast enough she was sure she was going to have a heart attack. Just being in his arms felt perfect and she was committing every feeling to memory for when he was gone. She was certain she was going to get him out of the Mavkas territory and free to go home. Once they were able to talk.

Leo began to hum one of his songs from the band he was in with Sam. He didn't sing the words as that would worry every single person who could hear him. With just music, no one cared.

Zia closed her eyes as he hummed and tried to picture how her life with him should have been. She could imagine the crystal clear shores of the Siren island, and could even picture walking on the beach with Leo. He would be dressed the same as now, but without his shirt. No one wore shirts on the island. It was a tropical paradise. It was all bathing suits and sun dresses. Zia had peeked at his blue tail when he went swimming before, and she was certain it would look perfect in the beautiful shores of the island. They would be free to come and go. She could even go to land with him and attend school if she wanted. Life would be perfect. If only she wasn't stuck in with the Mavkas. There was no perfect life for them here under the sea, and she was going to make sure Leo didn't stay.

By the time lunch was done and most of the people went back to their day, Leo didn't have much time left before it would be bedtime. Zia had pulled him off to their corner, and she reassured him that they were safe again.

"And how can you be sure?" Leo asked, wanting to stand up and look around the corner. He was pretty certain there was a guy following them around, and it was a little creepy.

"I can feel the people that are watching me," she told him, "and he's not right now."

Leo lifted an eyebrow at that to show his dismay. In the night human world, when you picked a mate and bonded to them, you could feel them. She made it sound exactly like she was already taken. Leo hadn't asked, and now was feeling a bit foolish that he was feeling so much for a girl who already had someone else.

"Who is he? Lan or Chris?" Leo asked, trying not to let the jealousy seep into his voice. Of course, a girl as beautiful as Zia was already taken.

"Who is who?" she replied, looking at him with confused eyes.

At least her mate didn't mean much to her. That still didn't help Leo any, but it was nice to know. Unfortunately, mating bonds were for life, and it was likely his life would be much shorter than anyone else's.

Maybe that was why Leo found himself caring so much. He had a few last days before he had to face Longray, and he had hoped he could just spend them with Zia, forgetting about his coming punishment. Mate or not, she was there with him now. He needed to just put it aside and enjoy the little bit of happiness he had left.

Leo didn't want to talk more about it, but Zia glared at him, waiting for an answer.

"Your mate," Leo finally told her.

"My mate?" she asked in shock, her eyes going large. "I don't have a mate!" she exclaimed and then quickly looked around the corner to see if the person following them had heard. Once satisfied they were still alone and not being eavesdropped upon she turned back to Leo. "I don't have a mate. Why would you think that?"

"You said you can feel who is watching us," Leo replied.

"It's a family thing," Zia quickly explained. "I can feel my adoptive family watching over us."

Leo looked at her and was relieved, yet confused. Her adoptive family was giving them plenty of space to be alone, yet they were keeping tabs on their conversations. Were they waiting for Leo to do something? Was it all a setup? Was that Zia's warning?

"Why would they be watching us that carefully?" Leo finally asked.

Zia opened her mouth, but nothing came out. She closed her mouth, thought something, and then tried again. But nothing came out.

"Yes or no questions, sorry," Leo told her as she had tried to answer. "Are you allowed to be alone with me?"

"Yes."

"Are they waiting for me to do something to be able to kick me out of here?"

"No."

"Is this a setup?"

Zia's eyes went wide again. She tried to speak, and no words came out. She shut her mouth in a pout, beyond frustrated. Leo couldn't get close to as mad as she was about the situation. It was obvious she wanted to tell him stuff and wasn't able to.

"Are you being forced to spend time with me?" Leo really didn't want to know the answer, but he had to ask. With all the strangeness with Zia, that was one of the likely reasons.

"They can't force me to like you, and I'm sure they have nothing to do with the connection between us." At least she could tell him that, even if Leo was now staring at her in shock instead of the other way around.

"You feel it, too?" he asked in a whisper, like he had heard her wrong and didn't want it to be untrue.

"And that's why you have to leave," she replied, not hiding the sadness in her voice. "They will…" Her words were gone again. It was like once she thought a thought, then she couldn't say it.

"They will do what?" Leo asked desperately. The game of yes and no wasn't getting him anywhere fast. "They will punish you?"

"No."

"They will punish me?"

"No." Zia looked as frustrated as Leo felt. "Let's try this. I will describe something else and see if you can get the word you need."

Thinking for a moment at what she said, Leo nodded. He didn't have any suggestions. He wasn't sure it would work, but it was better than doing nothing.

"When you go to school and pick up a pencil to write with, how would you tell someone to do that?"

"Write with your pencil?"

"No. Try another word for write."

"I don't know." Leo stared at her expectant face. She was trying, and he had to also. "Use your pencil."

Zia grinned. "That's it."

Leo waited and thought a second and put it back into the conversation they were just having about the Mavkas trying doing something to Zia if they knew about the connection. "They will use us?"

"Yes."

"Then I need to take you out of here."

Leo was certain that was his mission. If the Mavkas were following her around, monitoring her every move to use her, then he would have to free her. She had nothing tying her to the Mavkas. Mer law was simple: if you wanted to join another clan, you could. Most of the time the clans didn't mix, but Sam would keep her safe. That was the thing about Sam. He didn't specifically like being a Siren, but he cared for all mer.

"Be my mate, and then you can get out of here," Leo blurted out without any grace whatsoever.

Zia smiled, but then it turned to a frown. Tears began to well up in her eyes as she quickly stood and hurried back to the chairs. Leo followed her to find that she was already crawling across the chairs to leave. He had to follow that way also to not disclose her secret spot.

"I can't," she told him before running away.

Leo wanted to chase her, but stood there in shock instead as he watched her run away. The man he had suspected of following them stood up from the opposite side of the room and walked after Zia, but not without first glancing at Leo.

Staring after the girl of his dreams, Leo was confused. She seemed like she liked him, but she wanted him to leave. She admitted she felt the connection, too. He thought she would be happy that he would take her with him, but instead, she ran away. It made no sense. And now he had to go back and explain it to Sam. They were supposed to be looking for something, but he had a feeling it wasn't a mate. He hadn't done any searching of anything, and they only had days left. Sam wasn't going to be happy.

CHAPTER 7

Sam stared at his friend in shock. Part of the whole reason they wanted to leave the Siren was because neither one of them wanted a mate. It was hard to believe Leo asked the Mavkas girl he had known for less than three days to be his. Sam hadn't been expecting that.

"Let's try that again," Sam said, needing clarification. He held out his hand to make the blood connection between them.

Leo gripped his hand like they were going to arm wrestle as he stood face-to-face with Sam.

'I can't explain it, Sam. There's just something about her. From the first time I saw her, I felt it. Really, there isn't anything more I can give you on that.'

'And because you felt this, you want to be her mate and bring her back to the Siren even though you're facing death if we don't get our act in gear and find what my father is looking for?'

Sighing, Leo looked at his friend. Sam had no idea what Leo was thinking. He was supposed to be searching for something to save his life, not chasing a girl around. While it was technically allowed, the mer clans didn't mix. Leo was in enough trouble as it was, Sam was certain his father wouldn't be happy to take on a Mavkas mer. He'd see her as a spy.

'Once I bind myself to her, she will be considered a Siren. Your father would have to accept her.'

Sam wasn't certain of that.

'Didn't you say she ran off? I'd take that as a no.'

Leo shrugged.

Breaking the connection, Sam walked back to the clear wall looking out into the dark ocean. Sam had nothing. There was no evidence in Min's office, and there was nothing suspicious about anything in the Mavkas world. In fact, there was very little to the place at all. It was possible whatever he was searching for was outside. Sam planned to spend the next day exploring the area beyond the pods, but that was going to be hard with all the mer swimming around. They seemed to either fear, or be transfixed by, his blue tail. He wasn't going to be able to snoop too much.

"We aren't done," Leo told Sam from behind him.

Turning around, Sam raised an eyebrow at his friend. Leo wasn't typically assertive ... like ever. That alone made Sam hold out his hand for him. Leo took it, making their silent connection return.

'There's magic on Zia. She can't tell me what she thinks freely. She's being forced to hide a secret.'

Now *that* Sam could work with. Hiding secrets was enough of a lead that maybe he could back Leo's crazy idea.

'How can you be certain she isn't just dragging you along like I am with Cate?'

'They are following her around to make sure she does what they want. You can't tell me that if someone was in on it that they would need to do that.'

111

Leo did have a point there.

'And it doesn't add up,' Leo continued. *'Something makes her different than the rest of them. I didn't see it before, but I'm beginning to see it now. She doesn't act like them.'*

'Like how?'

Sam needed more information. Leo was already looking at punishment from Sam's father—he knew adding a mate wasn't going to make much of a difference there—but Sam still needed to know more. Leo was his friend, and more than anything Sam wanted to keep him safe, but he also wanted him to be happy. Leo was certain it was his last few days alive. If chasing after his dream girl would make him happy, Sam kind of had to go along with it. But if Leo had more information that could save them, Sam wanted to know that, too.

'She knows about the outside world. She talked about being in school and using a pencil. Do you see those around here? And she called this place an apartment. How does she know what one of those are? She's had to have been outside this place. She told me she was adopted by Min and his family when hers was gone, but she never said where they went.'

Leo was making lots of good points. All of that would make Sam question everything from her also, but if Leo was correct in that she was unable to answer questions, how could they find out more?

'I know you don't get it. But, Sam ... I have to save her. I need to save her. I know that my time is limited. Your father sent us here as torture for my final week alive. I get it. But I can't just let her stay here. She's in trouble. I just know. We need to save her and take her with us. If I bind to her, then we can do that. The Mavkas can't keep her because the Siren are

higher up. She would be free to come with us.'

Sam nodded but wasn't completely convinced. He was pretty certain Min's daughter, Cate, was sure that Sam was going to want to bind to her, too. However, he had no intention of doing that ever. Every time Cate mentioned binding, Sam just played along. What if that was the case with Leo? Sam had met Zia only once. He wasn't certain she could be trusted, or if she was just playing Leo. They needed more information.

'*We can't rush this*—' Sam began before Leo cut him off.

'*Rush this? We only have four days left.'*

'*We can't be sure her intentions are good.*' Sam held up his free hand to get Leo to not interrupt again. '*I get that you feel something. It isn't that I don't trust you. But we need to be sure she isn't just trying to trick you. We have to be able to talk to her before you do something crazy like bind to a mer of a different clan.'*

'*I told you, she can't talk about it, and doing a yes and no game takes forever. We don't have time to get the whole story.'*

'*She can't talk out loud but what about like we are talking now. Can't you try that first?'*

Leo nodded. '*I can do that. But once I confirm that she isn't a spy sent to ruin us, can I please ask to be her mate? I have like four more days to live, at least let me live them out happily.'*

Sam nodded, releasing his friend's hand. If she wasn't a spy, he couldn't deny Leo a bit of happiness, but Sam wasn't going to quit looking for something. With a mate or not, Sam was going to save Leo. He was his friend, and he wasn't giving up.

Leo walked to breakfast alone the next day. Upon waking, Sam decided to forgo breakfast and search the area outside. Sam was convinced there was something to find, even if Leo thought it was a lost cause. He did offer to go with Sam, but he said it was better for Leo to meet up with Zia.

The breakfast area was already full with people when Leo arrived. There were way more gathered than the day before, and it was probably good that Sam was using the time to look outside. It seemed possible that all of the Mavkas were inside. Leo joined the back of the line, waiting for the food as he casually observed the people. Zia's light green hair wasn't anywhere to be found.

Making it to the front of the line, Leo was disappointed she wasn't there to help him figure out what every food was. He kept glancing up for her every few moments, hoping he hadn't scared her away permanently. Without a clue as to what any of the foods were, Leo took a piece of everything. He'd try it all since he found out that some of the stuff tasted like real food. Now if only his new female friend would show up, she could tell him ahead of time what everything was.

Leo found a table and took the corner seat to himself. All around him groups of people sat together talking. Leo stared at his food, but listened. Since he remembered what silence sounded like, he was a little bit interested in the voices around him. Leo glanced around as he searched for the voices of the people he heard the clearest. It was a shrill female voice and a much softer one. Next to him were two groups that included males who were talking. He wasn't focusing on their conversations. Casually, Leo looked around the room again. It took several glances, but he found the pair of girls. When he glanced a second time, he could make out exactly which one was which. It was strange to find the clearest conversation he heard was from someone sitting three tables away, and at least another ten feet away beyond that. Zia and Sam were both right about the acoustics in this place. He'd never given it a second thought.

"This seat taken?" Zia asked as she magically showed up at Leo's empty table.

Leo shrugged. "Well, I was planning to save it for my dozen friends, but it seems none of them got the invitation." Leo smiled at Zia when her face broke into a smile, and she laughed. It was the first time he had heard her laugh, and he was already racking his brain for a good joke to tell her just to get her to do it again.

"Are you getting used to the sand beds?" Zia asked as she sat down next to him.

"I don't think anyone can truly get used to sleeping on sand. It just gets stuck in all the wrong places." And that was the truth. Leo had accidentally slid his head off the blanket he slept on the night before and woke with sand plastered to his skull.

"Oh, you get used to it," Zia told him.

"Like you?"

"Like everyone around here," Zia replied as though she didn't understand what he was trying to get her to admit to. "Are you up for a tour outside the pod today?"

He had expected to pull her back to the quiet alcove and tell her his plan, have her show him the answers he needed to reassure Sam. Now instead she wanted to leave the pod to go where they couldn't speak, but just swim around. Yes, Leo needed to hydrate his fin, but it was still weird. She didn't hint at wanting to talk to him.

"I was hoping we could just hang around today like *yesterday*."

Zia looked at him like she was lost. "Well it would be strange to give you a second tour of this place, but if that's what you want …"

Leo glanced around the room, specifically to where those two girls had been seated that he could hear. There had to be someone there listening in on them. To his surprise, no one was there. The girls were gone, and no one else sat at the table. Leo glanced around the room. There was no one paying attention to Leo and Zia as they talked, and the guy from the day before was gone.

"Is there someone else?" Leo asked, knowing Zia would understand what he was saying as he scanned around.

"You'd like someone else to give you a tour?" Zia suggested.

Now it was getting frustrating. She said she was the only Zia here and he knew he was with the same girl, but it was feeling like someone had taken away the Zia he had spent the day with previously. Leo watched her as she ate. When she smiled back at him, the smile didn't reach her eyes, and he scanned around the room again. People were clearing out, but he still didn't see anyone watching them.

"I wasn't looking for a new tour guide," Leo replied.

"So we can go for a swim?"

Leo didn't know how to answer. He really needed to get her alone to talk, but that didn't seem to be something she wanted to do. He'd have to play her game for now.

"Sure. Let's go for a swim."

Zia let Leo go first into the water, and he barely had enough time to turn around before she was zooming out of the pod and beside him. It turned out that swimming wasn't that bad of an idea. Like all mer, Siren needed the water as much as they needed blood, and Zia could see the relief on Leo as she dashed by him. Her orange tailed glowed in the water like the few Mavkas who were also enjoying the water courtyard, but his tail was the perfect shade of blue. She had wanted to see it since she had first met him and was completely right in that it was perfect like Leo. Pointing down, Zia waved for Leo to follow.

Leading the way around the courtyard, Zia stopped to point out the various edges of everything. She hoped he was paying close attention. They weren't kidding about being swept off to sea if you accidentally left the pod. When she was finally sure he would be safe, Zia made her way back to the center of the area. There were actual seats, which weren't on the floor like inside, and people sat around like usual. Zia typically only came out to refresh her tail; it was the first time for her to just sit. Leo followed and sat beside Zia. It was strange for the both of them. Zia found it easier to just glance around rather than stare at the mer beside her. Her feelings for him were only growing now that she had seen his night human side.

After lounging around for a while, Leo glanced over at Zia, who he had been doing his best to avoid looking at. She pretended not to notice as he now watched her instead of watching the various mer as the played around out in the water, or the ones that were doing their daily work.

Zia was content to sit around, but she felt the pull in her mind. Lan was going to be outside soon and staring at them. She was sure to finally be punished if he saw her not making progress. Zia tapped Leo's hand to get his attention off the world around him that he diligently stared at the moment she turned to him. She motioned for him to follow, and they went back inside. Leo went first again. Zia came in right behind him and accidentally bumped into him.

"What'd you think?" she asked

"Different than I'm used to. You weren't kidding about being caught if you left the barrier," he added.

No, she wasn't kidding, and it was good to see her tour had made a point.

Zia nodded as they walked back to the main area. Lan was still gone, but she was sure he wasn't far away. He was like a puppy who follows you around constantly. Zia had wanted a puppy as a child, but she sure didn't now. When she moved to sit at one of the tables, Leo ignored her and walked to the alcove outside of the main room. He sat down in one of the low chairs out of her view. Zia wasn't sure what to do. He seemed mad at her. She had a feeling it was because she was trying not to be alone with him. Every moment alone led to her wanting more from him. It was a dangerous game. He needed to be able to leave when the time came, and if she let her feelings out, he would get caught just as she did.

"It's a great view, but I figured you would be sick of the water after spending an hour outside," Zia commented as she came around and sat down beside Leo.

Leo shrugged.

Rolling off the chair perfectly to stay hidden, Leo made his way back to the secret spot. Zia remained in her chair. She had to stay strong and keep him away from her. They were way too close. His words would be hidden from anyone trying to spy on them. She remained where she was.

"I don't know why you're acting like you are, but I need to say something."

Zia didn't move from her spot. She stared straight ahead, trying to keep her face from his view.

"I can't give you a reason why, but I know we're meant to be together. I get that Siren and Mavkas aren't supposed to be mates. I get that we're supposed to stay within our clans. But that doesn't matter to me. I never wanted a mate in the first place, but there's something about you. I can't stop searching for you in this place. I can't stop wondering if you're okay and what you're so scared of. And I can't stop caring. I want to. I don't want to bring someone into my messed-up life. I don't want to tell you that I'm falling for you days before I'll likely be executed. I don't want any of that, but I want you. I can't stop it, and I can no longer keep pretending you're just some girl showing me around this place."

Zia had left her chair and was in front of him. Without a second chance to speak, she leaned forward and kissed him. Leo was slightly stunned but quickly gained his composure to kiss her back. All too soon she had to pull back from him. It was a mistake to do that, but she couldn't help it. He didn't understand at all. He wasn't the problem; she was.

"I get it," she said quietly. "I didn't want to fall for you either. And I get that this can't be."

Zia let Leo pull her back to sitting beside him, tucked under his arm. She was only going to get a moment with him and she'd savor it for the rest of her life. There was no way she was getting free of the Mavkas, no matter how much Leo liked her. She couldn't tell him the truth, and therefore she was stuck, but she surely wasn't going to let him get stuck, too. She was going to keep him safe.

"You talk about not wanting me to have your fate, but I promise you the fate associated with me is much worse. I wish I could tell you more. I really do." Zia gazed up at him with her big, sad eyes.

"I know you can't talk to me, but I have a different idea. Do you trust me?"

Zia nodded. She didn't just trust him, she was pretty sure she loved him. That was what made it hard.

Leo took her hand and placed a finger into his mouth. Using his sharp night human teeth that he normally used only to feed on day humans, he poked a hole in her finger. Zia hadn't been expecting that, but she waited. Then, still holding her hand to his mouth, Leo cut along his own finger, being careful not to spill any blood before pressing his own cut to hers. Zia really hadn't expected that. They were in a place filled with night humans and blood would draw everyone to them. He had expertly kept it a secret as he made a blood connection between them.

Zia's eyes widened in surprise when she felt him in her head.

Leo waited for Zia to yell at him, but she didn't. She continued to stare at him. He smiled as he felt her inside his own mind. There was so much he wished he could share with her, but he was afraid she would bolt again. It was better to make use of his time for what he needed.

'I wanted to be able to talk to you, and since you said you can't tell me what is going on, Sam and I thought you might be able to show me,' Leo explained, worried since she hadn't said anything.

'This might work,' Zia replied. *'I don't know why I didn't think of it.'*

Because you were too busy acting weird, Leo wanted to say, but kept his mouth shut. Unfortunately, his mind wasn't shut, and a hurt expression crossed Zia's face. Leo immediately felt bad for thinking it.

'Sorry.'

Zia shrugged. *'I'll show you what I can't tell you if you promise one thing,'* she told him. Leo nodded. *'You won't get mad at me or anyone else involved. Anger won't make it better. My fate is my fate, and it can't be changed. I've accepted it, so I need you to also.'*

Leo raised an eyebrow. What was she keeping from him? Why would he get mad?

'*Promise?*' she asked a second time.

'*I promise not to get mad,*' Leo replied.

'*Okay,*' was her tentative reply.

Leo waited as patiently as he could. She was acting strange, but not the sort of strange that might make him mad. Strange enough that it piqued his curiosity. Before he wanted to know what she was hiding, but now he *needed* to know.

Leo watched Zia remember her past.

Zia was swimming. That was how most mer stories started; nothing strange there. Breaking the surface of the ocean, she giggled at the sunlight. Not typical of the Mavkas, but still not strange. She turned around and smiled at the Mavkas, Lan, who seemed to be her constant shadow for the entire time Leo had been there. Dipping under the water, Lan pulled her down into his arms. Zia watched him smile as he leaned into kiss her.

Pulling back from the memory, he glared at Zia. '*If this is a story about you falling in love, I'd rather not see it.*'

Zia shook her head vehemently. '*I didn't fall in love. I thought I had, but it was all a trick. Lan tricked me. Because I didn't understand what love felt like, I fell for it. I knew the moment I was trapped here, but by then it was too late.*' Zia froze as she stared at Leo. '*I can tell you. My words aren't stopped in my head. Their power doesn't work in here. I can tell you everything.*'

Leo hadn't been expecting that. His problem had been solved the moment he had connected with her and had wasted precious minutes watching something he didn't need to see.

'So tell me the truth. Why can't I be with you? Why are Sam and I in danger? Why the heck do you like me one moment and hate me the next?'

Zia grinned at him. 'I'll tell you everything, but can we make it back to the chairs without breaking the connection? I feel Lan heading this direction.'

Leo made a sour face at the mention of the mer he had just seen about to kiss her.

"Come on," she said out loud to get his attention, and it worked. Her voice was softer outside their heads, and it melted Leo's heart. He wanted to know more. She was ready to give him answers; there was no way he was breaking the connection now.

A little clumsier than Leo wanted, they both made it back to the chairs facing the ocean. Leo kept his free arm wrapped around her, holding her in place so that she couldn't bolt and stop the story he was desperate to hear. He wanted answers, and he wasn't letting her slip away.

'Last year when I was sixteen, I was dropped off by my parents to find my way home like all the Siren do,' Zia began.

'Wait, what do you mean "like all the Siren do"?'

'No questions until I'm done,' Zia replied as she shook a finger at him for interrupting him.

Sighing, he let her continue.

'I was dropped off not too far from home, but got mixed up in my directions. Instead of heading south west, I went south east. I didn't notice for quite some time, and when I finally did, I was far from home without food, drink, or blood and was completely lost as to what to do. That's when I met Lan. He brought me back here and got me all situated and promised to *return me home. I was the first outsider who had come to the Mavkas home in decades. It was like I was a celebrity. I needed to get home, but was a little mad that my parents hadn't left me where they said I'd be. I decided to take a couple days and enjoy the Mavkas.'*

'*Just answer this,*' Leo said, finally interrupting her. '*Are you a Siren?*' She had an orange tail, but her story was making him think otherwise.

'*I was a Siren coming of age,*' Zia replied. '*And I was foolish enough to think the feeling I felt growing for Lan was love. In two short days, he convinced me to make a blood oath with him that I'd come back. He said we couldn't bind without permission from our clans, but it would be like a binding. We would be connected. He said I was everything to him, and I believed him. Turns out that the Mavkas keep witch-enchanted objects on hand. Lan was busy making me feel things that weren't true just to get me to do the blood oath. On the day I was to go home, it all changed. Everything inside of me felt like it was off, but I did it anyway. I made the blood oath, but didn't know that by making it I was cursing myself to stay here forever. That blood oath was just a plan to keep me.'*

'*Keep you?*' It wasn't making a lot of sense, but Leo was getting a little angry.

'*You promised to keep your cool. Remember?*'

Clenching his teeth, he nodded. Zia wasn't an object to keep. She was a person.

'*The spell changed my outer appearance to a Mavkas so no one would be able to know it was me. But I still have my Siren voice. The magic around here makes it duller, but I can control people to some extent. Unfortunately, the blood oath bound me to Lan's family; they aren't affected by my voice. Lan acts like we are bonded, but we aren't. There's no love between us.'*

Leo was having a hard time wrapping his head around everything. Zia wasn't a Mavkas, and she wasn't forbidden to him. She was a Siren. From what he had felt in the last couple days, Leo was certain she was *his* Siren. She was meant to be with him and not caught in the underwater world of the Mavkas.

'I can't leave. They bound me to them and can find me anywhere I go. With an orange tail, all the mer will think I'm crazy if I tell the truth if they find me. I'm stuck here for life, and they want me to get you and Sam stuck here, too. The Mavkas don't want to be beneath the Siren; they want to lead the mer world. They think Sam is the perfect way to do that. They don't tell me the details, but I know what they want. They've all done a great job acting these past few days, but the Mavkas hate Siren.'

And that was exactly what King Longray was looking for. The Mavkas were proving to be a problem for the Siren and had gone so far as to have kidnapped one. Leo needed to tell Sam, and they had to figure everything out. There was no way Leo was leaving Zia behind in the Mavkas world.

CHAPTER 8

Sam wasn't one for going through someone else's memories, but he had done so today for a second time. Even worse was he was going through someone else's memories that had been given to another. Leo said Zia was fine with him doing it, but Sam still felt a bit creepy. His father loved to see what he could find, but Sam strongly believed your mind should be your own.

After analyzing Zia's exact memories three times—which Sam was now grateful that she had shown Leo—Sam was starting to form a plan. He had very little experience with witch magic, and didn't know anyone firsthand who dealt with witches, but he wasn't about to let that stop him from trying to get Zia back to the Siren clan. The one thing Sam did know was that magic couldn't trump a bond of real love.

Sam had little hope left of finding a way to save his friend from his father's wrath. He had searched the whole outside area of the Mavkas, and there really wasn't much to search. He spent the whole day in the water looking around. It just about drove Cate nuts to have to wait for him, but Sam really didn't care about that. She lost her usefulness when he didn't find anything in her father's office. Yes, maybe it was a bit cruel, but he really had no intention of pursuing things with her. And now he felt less bad about it. She was likely trying to trap

Sam in the same way as they had Zia.

From what he could tell, Zia was trapped by some sort of blood bond. It wasn't the same as the mate bond that Sam had witnessed several times with the Siren, but something different. As he could see, it involved the same blood sharing, but it didn't link the people as one. He wasn't completely sure how it happened, but one thing he took notice of was the knife they used. Beyond the knife, it was a simple blood share, really as uncomplicated as talking to another night human in their mind.

Night humans were all equipped with sharp teeth to feed on normal humans. They rarely had a need for a knife unless doing something ceremonial. Zia likely just thought it was a ceremonial knife, but Sam figured it had to be the key.

After sleeping on everything, Sam came up with a plan. He would make the most of his time left with the Mavkas and make sure there was nothing else to find, but he was happy to have what he had. It might be enough to convince his father to leave Leo alive. Now he just had to be certain his plan would work. What better way to check it out than to use Cate one more time? Now that he knew he was the target, he knew he could get away with doing more. He was willing to play with them a bit to get what he needed.

Sam nodded to Leo as his friend left. He was positive his plan was going to work, but even if it didn't, Sam was free to go home and inform his father about everything. Leo already assured him that if he got stuck in the Mavkas home, he wasn't going to be sad about it. He would have

Zia, and that was all that mattered to him. Sam couldn't quite understand his reasoning. His friend had always had a bigger issue with having a mate than Sam did, but he knew that Zia was the reason. She was what would keep Leo safe and alive as a Siren. He was willing to believe Leo, even if he was crazy.

Though Sam couldn't understand Leo's new feelings, he did understand Zia. She was a Siren. She needed to go home where she belonged, and it was Sam's duty to bring her back. It was considered weak to not make it home after your coming of age ceremony, but they never factored in another clan taking you away. It wasn't her fault, and Sam was sure she would be welcomed back.

Ready to do his part, Sam stood and stretched. It was going to be a day of deception, but he was ready to play the game to get his friend and the lost Siren home.

Leo ate breakfast beside Zia, and she talked like nothing else was the matter. How she had acted on and off the days before didn't annoy him now that he knew she was trying to protect him. He found it sweet because he understood better now that her moods mirrored the stress of the people around her. Lan was off at the far table where he could listen in on their conversation. Nothing like tricking a girl and then keeping tabs on her. Just seeing the other mer made Leo want to punch him in the face.

"Remember, you promised," Zia said lightly, picking up on the anger Leo had.

"And I wish I hadn't," Leo replied as he stabbed his

food forcefully, causing the fork to clink on the plate.

"And I wouldn't do that unless you like sand in your food," Zia advised, pointing to the food he had stabbed too hard.

The plates were ceramic-like but made of something more like coral. Of course, Zia was right, and small shards of the plate were in his food now. Leo wiped off his food and continued to eat, trying his best to ignore Lan. It was hard to do until Zia reached over and took his hand in hers. His whole world stopped at her touch. That was exactly the distraction he needed.

"How do you want to spend today?" she asked.

Leo slowly chewed his last piece of food while he thought. He really wanted to just go to their secret corner, but he knew it wasn't an option. Lan was keeping closer tabs every day as the week went on. The first day Zia dragged him off, they had all morning together without Lan interrupting. Yesterday they talked for only minutes before he was ready to check on them. Leo worried that he knew something was up.

"What do you suggest?"

Zia smiled. "I think we should go for a swim again."

Leo nodded. That worked for him. Less talking meant it was less likely for them to get caught. And pulling Lan outside was better. Sam claimed he had a plan, but needed to double check everything. Chris wasn't a problem, but Lan seemed to be the one who was the most suspicious. Taking him outside would work well to keep Sam safe, too.

"I could use a swim. Siren never get sick of being in the water," Leo told her.

Zia smiled as she understood that he was including her in his statement. "Then let's go swimming."

Swimming was the perfect distraction for Leo. He needed to wait until Sam had everything set up before they could do anything anyway. His friend was off using his Siren voice on Cate to find out the few details they didn't get from Zia. Sam was certain the knife was the key, but they had to be sure there wasn't something else as well. Though it was hard to persuade someone with their Siren voice if other people could hear, Sam was getting information out of Cate already. He was pretty good at what he did. Leo didn't have the same level of control, and he admired how strong Sam was, but then again, that was the reason the Mavkas wanted Sam.

By the time they finished swimming, it was already time for lunch. Leo and Zia returned to a full room of Mavkas. Leo searched around for Sam and got a nod from him. Everything was a go to put their plan into action. Reaching out, Leo took Zia's hand. She looked surprised.

Without asking her or telling her a thing, Leo marched over to where Min was seated on the floor, bringing her with him.

"Since you're Zia's family now," Leo began as Zia still watched, uncertain if she should stick around, "tradition states that a Siren must pick a mate before they are eighteen. I'll be eighteen next year, so I want to ask permission to have Zia as my mate. I know that inter clan mates aren't always allowed, but I believe King Longray would be happy I finally found someone to bind to. He's a fair and kind king, and Sam assures me that his father would welcome Zia with open arms."

With Siren being the higher tier clan in the mer world, Zia would move to live with Leo. While Sam was certain that the Mavkas didn't have any intention of letting Zia go, he did think that they would jump at the chance to use a mating bond to trick Leo into becoming a Mavkas.

Min grinned at Leo as he stood.

"What a great honor you offer her," Min proclaimed. The whole room silenced to listen in on their conversation now. "My own sons haven't chosen mates yet. I can assure you King Longray will be happy at your choice."

As Sam suspected, Min was graciously taking the news. Leo didn't even glance at the hand clasped in his own. He was sure Zia wasn't going to take the news well. They didn't have time to tell her about the plan and the slight risk that binding might transfer the magic to Leo. He was fine taking the risk. If they didn't get Zia home to the Siren, Leo wouldn't have a life to live anyway. Now he just needed to get her to see that. Zia squeezed his hand tighter.

"We would love for our little Zia to be taken care of by the Siren. It's a great honor you offer her, right, Zia?" Min directed his gaze at Zia, and Leo finally looked down at her by his side.

"Yes, a great honor," she replied, her voice dead and there were tears pricking at the corner of her eyes.

"Good. Then let's do this all tomorrow since the boys only have two days left here. We don't want to make him come back. Do you think your father would mind if I was the one overseeing the mating?" Min asked Sam.

"I can go ask him, but I'm sure he will agree that it works best this way so that we don't have to come back," Sam agreed with the older man.

"Then it's settled. We will celebrate the mating of my adopted daughter, Zia, to Leo of the Siren clan tomorrow," Min told the room. Cheers erupted around them.

Zia dropped Leo's hand before leaning in close to him.

"I have to go," she said, her voice on the verge of crying.

Leo wanted to say something, or at least chase her, but Min was already moving and making a seat next to him as he waved Leo to sit down.

"Girls always get nervous about this stuff. They want everything to be perfect and feel like if they can't plan it out for months that it won't be what they dreamt. Don't worry about Zia. I'm sure she's just stressing about everything," Min explained.

Leo looked across the way at Sam. Smiling, he nodded like Min was correct. Leo wished that he could have told Zia, but he was pretty sure she wouldn't like their plan. She didn't seem to truly understand that his life was over if they came back without proof of something going on with the Mavkas. She still clung to the thought that Leo would be forgiven for wanting to leave. What she didn't seem to get was that Leo would certainly not stick around the Siren now. He wasn't going to bind to anyone when he turned eighteen unless it was Zia.

Zia spent the remainder of the day without Leo. At first, she ran because she was going to cry. She had no explanation for Leo or Min on why she was crying, or at least one that she could speak aloud. Then, when she was finally composed enough to go back and see him, the plans for the binding were already in order. Zia was forced to sit through a manicure, a haircut, eyebrow plucking, and a pedicure which was pretty pointless because the ceremony would be in the courtyard, and she'd have no feet. Zia tolerated it all, just waiting for a moment to find Leo.

With all the planning and prepping, Zia didn't get a chance to see him before she went to sleep for the night. And sleeping was a hard thing to do while her mind kept racing, trying to find a way to get him out of it. There was no reason for Leo to be trapped as a slave to the Mavkas, too. Already Zia had been forced to make dozens of Mavkas bend to Min's will. She was sure Leo would be in the same boat. He would become a servant to the Mavkas leader alongside her.

Zia couldn't condemn Leo to the life of a Mavkas. They didn't seem to mind communal living and never seeing the sun, but Leo was a Siren as Zia had been. He would miss the sun and swimming freely. The small courtyard was nothing compared to the whole ocean. While the mer clans kept to their own waters, Siren were the highest-ranking clan and could go anywhere. Now she was in a cage.

When morning finally came, and the mer all started their day, Zia was free to walk around. She had only hours to get Leo to leave, and she planned to do just that, even if she had to be mean to him.

It was easy to find Leo. He was staring at the breakfast buffet, just as he had every morning. This was one more thing she didn't need to force on him—the weird, limited Mavkas food. Zia missed the Siren island—every last part of it, even the boring, bland vegetables that she couldn't eat now.

Zia planned to march up to Leo and tell him she refused to bond to him, but watching him poke each item before deciding what to eat was too cute. It made her smile instead.

"They only save the live food for dinner, not breakfast, right? People are never awake enough in the morning to have to fight their food to eat it," Zia teased.

"You shouldn't ever have to fight your food," Leo replied as he went to grab a spoon.

Reaching forward, Zia stopped him. "Not that one. I don't know if it's animal or vegetable, but it tastes like it came from a toilet," she added. Leo pulled back at that comment and Zia took her hand in his. "You can't do this."

Leo turned, smiling at her. "Yes, you're right. I can't eat food if it's that bad." He pretended like he didn't know what she was talking about.

"Le-O." She made his name into two syllables to emphasise that she knew he was avoiding the real topic.

Reaching up, Leo brushed back the stray hairs that fell around her face now as she couldn't fit them in the lose ponytail at the base of her neck. Zia froze as his thumb touched her cheek.

"Let's have breakfast, and we can talk later," Leo

suggested.

Zia wanted to say no to him, but her stomach rumbling reminded her that she didn't eat the night before. She had been too upset to eat anything.

Grabbing a plate, Zia quickly added food to it to keep up with Leo. She had to be sure he remembered not to eat the gray-and-red-colored one. It really did taste horrible.

Zia found the meal was exactly what she needed. It wasn't just that she was hungry, but listening to Leo talk about his life on the Siren island and growing up with Sam was calming to her. Studying him as he talked, she found that he was confident and relaxed even though she had told him the day before that the Mavkas planned to bind him to her to make him stay. Zia tried to figure out why he was so calm, but his story made her laugh again. She had to cover her mouth so food didn't fall out. Leo and Sam had been quite the children. She had grown up a Siren, but she had lived on the other side of the island from where Sam and Leo had been.

The meal was finished, and Leo led the way to their little alcove. That was exactly what Zia was thinking, too, and she didn't wait to pull him back to her spot.

"What the heck are you thinking?" she asked, trying to keep the anger out of her voice.

Leo smiled at her anger and just leaned down to kiss her instead. Zia momentarily forgot she was angry and kissed him back. She was going to miss him when he was gone.

Pulling back triumphantly, Leo smiled at Zia.

"We have a plan," Leo said.

Of course, they had a plan, but neither Leo nor Sam had run it past her first. They didn't know the Mavkas like she did. They could easily be making a mistake.

"I showed Sam the memory of how you were turned by magic. He used his voice to question Cate and get answers from her. He said the plan will work, and we just need to follow the steps exactly." Leo wrapped his arms around Zia to hold her close.

She wasn't falling for his distraction this time.

"How about you tell me the plan, and I can tell you if it will work," she replied, giving him her best I-mean-business eyes.

Grinning wider, Leo bent down to kiss her again. Zia turned her head to avoid the distraction that was Leo's lips.

"The plan is for you to do what we ask and trust me," Leo replied, removing a hand from her waist to allow him to turn her face toward him instead.

"Really? Trust you? Leo, you've been down here for what, five days now? You don't understand them. You don't get how much they hate you and will do everything to trap you here for their use. You don't know what it's like to be in this cage. I don't want you caught here."

Zia could feel her anger melt into tears as they gathered in her eyes. She was trying her best not to cry, but it wasn't going to work. She really needed to know Leo was off free somewhere. She couldn't keep him in the Mavkas world with her. She just couldn't.

"They will use magic to do this to you, too. They can't let you leave. You and Sam are too valuable." Zia was desperate to get Leo to understand he couldn't go through with the bonding.

Zia felt the pull of Lan close by. She wasn't finished with Leo, but she didn't want Lan to know about her quiet corner.

"We have to go back and sit down."

Leo nodded and led the way back to the two seats facing the ocean.

"Zia, you need to get ready," Lan said from the doorway to the outer room.

Zia sighed. She wasn't done with Leo, but she was being pulled away. Regretfully, she stood to follow Lan. Leo stopped her before she was too far and pulled her in for one more kiss, surprising her. Leo laughed as she pulled back and hurried past him.

"Can't wait to see you in a few hours," Leo called to her as he made his way to the hallway where his room was.

Zia could wait. In fact, she was thinking about how she was going to refuse to do the bonding. Leo would be hurt, but he would be safe. That was all that mattered. Maybe she would even have to push him out of the Mavkas home. He had said Sam was excellent with directions and finding his way home. Zia kept her thoughts to herself as Lan waited for her.

Lan led the way to the first hallway where Min's family lived. He walked past the outer waiting room and over to Min's office. Zia wasn't surprised to find her *adoptive* father sitting there with his maps. He had been obsessing about the ocean as long as she had been there. Every once in a while she had heard him mumble about territories that should be split between different clans, but she had no idea what he was up to.

"Oh great, my daughter, Zia," Min said as she followed behind Lan.

The way he said daughter gave Zia the creeps. There was nothing about their relationship that was anything like father and daughter. He was the man who had planned and orchestrated her kidnapping. He wasn't her father.

"You, my dear, seem a little worried about today. Don't be. Soon you'll have a mate and be a happy little mer. I can't wait to see if your babies will need to be converted or if the magic will transfer to them also."

Zia had told Leo there was one dead spot in the whole pod, but she had left out the second one. No one coming near would hear a word Min said as he spoke freely. Unfortunately, the magic that made her a mer bound her to him, and he forbade her to speak anything that was said within the room either.

"I won't do it," Zia replied. "You can't force him to stay here. He's a Siren and free to leave."

Min smiled at her. "He won't leave you. I've seen how that boy looks at you. He wants to be your mate. And you don't get to refuse. You won't stop this ceremony, do you understand? My word is final."

Zia glared at him. She had no control to go against his word. Her last-ditch plan of pushing Leo and Sam out to sea wouldn't work now. Without waiting for him to say more, Zia turned on her heel and marched out of his office. It was likely she wouldn't be able to ask Leo to call it off now. She had lost her chance to convince him otherwise.

Standing in the silent alcove, Leo listened to his own heart pounding. His life was going to change, and even if their plan worked, his life would be forever altered. He was ready for it but nervous at the same time. He had never wanted a mate, and all he could do now was pray she wouldn't do something to screw up their plan. Leo wanted to tell her everything, but Sam forbade him to. She needed to react the way they expected, or they would be following her around closely.

Sam had assured Leo he was almost certain a real bond would break the magic, but there was always the chance that the magic would go across the bond. If that was the case, then Leo would be stuck forever in the underwater Mavkas world. Leo didn't like that idea, but he'd be stuck here with Zia. Hopefully, it wouldn't be that bad. And that was *if* the bond didn't break the magic.

The whole key to it wasn't just getting the spell broke on Zia. It was getting her out alive. Sam had been in Cate's head and found they had multiple contingency plans in place to kill her off if she were to break free. The Mavkas knew that what they were doing was big enough to start a war over. They couldn't let her leave.

And there was the problem of the knife. If that was the magical object, which as far as Cate knew it was, they needed to be sure that the Mavkas didn't get to keep it. Sam didn't have the slightest clue how magic worked, but he wasn't about to let other Siren fall into the same trap.

Zia appeared before Leo, and he took her into his

arms immediately. He had wanted to share their plan all day but couldn't. Now he was free to speak with her.

Zia opened her mouth and then shut it again. Her smile at seeing him turned into a frown.

"I've wanted to talk all day, but we didn't have time," Leo explained. Time was a better reason than keeping her in the dark on purpose. She'd know soon enough he was telling a white lie, but he didn't care.

"Please tell me you have a plan you're sure will work." Zia was finally able to speak.

Leo grinned. He was as sure as he was ever going to get. At least the next part he could wholeheartedly say he was sure about.

Taking Leo's hand, Zia tried to pull him to the chairs facing the wall of water. Leo stayed in his place. The Mavkas pod was mostly empty. They didn't need to hide.

"Cate is coming," Zia told him and tugged harder.

"Yeah, I know," Leo replied, staying where he was.

Sam stepped into the doorway.

"We have like two minutes to do this. I have Cate ready to lie to her father," Sam told Leo and Zia.

Zia peeked out at Cate. She stared straight ahead like she didn't know what was going on. "What did you do to her?"

"I made her my puppet ... just like they were going to do to Leo. She doesn't have the slightest clue what's going on. I have her ready to play her role and not remember a thing. But we need to get this show on the road before someone comes back to check on you guys."

Zia turned to Leo. "What's the plan?"

"We bind for real, and then you leave," Leo explained

as short as he could.

Zia opened her mouth to protest, but no words came out.

"I get it, it's chancy. But you have to understand, if I become a Mavkas, then I'll be alive here with you. If I leave without you, I'm a dead man."

Zia eyed him over.

"Yes. My father plans to kill Leo if we don't bring back proof that the Mavkas are up to something," Sam interjected.

"But he can't kill someone for thinking something," Zia stated, gaping at him.

Leo nodded. "Yes he can, and he will. Please trust us and do this."

Brow furrowed, Zia seemed to think it over for a moment. "Okay, let's say binding works, and you don't become a Mavkas. What do we do then?"

"You leave, and we have Cate call the alarm that you slipped and fell out that wall," Leo explained.

Zia's mouth hung open.

"I get it. Leaving through the wall means death to you. And it would if we weren't already bonded. Once we bind our lives together, I can find you anywhere. Sam and I will save you no matter where you end up."

Zia glanced at the wall of swimming fish behind them and back at the two guys standing there, waiting.

"But we don't know how to do a binding," she added.

Leo was glad to see it wasn't taking much to convince her.

"I know how," Sam replied. "You only have to drink each other's blood within a certain time frame, and if you truly love each other, it will bind you. It's that simple. The complicated stuff is to bind two people who aren't in love, and even then it isn't really a binding."

Tugging on Zia's hand, Leo pulled her closer to him. "I never wanted a mate. I never wanted to be a Siren. I never wanted to stay, but now I do. I want a life with you. I want all of that for myself as much as I want to save you. Siren aren't meant to live this way. Come home with me. Please be my mate."

Leo held his breath as he stared at the light green hair flopping on Zia's cheek. He wanted to reach down and move it, but he was frozen in place. He never considered that she could say no, but now the thought was there in his mind.

Zia tilted her head, exposing her neck. Leo was stunned.

"Um, a little faster now, buddy," Sam instructed Leo as his friend stood there, staring at Zia. "We need to get this done and out of here like yesterday."

Leo wasn't exactly sure what to do, so he pulled Zia to the seats. They needed to be in their mer form to feed on another person. After transforming, Leo pulled Zia into his lap. She seemed surprised by his fin.

"I didn't know you could transform in here," she commented. "I can't without water."

Leo smiled at her. Lots of mer needed water, which was probably why everyone was outside in the courtyard waiting for them.

"You don't need to be a mer to drink blood," Sam replied from the doorway, still waiting for them. He was a little impatient.

Leo smoothed the hair from Zia's neck. She sat absolutely still as he leaned forward and bit down. When he pulled away, Zia looked shyly at Leo as he put his own wrist to his mouth and bit down with his sharp night human teeth. He held up his bleeding wrist to Zia. Now was her chance. If she wanted to bolt, she could. Leo wasn't going to force her to mate to him.

Holding Leo's wrist, Zia's gaze seemed fixated on the blood. It was only a second, but Leo sat frozen in his spot, his heart beating as loud as it had been just moments before as he waited for her. Zia didn't make him wait any longer as she licked the blood off his arm.

Pulling back, she stared at him. *'How long does this take to work?'* she thought.

'Instantly, I guess,' he replied, grinning.

The smile that spread across Zia's face lit up her eyes. It turned out that Zia wanted forever, also. She just didn't want to see Leo get hurt in the process.

"How do we know it worked enough to break the magic?" she asked Sam without turning to look at him.

Leo already knew. Her light green locks were now a beautiful golden color, which had to be a sign that her Siren side was back.

"Did it work?" Sam asked Cate to be sure.

"Yes," she replied in a monotone. "I don't feel linked to her anymore. My family is coming to see what is going on."

"Time to leave," Leo exclaimed, turning back into his normal self.

Rising, Leo walked Zia to the wall.

"I'll find you anywhere," he told her before placing a

kiss on her forehead.

"Well, you better, buddy. If I die, you die," she told him as she poked his chest. Leo grinned.

Zia reached up to the wall and placed a hand on it. She wasn't scared in the least. Leo could feel her excitement. She had been trapped in the Mavkas world and was now a free Siren. He had to agree that was exciting. Zia slipped into the wall and transformed. Leo only caught a glimpse before the current took her away, but he saw her blue fin. She was truly back to being normal.

"Time for the rest of the plan," Sam said to Leo, distracting him from watching as Zia was pulled from their sight.

"Dad," Cate yelled as she turned and ran toward her father and older brother who were also running into the main room. "Zia fell into the wall. She was pulled out to sea!"

Turning to face Min, Leo tried to put as much anguish into his face as he could. "She was right there. I thought I could pull her back, but she wouldn't let me."

"No, son, you can't stop someone from going through the wall," Min replied. There was actual devastation in the older man's voice.

"We have to go look for her," Sam said to Min.

"No. No one who was lost that way has ever been found that," Min replied. "It's safer for you to stay here."

"I don't care about safe," Leo growled. It wasn't hard to pretend to be mad because he actually felt anger. They were ready to cast Zia off when she didn't serve a purpose. "I have to find her."

"Your father wouldn't want me to let you be in such

danger," Min commented, appealing to Sam instead.

"It can't be helped. He will understand." Sam began to march to the tunnel leading out of the pod with Leo beside him.

"Cate," Min said, trying to get his daughter to help them stay. "Cate?" Min turned around, and Cate was already gone.

"Boys, please." Min hurried to catch up with them. "It's too dangerous to go after her, and even if you do find her, you'll only get your heart broken. She's already dead. I can feel my link to her gone."

Leo stopped to glare at him. "I'm not giving up on her."

Walking over to the wall, Leo pushed his way through into the water. Sam was right behind him. Both of them shot straight up to the surface. Not too far behind was Cate. Her head broke the surface right where Leo and Sam waited.

"Here it is," she said as she handed Sam the knife.

"Good. Now remember, you forget everything you saw today. Zia fell through the wall, and there was nothing we could do to save her," Sam told her, putting Siren force behind his voice. "Now go home and pretend to be heartbroken over me, but never come looking for me again."

Cate nodded to Sam and ducked back into the water.

"Let's go find that mate of yours," Sam told Leo.

Leo nodded as he closed his eyes. He wasn't sure how it worked, but when he opened them, he knew which direction to go. He felt a tug. She was far away but waiting for him. He knew she was safe, and he was ready to go get her and take her home. Never once before in his life did Leo want a mate, but he was so happy that he had found her. She made him feel something he didn't even know was possible, and he couldn't wait to spend his life with her.

He wasn't sure how King Longray was going to react, but they had done what he asked. They found what the Mavkas were up to and even had both Zia and the knife to prove it. Sam and Leo's lives were both saved, and even though Leo had already given up, he was glad to be getting his happily ever after.

'I'm coming for you, Zia,' Leo told her across the bond.

'By the way, my Siren name is Lila.'

Leo laughed. He hadn't thought about that. She was going to keep him on his toes. He couldn't wait to find her and wrap her back in his arms where she belonged. She didn't seem to care that she was lost. All he could sense was the pure happiness of a mer in the ocean, and Leo felt it all through their bond. He had been prepared to live life isolated from the mer and was glad to not be. Leo was never going to be alone again.

EPILOGUE

It was strange for Sam to just step back into his normal life. It was like nothing had happened, and nothing had changed. Longray was so pleased at what Sam and Leo had found that he held up his side of the bargain. Leo was free, and Sam wasn't punished. Sam had a feeling it was because of Lila, which he still found strange to call her. Having a mate meant Leo had something the king could use against him.

Watching Leo and Lila talk before their swim lesson was strange. Sam knew his friend never wanted a mate, and here he was walking around and holding her hand all the time. Love changed people, but with Leo, it was instant. The guy went from being a loner to having a shadow. Sam could have been jealous, but he was happy for his friend more than anything.

Sam didn't wait for their other friend and swim instructor, Mark, to appear. He dove into the water. He would prefer his tail to legs, but being in the water was calming even without it.

They had plans to escape the mer world, but Sam was certain now his friend's plans had changed. Leo wasn't going anywhere. And now that Longray knew, he was going to be keeping better tabs on Sam. That meant, unfortunately, Sam was seeing more and more of his pain in the butt brother, Tim. His escape was going to be hard to do, but Sam wasn't giving up. He just needed to make new plans.

"How many new students do we have?" Sam asked Leo as he swam over to the edge of the pool.

"Looks like six. Two new ones for each of us," Leo replied as he finally pulled himself from Lila long enough to come over to Sam. He showed Sam the list; four girls and two guys.

"You take the first two, Mark can have the second two, and I'll take the last two," Sam suggested. It was better to divvy up the students before they arrived so that Mark couldn't complain about getting stuck with the ugly ones.

"Sounds good, boss." Leo mock saluted Sam. King Longray had decided that their trip to the Mavkas home upgraded Sam to the leader of the Siren military, second only to his father.

Sam rolled his eyes.

"I'd punish you for insubordination, but I doubt it would mean anything to you. You've been all mushy since we got back. I don't think it would have any effect." Sam nodded over to Lila. Smiling, she waved at the boys. Her Siren hearing would make her able to hear every word.

"Hey. Don't knock it until you try it," Leo replied. Lila blew him a kiss.

"Not going to happen. My father is going to have to force me to mate, and it will be a trial of wills. I just hope I'll be stronger than him."

And that was Sam's plan if he didn't get out of the mer world. He was just going to have to fight his father every step of the way. He wasn't going to get stuck with a mate, and he surely didn't plan to fall in love.

"Someday a girl is going to walk into your life, and you'll just know. You'll know she's the one for you, and you won't be able to help it. Just wait and see."

Sam nodded to his delusional friend and dipped back under the water. When he came to the surface, Mark had arrived, and six people were seated on the bleachers waiting. Sam watched Mark as Leo handed him the sheet with the names on it.

"We have you divided up between each of us. I'm going to have Mike and Sara," Leo told the people sitting there. Two people raised their hands, and Leo nodded to them.

"I have Matt and Whitney," Mark said as he looked at the list.

Sam hopped out of the pool. Two people raised their hands, and he glanced at them and froze. The girl who had been called was a blonde he hadn't seen before. She was staring at the pool and not Mark, but he was grinning as he glanced at her. He preferred his food to be pretty, and this girl was no exception.

The girl peeked up at them, and Sam's heart skipped a beat. Her crystal blue eyes locked with his, and he was hooked. He wanted to know more. Heck, he wanted to know everything about her. Who was this girl and where did she come from?

"Um, no," Sam said as he took the paper from Mark. "You get Ellen and Liz, and I get Matt and Whitney. Leo must have written it wrong." It wasn't wrong. It was exactly what he'd told his friend to do.

Mark opened his mouth to complain.

"Right, boss," Leo added before Mark could say anything.

It seemed like Mark was ready to continue complaining, but Leo's comment reminded him that Sam was in charge. While Sam really didn't want to be in charge, he was grateful to be at the moment. He had no idea why, but he needed to start his private lessons with the girl immediately. He felt crazy for wanting to know her. She was obviously just a normal human, but he was going to go with it. He wanted out of the mer world anyway, and a perfectly normal human was just what he needed.

ACKNOWLEDGEMENTS

To you, the reader. Thank You for taking the time to read this story. If you liked it, please leave a review on your favorite online bookseller (or all of them!) and connect with me social media. The greatest help you can do to keep a writer going is to support them by spreading the word about their books. Writing is a long lonely road, but knowing that someone like you is out there reading this makes it all the better.

As with every book I would like to thank my editors and cover designers. Thank you so much, Kathie at Kat's Eye Editing, Melissa at There for You Editing, and Ashton Brammer. They work so hard to get you guys the best book. A thank-you to my *AMAZING* cover artist Jessica for such a pretty cover- doesn't she do great work!! I'm beyond fortunate to have found these wonderful professionals to work with.

I'd also like to thank my hubby – who is the only reason I actually even published. He encourages me to keep going each and every day on this adventure. And he does all the behind-the-scenes effort to make this work. This would be so much harder without his help. So thank you, B. for pushing me off the deep end (or the cliff as I see it sometimes). And a great big thanks to my little munchkins who keep me going from before the sun comes up 'til long after it sets. Love you AK, KB, and EM.

Thank you so much for taking the time to read my novel!!

ABOUT B. KRISTIN McMICHAEL

Originally from Wisconsin, B. Kristin currently resides in Ohio with her husband, three small children, and two cats. A former cell biologist, she now does the mom thing of chasing kids, baking cookies, homeschooling the kids, and playing outside while writing full time. She is a fan of all YA/NA fantasy and science fiction. Find her at www.bkristinmcmichael.com and Twitter, Facebook, Instagram, and Goodreads under
B. Kristin McMichael.

BOOKS BY B KRISTIN MCMICHAEL

- To Stand Beside Her

Chalcedony Chronicles
- Carnelian
- Chrysoprase
- Aventurine
- Chrysocolla

The Night Human World series:

The Blue Eyes Trilogy (series 1)
- The Legend of the Blue Eyes
- Becoming a Legend
- Winning the Legend

The Day Human Trilogy (series 2)
- The Day Human Prince
- The Day Human King
- The Day Human Way

The Skinwalkers Witchling Trilogy (series 3)
- The Witchling's Apprentice
- The Wendigo Witchling
- The Witchling Seer

The Merworld (series 4)
- Waves and Secrets
- Water and Blood
- Songs and Fins
- Scales and Legends

The Hunter Trilogy (series 5)
- The Night Human Hunter
- The Night Human Heir
- The Night Human Siblings (coming in 2018/2019)

MIRROR-WALKER
The President's Wife Is Missing

I0452248

Mitchell Micone

MIRROR-WALKER
The President's Wife Is Missing

Fiction4All

Chapter One
"Alice Wilson"

David Malone walked carefully around his house checking that all the doors and windows were closed and properly locked. He stopped in his office, which had a separate door on the side of the brick ranch-style home, and made sure that the sign in the door window said, "Out of the office, will return at..." He turned the red plastic hands on the printed clock face to four o'clock. That should give him enough time. This was a local case. He would be back by then.

Walking back through the house toward his bedroom, he stopped and set the perimeter alarm system to 'on'. It wasn't that he was paranoid, but he was, after all, a licensed private investigator. Even limiting his practice to his unique specialty, he had upset enough people through the years to justify being careful, especially when he would be so vulnerable.

Satisfied that all was secure, he entered his bedroom, closed the blinds and then pulled the heavy curtains. After his eyes adjusted to the semi-darkness, he stripped off his clothing and stood naked before the large, bullfighter tapestry which hung from an especially large and ornate iron bar mounted on one wall of the bedroom. After taking a few deep breaths, he reached up and released a latch hidden within the iron filigree.

The bar swung open and David carefully pushed it around so the bullfighter was now facing– and covering– his closet door. Mounted on the wall behind the tacky tapestry was a huge mirror. Except it wasn't really a mirror. It was just a large sheet of automotive glass which David had ordered cut to size with slightly rounded corners. He, himself, had applied the several layers of spray paint to the back side of the glass to create the black mirror which he then carefully hung on his bedroom wall.

He relaxed and stared into the mirror, shuffling on the carpet and moving his legs slightly outward to a more stable position. His arms, seeming to move on their own, raised up and out until he was standing in a cruciform position. His body relaxed further and his breath became more and more shallow as he concentrated on looking into his own eyes.

He waited until the iris on his left eye seemed to open more fully and invite him to gaze into himself. Focusing on his own open eye, the image of the rest of himself in the mirror began to slowly dissolve and he started repeating slowly, "Angela Wilson, Angela Wilson, Angela Wilson..."

There was a pulling feeling as if he were being sucked into the black mirror and suddenly he was looking up at a bright blue sky. Green stems of reeds stuck up in front of him. Light brown cattails were swaying in a light breeze above him. The strange pulling feeling came again and he was standing on the smooth, still surface of the water.

Looking quickly around, he sought any familiar landmark or building that would tell him where he was. As he slowly turned three hundred sixty degrees, nothing was visible but trees and a vast stretch of wetlands which seemed to surround him. He could be anywhere– well, anywhere with shallow water and cattails. Then the sound of laughter caused him to turn suddenly. Three young women on bicycles raced past in the distance on what had to be a bicycle trail. "Three miles to go," one of them yelled. "Last one to the Old Mill buys lunch."

David Malone now knew where he was. He was on the Old Mill Bicycle Path south of town. He slowly exhaled as he looked at the body floating face down in the shallow water. The high reeds hid her from anyone on the bike path. The sound of traffic was so faint that he was sure she was also not visible from the distant highway. In all likelihood, with the thick reeds, she wasn't even readily visible from the air unless you were low... and right over her.

In his mirror form– invisible to those on the bike path– he couldn't move her... or the reeds. But he didn't have to. He had seen her face before he emerged from the mirror surface of the still water. It was the face in the photograph taped to the edge of the mirror.

He closed his eyes and said softly, "Home."

When he opened his eyes, he was once again standing in his bedroom. David Malone, private investigator who, at age 27, could find almost anyone, anywhere in the world, had once again succeeded when everyone else had failed.

He did not, however, celebrate his success. His voice reflected his sorrow as he called Mr and Mrs Wilson to report his find. He spoke slowly and softly. He had learned the hard way to be careful with his words in these circumstances. Several times parents or husbands or wives had responded joyously when he informed them that he had found their loved one, only to realize belatedly that he was not speaking of the living.

"I'm very sorry," he said softly, "but I think I have located Alice's body."

He waited for the sobs to quiet before continuing. "Tell the police to look in the shallow water west of the Old Mill Bicycle Path about three miles south of town. The body should be visible from a helicopter or a search drone now that they know where to look." He paused and said sincerely, "I was hoping it would work out differently, but..." He let his voice trail off.

"Thank you," came the quiet response from Mr Wilson. "We will call Detective Nash and tell him what you've told us."

He set the phone back on the small table next to his bed and began to dress himself. He left his casual clothing on the bed where it lay and pulled dress pants and a suit coat from the closet. He also put on a dress shirt and tie. It is always a good idea to make the best impression possible when the police think you are meddling in their business.

***

When Detective Robert Nash knocked on the door to his office, David was sitting behind his desk appearing to do paperwork. "Come in," he yelled as the detective opened the door.

Detective Nash stepped into the room and almost immediately dropped himself down into one of the two padded chairs which sat in front of the desk. "OK, nut job," he said, "you know the routine. I ask you the official questions. You give me your bullshit answers, and then I take you downtown so someone higher up on the food chain can listen to your fairy tales for the rest of the night."

"I assume you found the body," David said softly.

"Right where you God-damned said it would be!" Nash replied gruffly. His voice was just below a shout.

"Official question," he said a little more softly. "How in the hell did you know where the body was?"

David sighed. He had been through this many times before. "I saw it in the mirror," he said flatly. "Just like I see all the other people I find– dead or alive."

The detective stood in front of the desk. His six-foot-three frame blocked most of the sunlight coming through the window. "Official question number two," he growled out without moving his jaw or his lips. "Will you come willingly down to the station house to discuss

8

your involvement in the murder of Alice Wilson?"

"I always come willingly," David answered politely as he got up from his chair. At six foot even, his slim build was dwarfed by the muscular detective. "The house is all locked up," he said firmly. "We can go out through the office door."

"Gotta put you in the back," Nash said as they walked out onto the driveway. "They've gotten real picky since that wack job got hold of Parker's gun last month. I even have to put little old ladies back there now."

"I understand," David said. He did understand. He had been through this many times before both in Plain City and with other law enforcement agencies. The police anywhere are very suspicious of someone who can tell them where a dead body is located. They don't believe that anyone can see dead people in a mirror. And they especially don't believe that someone who knows where the body is knows nothing at all about who killed them or why.

They both remained quiet during the drive to the station house. Once there, Detective Nash turned him over to the division head who would handle the "interview."

"I just find people," he said quietly to Inspector Dwayne Harris. "I don't know anything about the crime. I don't know why they were killed or what happened to them yesterday or even one minute before I see them."

"You've been saying that for the last two hours," Dwayne said with exasperation. His voice reflected his anger as he said, "You've been saying that for the past eight years." He then bent over the table so that he was at eye level with David and said very firmly, "But you know– and I know– that your story is bullshit!"

He slammed his fist on the table and shouted. "You know more about this than you are telling us."

9

Turning so that he was standing sideways he jabbed his finger through the air like a sword pointed directly at David's nose. "And one of these days," he growled out, "we are going to find out how you really do this and charge you as an accessory."

"I assume," David said quietly, "that means you have no further questions... or charges. So I think it is time for me to go home."

Inspector Harris drew his hand back toward his body and made a rather rude sound with his lips as he slapped his own thigh in anger. "You are free to go," he said through clenched teeth. "But one day... one day you will make a mistake. And then we will have you."

"Always happy to be of service to the police," David said as he stood and walked toward the door of the interrogation room. "I assume," he said as he stepped into the hallway, "that Detective Nash can take me back to my office?"

"Whatever!" was Dwayne's only response as David let the door close behind him.

Just before they got back to his office, Nash finally broke the silence of the ride and said, "You know, it would be a lot easier if you would just tell the truth– or at least tell some believable lies about how you know about these things."

"Sometimes," David responded with a sigh, "the truth isn't that easy." He sighed again before saying, "Everything I have ever told you is the absolute, honest, hand-to-God truth." He paused. "I can't help it if that truth isn't believable."

"Yeah," Nash said as they pulled into the driveway. "Now all you have to do is convince Inspector Harris of that."

As the detective opened the rear door to let David out of the car, he said, "Until next time... I guess."

"Until next time," David replied as he walked

toward his front door.

He still had one unpleasant task to perform. He had to prepare the billing for the Wilsons. His standard fee was five thousand dollars plus expenses if he found the missing person. There was no fee if he didn't succeed. Often he would cut the fee in half if the person was not found alive. Once in a while, he would waive the fee entirely.

He always felt like a ghoul when he charged grieving parents for the recovery of their daughter's or son's body, but he was giving them closure when no one else could. And he had to eat and pay the mortgage like everyone else. His rather specialized practice meant he had only a couple dozen or so cases a year that he could solve. Sixty to ninety thousand a year sounds like a lot until you subtract off all the taxes and fees and licenses and bonds and insurance that are required to be a private investigator.

He sat at his desk for a long time before finally crossing off the $5,000 that appeared on the computer-printed bill and writing $2,500 beneath it. Then in his barely legible handwriting he wrote, "In consideration of your loss, I am cutting my fee in half. You may need the funds for a different investigator to find Alice's killer."

He knew that the police would have a good chance of catching the killer now that they had the body. Whoever it was had probably assumed that the rodents and raccoons and other small mammals would devour much of the evidence before her body was eventually found. That expectation might have made them careless and possibly they left traces of themselves behind. Hopefully the Wilsons would not have to resort to a private detective to find justice for their daughter, but the note– and the reduction in the bill– was his way of helping them if they needed to resort to that.

The note had a second purpose. He clearly said, "a

11

different investigator." He did not track down killers... or robbers... or other unknown miscreants. His was a special skill. If he knew a person's name and had a picture of their face, he could find them anywhere in the world. If the person were unknown, David's gift was useless. He could not, after all, pop in and out of every mirror and reflective surface on earth looking for some unknown person.

He set the bill on the table by the front door. It would go out in tomorrow's mail. For now he had to visit an old friend. There was no one else who would understand.

He again went through the ritual of checking everything to ensure that the house was secure. The suit and tie and dress shirt and slacks were hung carefully in the closet. Then once again standing nude in front of the black mirror he relaxed his breath and held out his arms and went into himself. As the image faded this time, he was saying softly, "Chou, Chou, Chou, Chou..."

He didn't know Chou's full name, or even if Chou was his real name. But it was a name, and that is all that mattered. He had met Chou when he was a teenager. Since he was a small child he had found that there was something about mirrors that seemed to draw him into them. One day, he went into the bathroom of his parents' house to take a shower. There was a large mirror over the sink counter. It was late in the day, but he hadn't turned on any of the lights, so it was rather dim in the bathroom.

As he stood looking at himself in the mirror, for some reason he found a need to stare into his own eyes. As he stared deeper into his own eyes, it was as if his left eye opened wide and swallowed him. The bathroom seemed to fade away and suddenly he was standing on a rocky beach somewhere. Large pools of quiet water reflected the clouds and sky above him. The sea was breaking against the larger rocks farther out. A naked man was standing looking out at the water.

"Where am I?" he asked in amazement.

"You are standing in front of a mirror," the man answered, "as am I."

He turned and faced David. He was Oriental of some sort, most likely Chinese or Korean because his eyes were almost round. "If my nakedness offends or frightens you," he said softly, "I will turn back around."

He laughed lightly and added, "But we are not really here, are we? So what difference does it make?"

"What's happening?" David had asked.

"You are mirror-walking," the man replied. "My name is Chou. I thought I was the last of the mirror-walkers, but evidently you also have the gift." He paused before saying quietly, "or curse."

"What do you mean?"

"You stood before a mirror and looked deeply into yourself and you entered the mirror," Chou explained. "Since you did not speak a place or name as you entered the mirror, you were– for some reason– drawn here, to me."

"Where is here?" David asked.

"Does it matter?" Chou replied. "I came here because I am dying. I have come here many times, and I wanted to see this beautiful place one last time before I die." He smiled at David and said, "But it looks like I will have to spend my final hours teaching you how to walk safely in the mirror."

David and Chou sat on one of the rocks for what seemed like many hours as Chou explained the long history of mirror-walkers. "As long as there have been reflections on the water," Chou said, "there have been mirror-walkers."

He explained that going into the mirror was easiest in a dim place and easier if the mirror was dark rather

13

than bright. He also warned of "stepping into nothing," as he called it. "If you step into nothing too many times eventually you will find yourself somewhere from which you cannot return. And that may not be a very pleasant place."

David wanted to stay there forever, but Chou said, "The mirror extracts its price. I must rest for now. Return tomorrow at this same time."

So, over the next several days, David returned to the serene cove and the strange man whom he considered his mentor. Each day, Chou would speak a little about walking in the mirror, but mostly he spoke of law and love and trust. "Those are the three most important things in the mirror," Chou said. "You must obey the laws of the mirror. You must love those whom you seek. And you must trust yourself and others who love you."

On the tenth day, rather than telling him to return again tomorrow, Chou said, "There are many other things I could teach you about the mirror... and about life, but my time grows short. I must leave. Come visit me when I have joined my ancestors. My spirit will hear you even if I cannot respond."

Chou was laid to rest in his family tomb. Although it was not part of their tradition, the family honored his wishes that his tomb be sealed with a highly-polished stone bearing his name. It was from that stone mirror that David stepped.

"Chou," he said as he turned to face the tomb, "how did you handle it?" He walked back and forth within the small crypt. "You lived through wars and all sorts of horrors. Did you have to find people separated by chaos? Did you have to tell wives they would never see their husbands again? Did you have to tell parents their child was dead?"

He sobbed before wailing out, "How many times

14

did you have to look into the faces of the dead whose names you had called?"

David was on his knees before Chou's tomb as he continued between his sobs, "How did you stand being alone? How did you handle being the only one who could understand what you did?"

He startled as he heard a soft voice. It was so soft that it sounded like it was far, far, away and yet somehow David knew that it was right beside him. "I was not always alone," the voice said. "Maybe you will not always be alone either. Look for one whom you can see, and you will no longer be alone."

David looked up. He was back in his bedroom. He was kneeling on the floor in front of the black mirror. His face was wet with his tears. "Or maybe I will always be alone," he said softly to himself as he stood and breathed deeply, trying to pull himself fully back into the real world.

Chapter Two
"A New Case"

As he stood in front of the black mirror with his breath slowly returning to normal, a sound from behind him caused him to freeze in place. There was someone in the room with him. "Son of a bitch," a familiar voice said, "he's been telling the truth all along."

David spun around to see Detective Robert Nash standing in his bedroom doorway. Standing next to him was a slightly larger, much better dressed version of the detective. Nash nodded his head toward the stranger and said, "This is my little brother, Mark. He's a Fed."

Mark gave a short huffing laugh and said, "Actually, I'm Secret Service. I'm Field Agent Mark Nash." He reached into the inside pocket of his black suit coat and pulled out a flat badge and ID case. He flipped it so David could see both the badge and the picture ID. There was a bulge on the other side of Mark's coat that was obviously a weapon, but it, thankfully, remained in place.

"You really do see all this shit in a mirror," Robert said. His eyes were wide as he stared past David at the black piece of glass mounted on the wall." He pointed at it and said, "You weren't there in that mirror when we walked in... I mean you weren't here... I mean you were here, but it wasn't just a reflection of you standing there! You were in some mausoleum somewhere, weren't you?"

David's own eyes went wide. He hadn't realized that someone watching could see through the mirror while he was walking.

"It was there for just a flash," his brother added, "and then you were back here."

"How did you get past my alarms?" David asked

almost angrily.

"Sorry about that," Mark said quietly. "But you really shouldn't have an alarm system that is connected to the internet. I had my office disable it before we arrived in case we had to... enter quietly."

"So," David continued, "who have I pissed off so much that I have brought the wrath of the Secret Service down on me?"

"Intrigued would be a better word," Mark said, giving David a quick smile.

He then gestured toward David with both hands almost as if welcoming him and asked, "Would you be more comfortable discussing this in your living room? Perhaps after you have had a chance to clothe yourself?"

"Oh," David said, suddenly becoming aware of his own nakedness. He smiled nervously and said, "It works better if nothing separates me from the mirror."

"Please join us in the living room when you have had a chance to dress," Mark said politely and both men turned and walked down the hallway.

David shook his head several times trying to clear his thoughts as he gathered up his clothing. Agent Mark was being very polite, but despite the "Please," his invitation sounded much more like an order.

A few minutes later he walked into the living room. "May I get you gentlemen a cup of coffee or something?" he asked. "I, myself, prefer tea."

"Tea would be fine," Mark said. His brother just shrugged his shoulders and said, "Whatever."

David returned shortly with three cups and a steaming pot of tea on a tray. There were also sugar cubes, a small pitcher of milk, and lemon slices.

"You prefer the British way," Mark said as he took a cup off the tray.

"I picked up the habit somewhere," David answered as he filled Mark's cup and handed a cup to

17

Robert. After filling that cup, he filled his own and sat down opposite them. "What brings you here?" he asked.

"My big brother," Mark began, "has often spoken about this nut job that he has to deal with on a regular basis who seems to be able to find anyone, anywhere, anytime." He took a sip of his tea and smiled slightly at David. "He thinks you are totally nuts," he said matter-of-factly, "but he swears that you can somehow find people, living or dead, no matter where they are."

"Only if I know their name," David replied. "And only if I have an image of their face. And... this is the big one... only if they are near a mirror or a reflective surface."

"Alice Wilson was out in the middle of the swamp," Robert said loudly. "There were no God-damned mirrors out there."

"It was a calm day," David answered firmly. "The water was smooth and reflective. I'm sure it was a marvelous sight from the path with the cattails reflected off the water, but the important point is that it was mirror smooth."

"Oh," the detective said. He then startled slightly as he noticed the stern stare from his younger, but larger, brother.

"However you do it," Mark said slowly, "it appears that you *CAN* find people who are very well hidden, is that not right?'

"Yes," David answered. "Name, image, mirror, and I can find them wherever they are in the world."

He looked across at the larger of the two Nash brothers. "You said you are with the Secret Service. Who's missing? The President?"

"No," Mark said, shaking his head and again giving a huff that was almost a laugh. "He would be easier to find with his implanted tracking chips." He took a deep breath and continued, "It's his wife. She

18

refused to be implanted."

He took a deep breath and said softly, but firmly, "We think she has been kidnaped. We don't know who and we don't know how. There have been no demands yet, but the last thing we need is for a video to be posted of her in the hands of our enemies... or worse, her kneeling in the sand..."

His voice trailed off as if he couldn't finish the thought.

"And you think I can find her?" David said slowly.

"You are more of a 'Hail, Mary' pass in the last two seconds of the game," Mark replied. "Every US agency on earth is on full alert and looking for anything, anywhere, no matter how off the wall, that might help us find her."

His face became impassive as he stared into David's eyes. "I'm here officially," he continued, "but off the record. If you can just give us some clue as to where she is being held, it would help immensely."

"You heard what I need," David responded. "Name, Image, Mirror."

"You already know her name," Mark said quickly. "Helena Travis. I have a picture of her on my phone if that works."

He paused and shrugged his shoulders, "The mirror where she is held... that's another question."

"I'll try," David said firmly, "but I need to be alone while I do it." He looked up and turned slightly pink. "And it's not just because I'll be naked. I need to be able to concentrate. This isn't as easy as it looks."

"I never said it looked easy," Robert said. "I just said it looked crazy."

He then chuckled and said loudly, "But I will never doubt you again. And if Inspector Harris has any questions, I will tell him to not look a gift nut in the mouth."

19

"My older brother is a bit uncouth," Mark said, "but in his own crude way, he is promising that he will protect you from now on when you help with their cases." His voice became very formal as he continued, "And I will help you with this, but your involvement can never be made public. It would be... ... too difficult to explain."

"Tell me about it," David said. "Tell me about it," he repeated as he stood and walked toward the hallway. He stopped and turned back toward the Nash brothers and said quickly, "You two stay here in the living room. I will go back into the bedroom and see if I can mirror-walk to where she is."

He looked into the faces of the two officers. His own face was totally devoid of expression as he said softly, "You know, I don't always find them alive." He then turned and walked down the hallway to his bedroom.

Chapter Three
"Airborne"

It was nearly an hour later when David returned to the living room. He had a robe wrapped around his body. He looked like he had just run a marathon. His hair was slightly wet and stuck to his head as if he had been sweating heavily. There was a light sheen on his face and he was moving somewhat slowly.

"Are you OK?" Detective Robert asked.

"She's alive," he said quietly in response. He then slid into the chair opposite the couch where Agent Mark was sitting. He picked up his cold cup of tea and took a sip. He grimaced at the taste, but finished the cup in a couple of quick swallows.

"Where is she?" Mark said urgently.

"I don't know," David replied. "She's in a plane, but I don't know where it is or where it is going."

"What do you know?" Mark asked slowly.

"It was all bare inside," David began. "There were some huge metal containers that seemed to fill up the whole inside of the plane. They were more or less the same shape as the plane and there was only a little space between the containers and the walls of the plane."

He gestured with his hands as if he were pointing to something and continued, "There was a big open space up front. That's where I stepped out of the mirror. Farther up was a strange-looking ladder going up to a small room that looked more like a regular plane. There were two short rows of chairs up there behind what I think was the cockpit. Behind the seats was what looked like a set of bunk beds built into the back wall."

"Sounds like a seven-four-seven configured for cargo," Mark said quickly.

He then gestured for David to continue. David

again moved his arms as if pointing to something on the floor. "The back row had four seats," he said as he pointed. "There were two men sitting together talking. Both had on what looked like pilots' uniforms." He chuckled– almost a giggle– "I sort of wondered who was actually flying the plane."

His arm moved slightly forward and he said, "The front row only had two seats. Helena was sitting in one of them. Her legs were tied together with a wide black piece of cloth. Her arms were tied to the chair with the same kind of black cloth. She wasn't gagged, but she didn't say anything in the time I was there."

"What else can you tell us about the plane?" Mark asked. He was furiously making notes in a small notebook as David spoke.

"The markings on the containers were in English- primarily numbers with a letter or two in front of them. But there were stick-on labels all over the plane itself that were in some sort of foreign script. I think they covered up the original English labels. The only thing they left in English was a big red arrow on the wall that said, 'Rescue' in white letters."

"Was it Arabic?" Mark asked anxiously.

"No," David answered. "It was Oriental of some sort. I think Japanese or Chinese, but I'm not sure."

He paused for a moment then sighed. "The two men in the back row were not speaking English, but I don't know for sure what language they were speaking. It looked like maybe Japanese or Chinese. They were talking about the fact that Douglas Travis was sure to shoot first and ask questions later. They said he was crazy enough to send the missiles to China just because his wife was missing."

Mark continued to scribble rapidly in his notebook.

"They said something about when they released

the videos there would be no way that the government could deny their involvement." He paused and smiled nervously. "I think they were referring to the Chinese government.

"Then after the ash settled," he continued, "she would turn up in Texas and the world would be shown how it had all been a Douglas Travis scam just to have an excuse to go to war with China."

He startled and said, "Oh! Then they said Mother Russia would be the only bear unbloodied and would be able to roar like she did in the old days."

"Wait a minute," Robert said suddenly. "You said they were speaking Japanese or Chinese or something. How do you know what they said?"

"There is no language in the mirror," David replied. "I can tell they aren't speaking English because the words I hear don't match their mouths, but I have no idea what language they are really speaking. The lip movements didn't look right for Russian. They might have been speaking Chinese, but I really can't say. It's sort of like watching a badly-dubbed movie. I know what they are saying, but I also know it's not what they originally said. And I can't read anything written down unless it's actually in English because... well I don't know why, but I can't."

"But the writing on the walls and stuff was Chinese, not Russian?" Mark asked. "You're sure of that?"

"Cyrillic looks more like Arabic." David replied. "It's actually got letters. This was one of the pictographic languages."

"Great!" said Mark. "I need to convince my boss that FLOTUS is being held on a plane by a bunch of Russian agents who speak Chinese, and they are taking her to China so they can bring her back to Texas."

He slammed his notebook down onto the coffee

table in front of the couch. "No one is going to believe any of this unless I can get some sort of physical proof."

He looked up at David and said, "Did you look out the windows of the plane? Was there anything painted on the wings? Could you see anything that would tell you where they were or where they were going?

"No," David answered, almost angrily. "I said I don't know where they are or where they are going. I tried looking out the windows, but they were all painted over on the outside." He gave another nervous half-smile. "That creates a mirror. That's how I found her."

He looked down and sighed. "At least my mirror is painted black," he said softly. "These looked like poop smeared on the glass."

"What did you say!?" Mark shouted.

David jumped and pulled his arms tight around himself in shock. "I'm sorry," he said. "I was just saying that my mirror is painted black. The windows were painted brown, almost the color of poop."

Mark moved over closer to him and asked quietly, "Perhaps the color of a UPS truck?"

David's eyes turned up slightly as he tried to remember the color. "Yes," he said slowly. "It was very close to the dark brown of a UPS truck."

"Son of a bitch," Mark said loudly. He sounded a lot like his brother when he swore. "That's how they did it. We were watching all the passenger and cargo terminals and they just shipped her out of the country UPS."

He picked up his phone and hit a speed dial. "Jimmy," he yelled into the phone a moment later, "I need you to check UPS planes in and out of Dulles and Reagan and any other airport within a hundred miles of DC. See if there is a plane on the airport logs that isn't on the UPS schedule of arrivals and departures."

He set down his phone and looked over at David.

"The 'Hail, Mary' is in the air," he said quietly. "We may have our physical proof." He then sat back on the couch bouncing his cellphone nervously against his leg.

Less than five minutes later his phone chirped and he immediately answered it. Keeping it on speaker he asked, "What did you find, Jimmy?"

The voice on the phone said, "There was a UPS special delivery that landed at Reagan at oh-six-hundred yesterday. It was a seven-four-seven-dash-four-hundred. There is no indication of any cargo removed or loaded. It took off today at ten-seventeen."

"What was the destination?" Mark asked anxiously.

"Shanghai, China," Jimmy answered.

"Where is it now?" Mark nearly yelled into the phone.

"That's where it gets interesting," Jimmy replied. "Forty-five minutes ago, six hours after departure, the transponder beacon disappeared from the scopes. Air traffic control notified UPS at Shanghai, but they said they didn't have any planes overdue or out of communication, so it was put down as equipment failure."

"Equipment failure, my ass," Mark spit out. "FLOTUS is on that plane. UPS doesn't know anything about it because it's not their plane. These bastards didn't sneak in and out under the radar. They were hiding in plain sight painted up like a UPS plane. They sat there on the tarmac where everyone could see them until FLOTUS was brought out there in a delivery truck of some sort. They went electronic silent as soon as they were out of range of coastal radar so we wouldn't know where they were going. I'm willing to bet that they cancelled their flight plan just before they dropped out of sight."

"Ummm," Jimmy murmured. "Checking... damn.

You're right on that, too."

"Notify those sons of bitches at NSA," Mark growled. "They know where everything is that's in the air or has been in the air. They should be able to tell us where that plane is going."

"If they went silent and dropped to just above the water," Jimmy replied, "they're not going to show up on anything, but I'll rattle some cages and see if anyone saw anything."

"We'll be waiting," Mark replied.

"Ahh," Jimmy said slowly, "before I start calling people, can you tell me how you came up with this information?"

Mark laughed, "I could, but you wouldn't believe me, and then I'd have to kill you."

"OK," Jimmy said. "Need to know. I get it. But someone is going to want an explanation eventually."

"Eventually," Mark answered with a slight laugh, "I might even have one."

"Do you need me anymore?" David asked softly.

"No... Yes... not at the moment," Mark said. "You may still be our only hope of tracking the First Lady." He paused and chewed on his lower lip, "But right now you probably can't tell us any more than we already know."

He stood and walked over to David's chair. He could tell that the previous hour had been very hard on him. "How long before you can try again?" he asked.

David exhaled deeply. "I should be OK in an hour or so," he said with a sigh. "I've just been in the mirror too much today." He looked up at Mark, "And I wasn't sure whether I was finding her or locating a body." He looked down at the floor as he said, "I much prefer finding someone." Looking back up he said softly, "Locating a body is very hard. It is like they are still there and pulling energy out of you or trying to talk to

26

you or whatever."

He gave the wrinkled smile both Robert and Mark had seen before. "I need to talk to Chou," he said, "then I need to sleep."

"Who's Chou?" Robert said abruptly.

"That's who's in the mausoleum," David answered. "I met him in the mirror. He thought he was the last of the mirror-walkers." The wrinkled smile returned, "Now, I guess I am."

"Do what you need to do to recharge yourself or whatever," Mark said, "but be ready to go back if NSA and the other alphabet people with the spy satellites come up blank on telling us where she is."

"I'll come back out in an hour or so," David answered. "There's beer in the fridge if you want some."

As he started back toward his bedroom, Agent Mark said, "David..."

He turned around and looked back into the living room.

"Thank you for your service to your country," Mark said and gave him a short salute.

"Thank you," David mumbled and continued into the bedroom.

Chapter Four
"Chi"

The bed was beckoning as David walked back into his room, but there was one last trip he had to make into the mirror before he lay down. He had to talk to Chou.

He dropped his robe on the bed and stood before the black glass. It took several deep breaths before his mind was clear enough to even begin to look within himself. *"Don't push it,"* he told himself slowly as he tried to center in on his left eye.

It wasn't happening, and he was about to give up and go to bed when suddenly he felt the pull of the mirror and saw the opening of his iris. He wanted to ask Chou what to do. He knew that Chou wouldn't really answer, but it was more important to ask than to hear the answer. In asking the question, he would be able to feel how– and where– he was drawn. Chou had once told him, "The answer is in the question. Ask and you will see."

"Sounds like something in a fortune cookie," he muttered to himself as the mausoleum slowly appeared from the mists of the mirror.

David froze. He was not alone at Chou's tomb. A young woman was standing in front of the shiny stone... and she was naked. "Grandfather," she said through her tears, "when I was a little girl, you promised that you would tell me what I needed to know when the time came." She broke down sobbing. "You never said what you meant. Now, I know you were talking about going into the mirrors."

More sobs echoed in the tomb as she beat her hands against the marble. David was startled as he realized that her hands were not bouncing off the surface of the stone. They were instead sinking several inches

28

into the marble. "I am all alone," she wailed. "No one understands."

"I understand," David said. He then said quickly, "Do not turn around. I have turned so that I am not facing you. I remember when I first met your grandfather, how difficult it was to stand naked before him."

The young woman gasped. She may have turned to look, but David did not see her. He was facing the outer wall of the tomb. "Chou told me that since we weren't really there, it didn't matter," he continued, "but it did. It took me a long time to feel comfortable with both of us not wearing anything."

"You knew my grandfather?" she asked. Her voice sounded somewhere between surprise and hope.

"I met him when I was walking in the mirror," David explained. "I was drawn to where he was. He was on a rocky beach. There were some large rocks above pools of water where we sat and talked."

"That is our ancestral village," the young woman said, "or where it once was. I have visited it many times."

"I have never been to China," he said.

"Then how is it you speak Mandarin so well?" she asked.

"I don't," David answered with a laugh. "There is no language in the mirror. You can understand whatever anyone is speaking."

"You are younger than I expected you to be," she said quietly. "You appear to be only five or ten years older than myself."

"I'm twenty-seven," David answered. "I saw you for a moment before I turned around," he said. He felt himself blushing with shame or guilt as he admitted that he had seen her naked body even though she was now, obviously, looking at his. "I thought you were much younger," he said softly.

"A woman from China looks young until she looks old," she said with a light laugh, "but we look old for a long, long, time."

"I am from America," David said. "The Midwest. I only knew Chou for a short time, but he taught me much about mirror-walking. I am willing to share what I know with you."

"All I know for sure," she answered, "is that when I look into the mirror and say my grandfather's name, I end up here."

"Then you know what is important," David said. "If you say a person's name and know what they look like, and if they are near a mirror, you will go to them."

"There is no mirror here," she said.

"The polished marble," David said quickly. "That's why Chou had it used to seal his tomb rather than the traditional terra cotta."

"Are there others?" she asked. Her voice was trembling.

"Chou thought that he was the last," David answered quietly. "Then he found me. I thought I was the last, and now I have found you."

David wanted to turn around, but he had promised her that he would not. "He told me there was another when I was here earlier today."

"What?"

"I heard a voice," he continued. "It told me to look for one whom I can see, and I will no longer be alone."

"I don't understand," she said.

"When I am walking in the mirror," David explained, "no one can see me. Chou could see me and I could see him, so evidently only another mirror-walker can see me." He paused and said, "I can see you. And you can see me. So neither of us is alone."

He didn't intend to turn around, but suddenly he

was looking into her dark brown eyes. They both blushed slightly and looked down. "What is your name?" he asked.

"Chi," she answered. "What is yours?"

"David."

"If I call your name," she asked, "will I come to you?"

"If you wish," he answered, "but I will not know that you are there. We can see each other only if both of us are walking in the mirror."

"We could meet here," she said softly. "Since there is no language in the mirror, all you would have to do is write a note saying what time we should meet. Then when I walked to visit you I would know when to come here to my grandfather's tomb."

"That wouldn't work," he said dejectedly. "Writing doesn't work the same as speech. I don't know if you can read English, but I know for sure that I can't read Chinese."

"I can read a little English," she said with a giggle. "Mostly the menu words on the internet."

Her voice became somewhat firm as she said, "I can read Chinese, Japanese, Korean, and several other Oriental languages used by the fishermen who come into our village, but I have never learned English. They teach English to everyone in the bigger communities, but ours is a very small village, even today." Her shoulders seemed to droop slightly as she said, "And I am only a girl."

"Wait a minute!" David suddenly yelled out. "Chi, I need you to meet somebody. This is going to be a little hard to believe and I'm not sure it will work. If this doesn't work, come back here and I will meet you."

"What is wrong?" Chi asked. The concern was obvious on her face and in her voice.

"What is wrong," David replied, "is that our two

31

countries may be about to fire nuclear missiles at each other. And someone else is pulling the strings to make it all happen."

"What do you need me to do?" she asked.

"Go home," he said. "Wait three minutes and then come back into the mirror, but say my name."

She nodded to indicate that she understood.

"You should end up at my house in America," he said, starting to talk rapidly. "I will explain everything when you get there. ... except I won't know if you are there. You will be able to see me and Agent Nash, but we won't be able to see you. I won't know if you are willing to help until I get back on board the plane."

"What plane?" she asked.

"Just come to me in three minutes," he said.

David was standing in front of his black mirror. He was swaying slightly as he often did when he returned from his trips into the mirror. "Agent Mark, get in here!" he yelled.

Both brothers came running into the room. Mark had his weapon drawn. Robert had one arm behind his back, obviously ready to pull his pistol from its holster.

"What's up?" Mark yelled.

"I think I know how to find out where the plane is going," David said quickly. "But you are going to have to take a rather large leap of faith."

"How large?" Robert asked.

Extending his hand toward the mirror, David said, "Mark, Robert, I want you to meet Chi. She's a mirror-walker from China." He swallowed hard as both brothers stared at him. "I know you can't see her, but she's there... I think. I need you to explain to her what is happening. Then she and I are going to try to get back on board that plane."

When neither brother showed any hint of understanding, he said, "She's from China. She can read the Chinese writing." Turning to the mirror he said, "You can also read Japanese, Korean, and a couple other languages, can't you?"

"Can you see her?" Robert asked.

"No... not really," David answered. "But she should be here. Just tell her what is going on and then I will explain to her what we have to do."

"I don't know if I can get a Chinese national involved in this," Mark said slowly. "That might be a little hard to explain to my supervisors."

"And the rest of this isn't?" David said heatedly.

"Point taken," said Robert. "Mark, why don't you tell the nice ghost what is going on.'

"She's not a ghost," David said defensively. "She's a mirror-walker... just like me."

Mark cleared his throat and faced the mirror. "Is that where she is?" he asked.

"Come stand next to me, Chi," David said. Then he looked at Mark and gave him a very nervous smile. "If she's here, she's next to me," he stammered out.

"OK," Mark said. He turned to face just to David's left and said, "Miss Chi, I am Mark Nash. I am a Secret Service Agent. The Secret Service, among other things, protects the President of the United States."

He paused and looked over at David and then continued. "The President's wife has been kidnaped. David was able to go to where she is, but he cannot read the Oriental writing he found there. We think that someone is trying to make it look like China is behind this, but unless we can figure out where the plane is going, we can't know for sure. Will you help us?"

David turned to the empty space to his left and said, "Chi, if you are willing, go back home and then come into the mirror again seeking Helena Travis." He looked up and said "Mark, show her a picture of the First Lady."

Mark held his phone up to the empty space next to David and said, "This is Helena Travis."

"Chi, I'll meet you there," David said. Then he turned to the brothers and said, "I need to go back into the mirror."

As Agent Nash and Detective Nash walked back into the living room, David once again was taking deep breaths in front of the mirror. A few minutes later he was standing next to a cargo container aboard an airplane somewhere over the Pacific.

He heard a soft giggling and turned to see Chi standing behind him. "What's so funny?" he asked.

She pointed to the various words printed on the tape which covered the English signs on the walls. "This is Chinese," she said as she pointed to one large, two-symbol section which was taped over English wording above the side cargo door. "That is Japanese," she said as her fingers pointed to a long segment along the top of the bulkhead. "It explains how to wash your blanket." Pointing at a small sign on the side of the folding ladder-stairway, she said, "And that is Korean for 'Lady's Bathroom.'" Pointing back at the large section she had said was Chinese, she said, "That reads literally 'Clean sheets, Warm beds.' It would be used to mark a house of prostitution. Whoever created these labels had no idea what they meant."

Looking around at the other signs, she said, "I think I have seen some of these symbols before in tattoo books or on internet pages that make fun of Westerners who have no idea what their tattoos actually mean." She smiled shyly, "Most of them are too vulgar to speak aloud."

She then sounded almost angry as she said, "These would never fool someone from Asia. They are just badly done stage props to fool your president's lady into thinking this plane is Chinese."

34

"So we still don't know where they are going," David said sadly.

"Maybe something up there will help us," Chi said as she started up the stairway to the upper area.

David followed her up the ladder, trying not to stare at her naked behind. He was totally red by the time they reached the flight deck level.

One of the pilots was now asleep on one of the bunks. Helena Travis's head was lolled forward as if she, too, were asleep.

David looked around and said, "Nothing here to tell us where they are going."

"Why not just go see what the pilots flying the plane are doing," Chi said as she walked forward through the galley.

There was a heavy security door between the galley and cockpit itself. Chi reached out her hand and said, "Maybe it is unlocked?"

"You can't open a door!" David said. "You don't have a real body."

"Then I can go through it," she replied as she stepped into the cockpit.

David followed behind her. "I didn't know I could do that," he said in surprise.

"I didn't know I couldn't," Chi answered calmly.

Both looked around the cockpit. They were standing in a small area behind the pilot's and copilot's seats. A third seat was folded up into the side wall. One of the men David had seen earlier was flying the plane. Another man, dressed in a slightly different uniform, was in the co-pilot's seat.

"That's Chinese," Chi said softly as she pointed at a small slip of paper held in a clip on the pilot's armrest. "It says 'Singapore' and 'Air Cargo Flight 864'".

Pointing to another slip of paper, she said, "That also says Singapore, but there are some numbers after it."

David looked at the slip. "I can't read the Chinese," he said quietly. "But the numbers look like compass directions."

"Runways are numbered with compass directions," Chi said quickly.

"They are headed for Singapore," he said excitedly. "I need to report back."

He paused for a moment and said, "You can read American numbers, can't you?!"

"Actually, they are ancient Arabic," she replied, "but yes, I can read them."

"Come to me in one hour," he explained quickly. "I will write a time on a big piece of paper. Meet me at Chou's tomb at that time."

"But your time and mine are not the same," she answered.

"I will tape the note to the clock in whatever room I'm in," he said. "You can adjust for what time it is for you."

"In one hour," she said carefully, "I will go to my grandfather's tomb. If you are not there, I will come look for you."

"That works, too," David replied. "I will check in at Chou's tomb in one hour." He paused as if thinking, "If I can't, I'll do the note thing to let you know when I can be there."

Chi nodded her head and disappeared.

A few moments later, David was once again yelling for Agent Nash.

"They are headed for Singapore," David rapidly explained. "There was something about Singapore Air Cargo Flight 864."

"Got it," Agent Nash said and began talking once again on his phone.

Meanwhile, Detective Nash was standing looking

36

up and down at David's naked body. David suddenly grabbed for his robe and wrapped it around himself.

"What!?" he said almost angrily.

"Sorry," Robert growled out. "But you look like shit warmed over. Are you sure that going into the mirror this much won't kill you or something? I've seen people in the morgue that looked better than you do right now."

"I just need to lie down," David said wearily. "I told Chi I would meet her at Chou's tomb in one hour." He gave Detective Nash a weak smile and said, "Otherwise, I have to put a note on the clock that says when I will be there."

"There isn't anything you can do for a while anyway," Agent Nash said quietly. "I've notified our people about the flight and they are making plans." He looked across the room at one of the small pictures on the wall and added in a somewhat strange voice, "Not sure what they are going to do, if anything, but that's out of my hands."

He shook his head slightly and returned his gaze to David. "In any case, you have time to grab some shut eye. Best make use of it."

With that, he– and his brother– walked out of the room.

Chapter Five
"Changi"

David awoke with a start. Sunlight was illuminating his bedroom curtains. "Dammit, Detective Nash," he screamed out, "you said you would wake me!"

Both brothers again appeared in his bedroom doorway. Robert shrugged his shoulders and said, "We tried. You wouldn't wake up. I think going into the mirror takes more out of you than you realize."

"How long was I asleep?" David asked in a more civilized tone.

"About five hours," Agent Nash responded.

"Chi!" David exclaimed and Detective Nash pointed over at the clock above his desk. There was a large note taped beneath it with 07:00 on it.

"I figured you would be awake by then." He then turned slightly pink and looked down at the floor before saying. "I stood by the clock at two and told Chi what was happening." He looked back down at the floor and added, "At least I think I did."

His face– and his voice– regained their usual toughness as he pointed at a second piece of paper taped to the wall and said, "I also wrote down your cellphone number." He coughed rather nervously. "I told Chi to call you before she went back into the mirror. You might not be able to understand what she says, but you will know to go meet her wherever it is that you go to..." His voice again trailed off into nothingness as he finished. Evidently he wasn't really convinced that Chi had heard him.

As if to validate his claim, however, David's cellphone, plugged into its charger and sitting on his desk suddenly chirped indicating an incoming text.

"Speak of the Devil," Robert said as stepped aside to allow David to reach for his phone.

David laughed slightly.

"What does it say?" Mark asked.

"Return to Home Page," David said. Then he added with a smile, "She said her English was limited to menu commands on the internet."

"I need to talk to Chi," he said firmly. "I will only be gone a few minutes."

"Have her come back here," Agent Nash said. There was almost a frown on his face. "I think you both need to hear what is going on."

"Will do," David replied. Then he motioned toward the door and said, "I need to be alone."

"Call if you need us," Detective Nash said as they walked back into the living room.

***

Chi was waiting at Chou's tomb when David arrived. She looked very worried. "It's on television," she said in a slightly shaky voice. "Your President is very mad. He says that..." She paused as if thinking hard. "He says that the Chinese have stolen his wife."

She looked down as she continued, "That's not the word he used. I couldn't repeat what he called my people."

"Douglas Travis is an ass!" David said angrily. "But evidently the people thought he was the lesser of two evils and voted for him." He shrugged his shoulders and said, "That's the way our system works. It's not perfect, but it seems to have worked well so far." He gave her a smile before adding, "And win, lose, or draw, he's going to be replaced by someone else in two more years." He smiled at Chi and said, "That is also how our system works."

Chi laughed slightly but then turned back to very serious as she said, "But for now, we have to prevent war between our peoples."

"Agent Nash wants to talk to us," David said quickly. "I am going back. Join us there as soon as you can. He sounded really worried."

"I will meet you there," Chi said as he returned home.

"Chi is pretty," Detective Nash said from the doorway.

"Don't do that!" David said angrily.

"I apologize," Agent Nash said firmly, "but things are getting... tense."

"Give Chi a minute to get here," David said. "Then tell me what you need from us."

They stood silently for a moment waiting. David's phone chirped and he walked over to check it. "It says, 'Next Page,'" he said almost with a laugh. "I think that means she is on her way." He paused for just a second before saying, "... which means that she is now here with us."

Agent Nash took a deep breath and began, "You probably know that the President, despite advice to remain quiet, has spoken out." He let out a deep breath. "... quite dramatically."

He turned to face the empty space next to David. "But that is a problem for someone else to solve," he said firmly. "Our problem is that there is no Singapore Air Cargo Flight 864. If they were going to Singapore, they should already be there or be arriving about now, but there are no Singapore Air Cargo Flights expected in the next hour."

Robert said disgustedly. "They must be going somewhere else."

David's gaze slowly switched back and forth between the two brothers. "I guess Chi and I will have to go back into the mirror and see what is happening," he said glumly. "I was so sure," he said softly as he walked back over to his black mirror.

This time he didn't ask the brothers to leave. He just dropped his robe and stood in front of the mirror. After a moment the familiar pull took him into the mirror and deposited him once more in the space in front of the cargo containers where the poop-brown windows reflected the dim light of the main deck. Chi was already there.

"She's gone," Chi said quietly, pointing to the upper galley. She sounded confused.

"And we're on the ground," David replied. He, too, was confused. They raced up the stairs. The cockpit door was open and it was possible to see the ground through the front windshield. Helena Travis was nowhere to be seen. In fact, the only person in the plane seemed to be the copilot who was lying on one of the bunks at the back of the galley. He seemed to be deeply asleep.

The pilot's seat was empty. David noted that the small slip of paper was still clipped to the armrest of the chair. The numbers were definitely 864.

"How is this possible?" Chi asked.

"I don't know," David answered.

He then pointed excitedly through the windshield– literally, his arm and hand extended through the glass pointing at writing on a nearby hanger. "Can you read that?" He asked.

"No," she answered, "but I don't have to." She then pointed in the other direction and said, "We are at Changi."

"Changi?" David asked.

"Singapore International Airport," Chi replied. "I don't think there is another tower like that anywhere in the world."

41

David looked where she was pointing and could see a very tall, free-standing tower topped by what looked like a king's crown. The sun reflecting off the radar dome at the top made it look like a giant pearl.

"I have to go back and report," he said excitedly.

"Meet me at Chou's tomb in ten minutes," Chi said. "We have to ask him something." Her body shimmered for a moment and then she disappeared.

David looked at the spot where she had been standing. "I wonder if I look like that when I come out of the mirror?" he asked himself. Then he thought, *"Home,"* and was once again standing in front of the black mirror.

Both of the Nash brothers were waiting for him when he stepped back into the living room.

"They are on the ground in Singapore," he said slowly. "Chi recognized the control tower."

He took a deep breath before continuing slightly faster, "But I don't know for sure where the First Lady is. There was no one on board the plane but the copilot and he was asleep... or unconscious."

"I don't understand," Mark said. "We checked and no Singapore Air Cargo flights were arriving."

"Chi was sure we were in Singapore," David said, almost angrily. "The note was still attached to the pilot's seat. I don't know about the words, but the numbers were definitely '864'."

Agent Nash stood thinking a moment before slowly pulling out his phone. He put it on speaker as he spoke, "Jimmy, is there any way to do a search to see if anything with the number 864 landed at Singapore in the past half-hour?"

A short silence was followed by a loud, "Damn!" from the speaker. Jimmy's voice followed. "Shanghai Air Cargo Flight 864 declared an in-flight emergency and requested permission to land about twenty minutes ago. The copilot was evidently sick. He refused medical attention, but said he would not be able to fly. The plane was put in a holding area awaiting a fresh crew from Hong Kong. Since no one deplaned except the crew, and they remained in the holding area, they didn't show up as entering the country."

The phone went silent for a few moments before Jimmy's voice continued, "A Gulfstream G5 from Shanghai Air Cargo in Hong Kong landed about five minutes ago with a replacement crew. The crew with the sick copilot boarded immediately. It has already requested permission to take off and is probably rolling out as we speak."

Jimmy mumbled, "Just a minute," and the phone once again went silent.

"They are in the air," he said a few moments later, "but the plane is definitely not from Shanghai Air Cargo."

"How can you be sure?" asked Agent Nash.

"Shanghai Air Cargo," explained Jimmy, "sold off their G5s almost a year ago and switched their smaller fleet to Dassault Falcons. The plane's a fake."

"Shit, shit, shit, shit, shit," muttered Detective Nash. His brother gave him a severe look and said, "Bob, we're on speaker phone and this is all being recorded. Watch your language. It could end up in a history book someday."

"Well," Robert replied, "then they would know how frustrating this is. We were so close and now it's gone."

David interrupted, "I have to meet Chi at the tomb. She said that there something we have to ask Chou."

Mark's head snapped up and he said, "I thought you said this Chou person was dead."

"He is," David said with a short laugh, "but we still have to ask him something."

Detective Nash looked up at his younger brother and grinned. "I am really going to enjoy reading your report on this," he said as his grin grew broader. "This shit just keeps getting weirder and weirder."

Agent Nash looked over at his brother and then at David. "Do what you have to do," he said firmly. "I'll worry about explaining it later."

Jimmy's voice came from the speaker on Mark's phone. "I'm not sure I want to know what's going on or how you're doing this," he said. "But keep doing it. We need to know where FLOTUS has been taken."

Chapter Six
"Going Places"

Chi was pacing nervously up and down in front of Chou's tomb when David arrived. As soon as everything became clear, she looked up at him and asked, "You said that the first time you met Chou he was at the site of my old ancestral village?"

"Yes," David answered. He looked confused as he said, "I told you that."

"Who else was there?" she asked. There was a sense of urgency in her voice.

David stood silently looking around as he tried to remember everything about that first meeting. Finally he said softly, "No one. We were alone, just Chou and me."

"Then how did Chou get there?" Chi said loudly.

"I don't know," David replied, looking down. "There were pools of water that probably acted as mirrors."

Chi crouched down so that she could look up into David's face and said even louder, "There was no one else there!"

David looked at her for a moment and then suddenly his eyes went wide as he realized what Chi was saying.

"There has to be a way to walk to someplace without following someone's name," he almost yelled. Then looking at the smooth headstone which sealed Chou's tomb he shouted out, "How did you do it? How did you go somewhere alone?"

Chi started to say something, but David held up his arms to cut her off. That soft voice in his ear that sounded so far away and yet was still so near was speaking. Maybe it was just his memory, but he could clearly hear Chou's voice say, "I have come here many times."

Looking over to her, he asked, "You said that Chou took you to the site of your ancestral village many times?"

"Yes," she answered. "It is a beautiful place."

"He had been there before!" David yelled. "You can go anyplace you have ever been!"

He looked over at Chi and said firmly, "We have to get back on that plane." He grabbed her hands and said, "Now!"

Everything shimmered around them and suddenly they were standing just behind the cockpit on the fake UPS plane.

"I didn't know we could do that," Chi said with a surprised look on her face.

"I didn't know we couldn't," David replied with a smile.

"I meant I didn't know we could touch," Chi said and David suddenly looked down at his hands which were clasped around Chi's.

"Oh!" he said as he jumped back slightly. "I'm sorry."

"I'm not," Chi answered with a slight smile. "But we have other things we must do right now."

She turned and walked through the door into the cockpit area. David joined her.

The pilot and co-pilot were sitting in their seats going over some sort of checklist or report. David was leaning over the pilot trying to see what notes might be written on the pilot's clipboards when he felt Chi's hand on his shoulder. Looking up, he could see that she was pointing to the co-pilot.

"Does he look familiar?" she asked.

"More than familiar," he replied. "That's the same co-pilot as from before. He even has the same stain on the front of his shirt."

Both of them looked down in silence at the large food stain on the front of the co-pilot's uniform shirt. They remained motionless for several seconds and then turned toward each other and said in unison, "There were no stains on the sleeping co-pilot's shirt!"

There was another pause before David said, "That was the First Lady. They put her in some sort of really good disguise."

Then again speaking in unison they both said, "She's on that small jet."

"I have to tell Agent Nash," David said rapidly. "Meet me at the tomb in ten minutes."

Chi looked up at him as if she wanted to say something, but remained silent.

"What?" he asked.

She looked down. "I don't know if I can," she said with obvious emotional strain in her voice. "I was at your place while you slept. I feel like I have run a thousand kilometers."

"Oh," David said. "I forgot how badly this wiped me out before. We need to pace ourselves."

He stood silent for moment thinking and then said, "You go back to your home and rest. I will text you if I need you." There was another pause as he continued to think. "Otherwise," he said, "meet me at the tomb in five hours."

"Your day is my night," Chi replied. "I will try, but I may need to sleep more."

"Then text me when you awaken," David replied. "Join me at the tomb when I text back. ... OK?"

David laughed when Chi also replied "OK." It was obvious that she was actually saying, "OK."

"Why did you laugh?" Chi asked. She looked fearful... or perhaps hurt.

"Your mouth never matches the words I hear," he answered. "But when you said, 'OK,' everything was in

47

sync."

Chi giggled slightly. "I guess I know a few English words after all," she said. She then blew David a kiss and shimmered away.

David stood staring at the co-pilot for a moment as he thought of what that blown kiss might mean. Then he said loudly to himself, "Focus! You need to report back!" He silently thought, "Home," and was almost immediately standing in his bedroom.

Grabbing his robe and running towards the living room he shouted, "Found her!"

As he rounded the corner from the hallway, he suddenly skidded to a halt. His living room was full of people and equipment– at least that's the way it seemed to him. Mark stepped forward and said, "I'd like you to meet Special Agent in Charge Patricia Woods."

He coughed slightly and looked down at the floor. "She's my boss," he said.

"Actually," Patricia said in a rather strong voice for a female, "I'm in charge of this whole Midwest sector." She looked around the room and gestured toward the several technicians setting up equipment and said, "I flew in because Agent Nash had evidently found a reliable source of information regarding FLOTUS."

She looked back over at David and said in a much harsher voice, "Now, I'm not so sure."

David looked back at her in silence for a few moments and then turned to Agent Nash. "The First Lady is aboard that small jet. They disguised her as the sick co-pilot. The co-pilot currently on the plane is the same man who was there before."

"Are you sure?" the Special Agent asked.

"The co-pilot must have spilled something down the front of his shirt," David answered rapidly. "There is a large stain. The sleeping– or unconscious– co-pilot was wearing a clean shirt. The current co-pilot has the same stain."

He took a deep breath and continued. "It had to be her sleeping on that bed when they first landed. She was the only one on the plane, and that was before Chi and I figured out we could go to places as well as to people."

Special Agent Patricia Woods stood silent and unmoving except for her lower lip which she was moving back and forth across her upper teeth.

"I know this shit sounds really weird," Detective Nash said as he stepped between the boss lady and David. "But everything this nut has ever told us has checked out one hundred percent. And when he comes out of the mirror, for just an instant, you can see where he is... or was... or whatever. He was at some tomb somewhere and there is a naked Chinese chick who is helping him with the language."

"What?!" Patricia screamed. "You have involved a Chinese national in this!?"

"Little brother said that was going to be a problem," Robert said. Then he pointed his finger directly at her and his voice got louder as he said, "But I think you'd better make a decision... fast. Do you go with what this nut can give you and deal with the weird shit latter... or do you let these terrorists start a war between China and the United States of America? Right now, he's the only hope of preventing a catastrophe."

Patricia took a deep breath and turned to look at Agent Nash. "Mark," she began, "you've always said your big brother was crude but effective." She gave a nervous laugh and said, "So, what do we have?"

One of the technicians looked up from a large computer monitor and said, "We've pulled the radio chatter from the plane before and after the emergency landing in Singapore. One of the voices is definitely the same... 95% probability that it is the co-pilot."

"Where did the G5 go?" Special Agent Woods

asked hurriedly.

"Hong Kong," answered a different technician working on a table which had been setup where the couch was supposed to be.

Patricia turned again to David. "Can you get on that plane?" she asked.

"We tried," he answered. "But evidently there were no mirrors... or mirrored surfaces." His shoulders raised and lowered as he took in a very deep breath. "To find a person," he said in a more-or-less flat voice. "I need to know who they are. I need their name... or at least a name that I can think of while I'm going into the mirror. I need an image of them. And, I need them to be near a mirror or a mirrored surface."

"The inside of G5s," Mark said, "are often covered with soft materials to minimize noise. If the window covers are down, there might be nothing reflective in the areas where the First Lady is being kept."

"You said something about places," Robert interjected. "Would what you said work for a place? If we gave you a name and a picture could you go there?"

David stood thinking for a moment. Then he said softly, "I don't know that I can't. ... But I don't know that I can either." He raised his hands and said in a frustrated voice, "I just don't know."

"Then we need to do a test," Agent Mark called out from over by the table. He picked a piece of paper up out of the printer and walked over to David. "This is the arrival area of Hong Kong International Airport." he said gently. "See if you can go there. ... Please?"

"I'll try," David replied as he walked back toward his bedroom.

As he entered the hallway he could hear Agent Woods' voice saying, "How are we ever going to write this up?"

Robert's laughter echoed down the hallway as

David closed his door and positioned himself in front of the mirror.

He taped the printed image on the edge of the mirror and began softly repeating, "Hong Kong Airport... Hong Kong Airport."

The familiar tug pulled him into the mirror, but when things began to clear he was not in an airport. Flames were all around him and strange snarling beasts snapped at him from all directions. He looked for some path of escape, but beyond the flames was nothing but a deep, unnatural, darkness that somehow appeared cold, almost frozen.

There was a slight break in the flames and he ran toward the opening. He skidded to a halt as two huge, laughing men with large swords stepped out of the flames to block his path. They forced him back into the center of the flames. The snarling beasts joined them and they now began herding David slowly toward the opening in the flames.

David closed his eyes and thought, "Home," but nothing happened. He could now see that the path led toward a flaming pit. Huge flames shot out of the pit into the frozen darkness.

He shouted "Home!" but the laughing men and snarling beasts remained in front of him forcing him slowly down the path.

He was at the edge of the pit. He could feel the flames against the bare skin of his back. Chou's words from the first time they met rang through his mind. "If you step into nothing too many times eventually you will find yourself somewhere from which you cannot return. And that may not be a very pleasant place."

This was definitely not a pleasant place. "Chi!" he screamed. "Chi! Help! I need you!"

Chi was suddenly standing before him. "Take my hand," she said urgently.

He reached out and grasped her hand. Instantly they were in a small room standing next to a cot or bed. Chi was lying on the cot asleep. But at the same time, Chi was standing before him.

"You can go home now," the Chi who was holding his hand said firmly. Then she shimmered and disappeared.

"Thank you," David said to the sleeping Chi. She moved slightly on her bed and mumbled something in her sleep.

"Home," David said quietly.

As soon as he was out of the mirror, David collapsed. He would have fallen to the floor, but the strong arms of the Nash brothers caught him as he fell.

"We heard you screaming," Mark said as they laid him on the bed.

"I don't know where you were," Robert said, "but that sure as hell wasn't the Hong Kong Airport."

"I think it was Chi's room," David replied. His voice was soft and he had trouble forming his words.

"Yeah," Robert said, "but before that it was all flames and two really mean sons of..." He coughed and let his voice trail away as Special Agent Woods stepped up.

"I assume this means," she said brusquely, "that you can't go to the airport."

David looked up at her and said weakly, "I didn't have a link because I had never been there. I stepped into nothing." He shook his head as if to clear it and continued, "Chou warned me that if I stepped into nothing too many times, I might end up someplace from which I couldn't return. He hinted that it would be a bad place."

"I think that qualifies," Detective Nash said with a rough snort as he pointed at the mirror.

"Chi saved you," Agent Nash said softly. "But it

looks like the effort drained you pretty badly." He looked up at his boss and then said, "For now, you sleep. We will try to use... more conventional means... to locate the First Lady.

Chapter Seven
"Lost"

David slept heavily for several hours. His dreams alternated between images of Chi and images of the laughing men with swords. Whenever the men, accompanied by the snarling beasts, would get too close, Chi's voice would call out to him, "Take my hand," and suddenly he would be back in her bedroom gazing down on her as she slept peacefully on her cot.

He was looking down at her when suddenly she turned to face him and said harshly, "Awake, now!" But the voice was wrong. It wasn't her voice. It was the voice of Agent Nash.

The dream began to fade, but the voice continued, "David, please wake up. We need you." David could feel someone shaking his shoulder.

A different voice, this time the older brother said loudly. "Come on, kid. We need you. Shit's getting serious."

David pushed himself up to look around his bedroom. The Nash brothers were standing next to his bed. Both were looking down at him. Their faces showed their concern and urgency.

"We need you to find the First Lady again," Agent Nash said softly. "The... her husband... is about to go nuclear unless she is returned."

David shook his head slightly and muttered, "And I voted for that idiot." He smiled up at Agent Nash and said flatly, "Lesser of two evils."

He slowly got out of his bed and grabbed his robe. "What happened?" he asked.

"A lot," Robert said with his characteristic short snorting laugh. "Give him the highlights, little brother."

"We put out a terrorist alert on Helena Travis,"

Agent Mark said.

"That was my idea!" brother Robert interjected.

"Yes, it was," Mark answered sternly. "Only you would be that crazy."

Pointing over at the black mirror, Detective Nash said, "After all this, *nothing* is crazy."

"Why did you do that?" David asked.

"Because they thumbprint everybody going through any airport or border crossing," Robert answered. "Anyone on our suspected terrorist list gets flagged to us immediately."

"Oh," David said. "... and..."

"She flagged going through customs from Hong Kong to mainland China," Agent Mark answered. "We got the video, and the person with that thumbprint was a semi-conscious man in a pilot's uniform. He was in a wheelchair. His nurse, or whatever, pressed his thumb against the pad."

He blew out a long breath. "You were right. They disguised FLOTUS as the co-pilot to smuggle her into mainland China."

"And this is where it gets really hinky," Detective Robert said.

Agent Mark shot him a glaring stare and he immediately shut up.

"About ten minutes ago," Agent Mark continued, "these images were taken at the embassy in Beijing."

He held up his cellphone with an image of a limo sitting on a street. He flipped to a new image to show a close-up of a woman's face. It was Helena Travis. The obviously Chinese man next to her was holding a gun to her head.

"Those're from security cameras at the main gate," Agent Mark said firmly. "Douglas blew a gasket when he saw them and made a direct phone call to the Chinese Premier."

"I assume he was not very diplomatic about what he had to say," David said softly.

"We are now at DefCon Three, ready to go to Four," Robert said harshly. "Does that answer your question?"

"So what do you need me to do?" David asked.

"Find the First Lady," a voice said loudly from the doorway, "... before we go to DefCon Five."

David looked over to see Special Agent Patricia Woods leaning against the door frame. "You were right about the co-pilot. I don't know how you do it, but it works." Her voice softened greatly. "We really need you to find the First Lady again so we can defuse this."

"I will try," David said. "But first I have to talk to Chi. I... we... may need her help."

"Keep it short," Agent Mark said. "We'll leave you alone for now so you can..." his voice trailed off as he pointed at the black mirror mounted on the bedroom wall.

"And watch out for that flame place," added Detective Nash. "We really wouldn't want to lose you." His face and body language showed that he was honestly concerned.

"I'll be careful," David said. "I'm pretty sure I'm safe as long as I don't step off into nothing."

"Remember," Special Agent Woods said from the doorway, "time is of the essence."

"Please close the door on your way out," David replied.

Robert grinned at him as they all turned to leave. The detective was the last to go through the door. As he reached back to grab the doorknob, he again grinned at David and gave him a thumbs up sign.

"I wonder what I did that get that response?" David thought to himself. As he turned to the mirror he suddenly said "Oh! I didn't ask them to leave. I *told*

them to leave."

He walked across the room to where his phone was sitting in its charger. His simple text said, "Return to Home Page."

A moment later, a single Chinese character appeared in a response.

He returned to stand in front of the black mirror and smiled at himself before taking a deep breath. It took longer than normal to clear his mind and enter himself, but eventually he felt the tug as he was pulled into the mirror. Soon he was standing with Chi at Chou's tomb.

"Things have gotten worse," he told her. He stood looking at her silently not able to form what he knew he had to ask.

"What is wrong?" she asked.

"I don't want to put you in danger," he answered.

"I don't understand," she replied.

"I think we might be the only ones who can stop this war," David said softly, "but no one will believe us."

He took Chi's hands and looked directly in her eyes. "Is there any way that you can speak with someone in your government and get them to understand what is happening?"

Chi laughed. It was a light, almost silvery laugh. "I'm sorry," she said, "but who would believe a peasant girl from a little village?"

She turned very serious and said, "What would your President say if you tried to tell him directly what was going on?"

It was David's turn to laugh. "Point taken," he said. "That means our only hope is to find the First Lady and get her freed before her impulsive husband triggers World War Three.

"We need to find the First Lady," David said as he once again took Chi's hands. They both took a deep breath and closed their eyes... but nothing happened. They tried again... and again... and again, but both remained standing in Chou's tomb.

"There must still be no mirrors near her," David said dejectedly.

"Or," Chi said slowly, "she could be dead."

"No," David answered with a short, joyless, laugh. "If she were dead, it would be easier. I don't know why, but if the person is dead, the mirror only needs to be somewhere close. It doesn't have to be in the same room or even an adjacent area. It's like the spirit of the dead person knows we are searching and helps draw us there. She's alive, but cut off from all mirrors."

He released Chi's hands and said, "I need to report back."

Chi nodded at him and pulled her hands away. "What do we do now?" she asked.

"Pray," David answered, "and try to think of something really outside the box."

"Text me," Chi said, and then she shimmered slightly and was gone.

***

When David walked slowly into the living room everyone turned to stare directly at him, he said simply, "I couldn't find her. She must be back on the small plane or somewhere else where there are no mirrors."

In response Agent Nash pulled out his phone and tapped the screen. Almost immediately Jimmy's voice answered, "Yeah, what do you need?"

"The G5," Mark replied. "Where is it now and where has it been?"

"That's a little difficult to say for certain," Jimmy replied. "The transponder codes have been changed several times. We are having to rely on satellite

58

maintenance pings."

There was a short silence before Jimmy continued, "We're pretty sure that it hopped from Hong Kong to Shenzhen about forty klicks into mainland China. No one deplaned, but an elderly woman along with her nurse were taken aboard."

"Did you get any security tapes?" Special Agent Woods asked from across the room.

"Private arrival," Jimmy answered quickly. "Didn't have to go through security." He paused and said, "We assume it was the First Lady with a new disguise."

"Or they just put her in a dress and added a wig," Detective Nash said abruptly.

"Where did they go after that?" Agent Nash asked.

"Surprise, surprise," Jimmy answered. "They went straight to Beijing."

"Now we know how they got her to the embassy," Agent Woods replied. "It's about a three-hour flight. Timing would be right."

Walking over next to Agent Nash, she leaned toward the phone and asked, "Where is that plane now?"

"I'm not sure," Jimmy answered. "They must have cloned something in the automatic ID programs because there are three different aircraft pinging satellite maintenance logs with the same ID. None of them are G5s. They all read as G6s. One is heading to Shanghai, one to Singapore, and one to Moscow. The real plane could be any one of them, or none of them."

"Follow them all," Special Agent Woods barked out. "And let us know as soon as any of them land."

"What do you think?" she asked as she turned toward Agent Nash.

"Like Jimmy said, it could be any of the three," he replied as he shook his head, "... or none of them. I guess since David can't find her all we can do is wait and see what happens at the other end."

Turning to David, he said, "It might be best if you just rested for a while. Once these planes are on the ground we will have you try again. There's nothing you can do 'til then, so grab some sleep."

David walked slowly back into his bedroom. He mind wasn't sure that he could sleep, but his body was pulling him toward the bed. A few moments later he was face down on his pillow, snoring softly.

Chapter Eight
"Found"

The soft ping of David's cellphone receiving a text normally would not have awakened him, but nothing was normal about the past day. He sat bolt upright on his bed as his mind processed what had happened. A second ping brought him out of bed. The text said, "Return to Home Page."

Chi was once again pacing back and forth in front of Chou's tomb when David arrived. "What's up?" he asked as things cleared.

Chi held up her hand with one finger extended. "How will they get Helena back into the United States?" she asked. "They don't know that we found their planes. So they might use the same plane to bring her back."

"And..." David said.

"We need to go back to that plane and see what they are doing with it now." Chi answered.

She reached up and took David's hands in her own. David joined her as she said, "The plane."

A few moments later, they were once again standing in the main cargo deck area on the fake UPS plane. Both startled slightly at the expansive space they found themselves in.

"The plane's empty," Chi said.

"The important question," David replied, "is where are we?"

Chi turned and stuck her head through the window on the side of the plane. When she pulled herself back in, David shuddered and said, "Don't do that. It looks too... weird."

Chi smiled and said, "Maybe I should try that while we are flying."

David shuddered again and asked, "Can you tell

where we are?"

"Shanghai," Chi replied. "The Hongqiao Airport."

She paused for a moment and then said, "And the plane's a different color."

David stepped toward the fuselage wall and then stopped. "Oh, well," he finally said. "Here goes."

He then stuck his head through the wall and looked around. The airplane was now obviously white. There were Chinese characters above the painted-over windows and a symbol that looked like a blue boomerang hitting a larger red one on the tail.

"That says 'China Cargo Airlines," Chi said. David startled as he looked to his right to see the top portion of her body sticking out from the side of the plane.

As they pulled themselves back inside, she added, "It should say it in English just below the Chinese characters. I don't know why it doesn't."

"Plausible denial," David said. "They are probably going to claim to be somebody else when they get to the US."

"You need to go back and report," Chi said. "I am going to try to find the First Lady."

"How?" David asked.

Chi gave a shy smile and said, "I'd rather not tell you unless it works." She then stretched her head up slightly and gave him a quick kiss on the cheek.

"Wait... wait," David sputtered as she shimmered and disappeared. He then sighed deeply and said, "Home."

He half-way expected the brothers to be waiting for him in his bedroom, but when he turned from the mirror, he was alone. He took the time to put on a pair of blue jeans and a shirt before going out into the living room.

More equipment had been added to the tables.

Agent Nash and Special Agent Woods were hunched over a monitor talking softly. They looked up when David said, "I think they are taking her to Shanghai."

"What makes you think that?" Agent Mark asked.

"That's where the fake UPS plane is," David answered. "But now it's a fake China Air Cargo plane. They wouldn't have gone through all the trouble of re-painting it if they weren't going to use it again."

"Jimmy," Special Agent Woods called out, "is there anything you can tell us about that plane headed for Shanghai?"

A sandy-haired young man stuck his head up over one of the monitors on one of the other tables. "Still pinging as a G6," he said. "Current altitude forty-eight thousand feet. All systems check as OK."

"That can't be," David said loudly, and then shrank back slightly as all eyes in the room turned to look at him..

"Why not?" asked Agent Nash.

"Only a G5 can fly that high," David answered. "The G4 can only go to forty-five thousand and the G6 can't even get that high. The G5 can go above fifty-thousand. If it's at forty-eight thousand it has to be a G5."

He shrugged his shoulders and added softly, "I saw it on the History Channel."

Jimmy, who had been typing furiously on his keyboard, exclaimed. "He's right. That has to be a G5 headed for Shanghai."

Special Agent Woods turned to face David. "We need to know everything that you can find out about that plane. You and your girlfriend go back there and look around. Try to find out where it's going."

Agent Nash added, "Then come back here and rest. The G5 will be arriving there in about three hours. We need you there when that happens so you can tell us if they transfer FLOTUS to the China Air Cargo."

"OK," David answered. "I'll bring Chi up to speed and then we'll go take a closer look at the plane."

"I think she already knows what is going on," Detective Nash said in his typical, loud voice.

David looked at him quizzically. "I think she has been hanging around here for the past hour or so."

Now everyone was looking at him with questioning looks on their faces. He shrugged his shoulders and said, "It's what I would do."

He then leaned over and said very softly to David, "Plus, I think I saw her face flash in the mirror about forty-five minutes ago." He pointed at an ornate mirror on the living room wall and added, "It was like when you came back from the tomb. It was there and gone in an instant, but it was her."

"Oh," David said. He had never considered that he might be seen as he entered somewhere from the mirror.

Robert continued, "If I hadn't seen it before, I would've thought it was just my mind doing strange things with a reflection." His voice softened as he continued, "I don't think anyone else would have caught it even if they were looking directly at the mirror when she stepped out."

He then shrugged his shoulders once again and raised his eyebrows.

"I'll ask her if she was here when we talk at Chou's tomb," David said.

His phone chirped and he pulled it from his pocket. The text message said, "Return to Home Page."

"That's Chi," David said. "She wants me to meet her at the tomb."

"She was here," Robert said. "She must be one sharp little fortune cookie."

"She's not that little," David replied, and then suddenly felt himself turning a deep shade of red. "I

64

mean..." he sputtered out but was interrupted by Agent Nash who said firmly, "Just go get her and check out the plane."

When he arrived at the tomb, Chi was waiting for him. "Yes, I was there," she said. Then she held up her hands and said, "Grab on. Let's go."

David took her hands in his own and together they said aloud, "The plane."

The tugging feeling when they moved from mirror to mirror was different than when they were drawn into the mirror. Being pulled into the mirror was like something grabbing your belly and tugging you forward. When they moved from the tomb to the plane, David felt like he was being tugged sideways.

As they appeared in the plane, David had the quick worry that their faces might have appeared in the painted-over windows for just a moment. The plane, however, was empty.

Chi walked slowly to the side of the plane where a large stairway was pushed up against a door. "I wonder how far away from the plane we can walk?" she asked as she stepped down the stairs.

"Only one way to find out," David answered as he joined her.

As they walked away from the plane, voices drifted toward them from the wing. A wide, flat fuel truck was parked next to the plane with a hose attached to the wing. Two men were standing next to the truck.

One of them looked down at his clipboard and asked, "Are you sure they ordered this much fuel? Their tanks will be close to completely filled."

"It's flying empty to the ivory field," the other man answered. "So there's no cargo weight. They want to make it non-stop."

"It's a shame to see a plane like this sent to the ivory field," the first man said. "But they are switching the entire fleet over to more fuel-efficient planes and evidently couldn't get a buyer for this one."

The second man laughed and said, "We all end up in the ivory field eventually. Some of us just go there sooner than others."

Both men laughed for a moment. Then a loud beep from the side of the truck cut short their laughter. "110,000 kg of fuel," one of them said as he read a panel on the side of the truck. "With an empty plane, that should get them at least seven thousand nautical miles." He closed the cover on the meter area and said, "Log it and bill it."

"Already done," the other said as he set a notepad of some sort back in a holder inside the cab of the truck. "We're ready to roll as soon as ground traffic gives us clearance."

David suddenly realized that Chi was no longer at his side. She was walking slowly away from the plane. She was about a hundred feet away when the top half of her started to shimmer slightly.

She screamed and struggled to pull herself backwards. The mist seemed to be pulling her in as David ran toward her. "Chi!" he yelled, and she turned toward him, straining to pull herself out of the fog. Finally she broke free of the mist and stumbled toward David. Her face was filled with fear.

"Are you OK?" he asked loudly as he reached where she was standing.

She stared at him a moment and then said in a shaky voice, "There was fire..." she held herself tightly before continuing, "... and beasts. ... and two warriors with long swords."

"Been there... done that," David answered. "And I really don't want the T-shirt."

He laughed at Chi's very confused expression and said, "American idiom. It probably doesn't translate into

Chinese."

"It made no sense," Chi said, "but neither did what I saw."

"It is the nothingness that Chou warned me about," David replied. He gestured with his hands and arms moving in a circle around himself. "However all of this works," he said, "it is evidently not totally real... or not totally within our normal world... or something."

He pressed his lips together and continued. "We... or the mirror... or something... evidently creates a bubble of mirror world that overlaps the real world. We can jump into that bubble or from bubble to bubble, and as long as we stay inside that bubble everything is fine."

His voice became very firm as he said, "But, if we step outside that bubble, we are in the place of beasts and flame that Chou warned me about."

"Have you really been there?" Chi asked. Concern was evident on her face.

"Unfortunately, yes," David answered. "And I would still be there if you hadn't come and rescued me."

Chi replied in surprise, "I rescued you?"

David gave a short laugh. "You were asleep," he said. "I called out to you and you reached into the nothingness and pulled me back into your bedroom."

He looked down at the ground and said, "It was really weird standing there holding your hand while at the same time you were sleeping in your bed."

"I don't remember anything about that," Chi said slowly. Then in a much softer voice she added, "Sometimes the actions of the mirrors are very frightening."

"But you are no longer alone," David said as he took her hand, "and neither am I."

"You need to go back and report." Chi said softly. "We really didn't learn anything except that they filled the plane with fuel and that it is going to an ivory field somewhere."

"That's about it," David replied.

"I will text you when we need to come back into the mirror," he said. Then he looked Chi directly in the eyes and said softly, "Don't wear yourself out coming to my house. I will tell you everything when we meet at the tomb."

He suddenly stopped and said, "No. Better idea. I'll text you when it looks like things are heating up again. If I say 'Return to Home Page,' meet me at the tomb. If it is 'Return to Page One,' come to wherever I am. OK?"

"OK," Chi answered with a laugh. "You are 'Page One.'" She laughed again and asked, "Does that make me 'Page Two'?"

Both laughed again and David said, "See you soon." This time he must have left first because he didn't see Chi shimmer and leave. As he took several deep breaths in front of the black mirror in his bedroom, he said to himself, "This just keeps getting weirder and weirder." He gave a short laugh and added, "Or maybe I should say curiouser and curiouser."

Chapter Nine
"Lost Again"

Once again, as he walked into the living room he stopped in shock. This time it was because everyone was gone. The people... the equipment... the tables were all gone. All that was there were two men who were setting the couch back in place and Special Agent Woods standing near the door speaking with Agent Mark Nash and his brother.

"What... what happened?" he sputtered.

"What happened is DOSS Richards," Special Agent Woods said angrily.

"Who?" David asked.

"Director of Secret Service Andrew Richards," Agent Mark said evenly. "He demanded to know exactly how we were getting our information."

"And you told him?" David said incredulously.

"Yeah," Robert said, "she told him."

"We have been ordered to return all assets to our regional office in Chicago," Special Agent Woods said. Her voice was controlled, but obviously still filled with anger.

"You can't," David said, his own anger rising. "This is our only chance of finding the First Lady."

"I know," she replied shaking her head and sighing. "But when I objected, he made it a direct order." She paused and pressed her lips together very firmly. "We are now at DefCon Five, so refusal to comply with a direct order would be considered treason in time of war."

Her shoulders drooped and her voice dropped to not much more than a whisper. "I have no choice."

Taking a deep breath and squaring her shoulders, she turned to face Mark. "Field Agent Mark Nash," she said firmly, "for putting us in this situation, I am placing you on administrative leave starting immediately."

Mark looked back at her in shock.

"I will not demand your gun and credentials," she continued, "but as of this minute, you are to consider yourself to be on modified duty. As a condition of that administrative leave while on modified duty, you are not to participate in any actions or commands of the Chicago Field Office." She looked him in the eyes and said, "Do you understand me?"

Agent Nash looked back at her in shock and then suddenly his face changed to almost a smile. "Yes, Ma'am," he almost shouted back. "I understand you."

He looked over at his brother, Robert, and then back at David before once again facing her and saying, "And I will report anything to you that may affect my status while on modified duty."

"You do understand me," she said, also almost smiling. "I look forward to hearing from you," she said as she walked toward the front door. She paused before leaving and turned back, "I have told Jimmy that he may assist you in whatever you might be doing while out of the office."

"Thank you, Ma'am," Agent Nash said as she closed the door.

Detective Robert walked up to Mark and said, "OK, little brother, I'm confused as hell. You look happy to have been relieved of duty."

"I wasn't relieved of duty," Agent Mark said firmly. "I was freed to do my duty."

"Oh," Robert replied, "that explains everything."

"I'm on administrative leave," Mark said loudly. "The direct order doesn't apply to me. I don't have to go back to Chicago with the rest of the team."

"Oh!" Robert said, nodding. "So you can stay here and work with David and maybe solve this whole thing."

"That means," David said slowly, "that it falls on us to stop World War Three."

"Actually," Agent Mark said, "it falls on you. The fate of the world is in your hands."

"No pressure," said Detective Nash.

Mark immediately shot him one of his nastier glares and then turned to David and said, "What do we have?"

"Well," David began, "we know that they have loaded the plane with as much fuel as it can carry and that their ultimate destination is 'the ivory fields,' whatever that means."

"A fully-fueled 747," Mark responded, "could reach almost anywhere in the world."

"But they said," Robert interjected, "that they would bring the First Lady back to the United States."

"OK," Agent Mark said walking over to David's personal laptop which had been returned to a small desk on one wall of the living room. "What does the internet say when we search for 'ivory fields USA'?"

He typed on the laptop keyboard for a moment and then turned back to face the other two. "Unless they are going somewhere named for a famous race horse or known for its linen ware, I've come up empty."

"Let me go back into the mirror," David said. "I will text Chi and we will go back to the plane. Maybe we can figure something out."

"OK," Mark replied. "We'll be waiting."

"Do you need to eat first?" Robert asked. "The team left a bunch of food in your refrigerator."

"No," answered David, "I'm good. I'll report back as soon as Chi and I figure out anything."

"Stay safe," Agent Mark said, and David turned and walked down the hallway back to his bedroom.

David texted Chi and then stood before his black mirror. It took several deep breaths before he could even begin to relax enough to feel the pull of the mirror. When he arrived at the tomb, he expected Chi to be there, but he was alone.

He stood in front of Chou's tomb and rested his hands against the cold marble. With a light touch, his hands remained on the surface, but if he pressed more firmly, they pushed into the rock itself.

"Chou," he said, "you knew war. Did you think your war was the last war? Or did you know that war is always lurking just over the horizon?"

"This war is not inevitable," Chi said from behind him.

David turned and Chi was standing looking at him. "We can stop this war," she said. "Even if all of the other people have left you, David, you and I and your two friends can stop this war."

"You were there?" he asked.

"Yes," she said. "I was there. Is your entire government that stupid?"

"I'm beginning to think," David said with a bitter laugh, "that all governments are stupid. Otherwise we would never have war."

He took her hands in his own and said firmly, "The plane!"

***

Once again they found themselves standing on the main cargo deck of the 747. It was apparently airborne. David looked around and startled slightly at the sight of the huge cargo container which seemed to fill most of the plane's cargo bay.

"I thought they said the plane would be empty," Chi said as she stared at the huge container.

"They had to have opened the nose to slide this one in," David said.

He pointed to about the center of the container and said, "There's no seam or separation like before. It's one container, not two or four stacked together."

"The ladder is up," Chi said, pointing at the space where the ladder had been before.

Looking up, David could see the ladder folded up into the ceiling.

"What's that area called?" Chi asked, pointing up at the ceiling of the cargo area.

"The galley... I think," David answered.

"It is whatever you think it is," Chi answered and took his hands in her own.

"The galley," she said firmly and with a sideways tug they were whisked to the space in front of the now empty seats behind the flight deck.

They quickly looked around and Chi pointed to where a man was sleeping on one of the bunks.

"Doesn't he ever change his shirt?" David asked as he recognized the co-pilot.

Chi walked forward and stepped into the cockpit. Her startled yelp caused David to rush to her side.

She was standing partially through the legs of a man seated in the third seat which was now fully deployed from its storage place in the wall.

"I walked right through him," Chi said, shuddering. "I could feel it." She shuddered again and said, "I don't feel anything when I go through the doors or walls, but there was something when I went through him."

"You must be feeling his life force or whatever," David answered. "I'll stay here. You look around and see if you can find anything that says where they might be going."

"It says row," Chi replied after looking over the pilot's shoulder. "Like in row and column. Those are two more English words I know."

"I don't know how helpful that is," David said.

"It also says s-h-a," she added. "I don't know what that word means, but it was written on some of the buildings at Hongqiao airport in Shanghai."

"They're not words," David almost yelled. "They are airport call signs. SHA is the call sign for Shanghai's Hongqiao Airport. All we need to do is find out where ROW is and we know where they are going."

He grabbed Chi's arm and pulled her back into the galley area behind the cockpit. "I need to go back and report. Follow me... come to where I am."

Chi nodded and David said softly, "Home."

Chapter Ten
"Curiouser and Curiouser"

When David stepped into the living room, Agent Mark was hunched over his laptop at the desk. Detective Robert was snoring loudly from the sofa. Mark gave him a quick hand signal and said, "Just a sec."

David walked into the kitchen and opened the refrigerator. A few moments later, he walked back into the living room holding a bottle of sports drink. "I don't need this when I go running," he said to Agent Nash as he walked over to the desk, "but after a little while in the mirror, I'm low on electrolytes."

"What have you found out?" Mark asked.

"Do you know where they are going?" Robert asked from behind him as he got up from the couch.

"There was a slip of paper in the cockpit," David began. "It had two call signs on it. One was SHA, which is Hongqiao airport in Shanghai. The other was ROW, but I don't know what or where that is."

"ROW," Mark repeated as he typed on the keyboard.

His brother, who was looking over his shoulder startled slightly and looked over at David. "Just when you think it can't get any weirder..." he said shaking his head.

"Where is it?" David asked.

Agent Mark seemed to be chewing on his lips as he read and re-read the screen. "Roswell, New Mexico," he answered.

"*THE* Roswell?!" David sputtered.

"None other," answered Detective Robert with a smile. "They are *REALLY* going to believe us now"

His voiced changed to a higher-pitched, almost sing-song quality as he bounced slightly and said,

"Mister Richards, your Directorship, Sir, the First Lady is being taken to Roswell to join the aliens in Area 51's fields of ivory."

"The key to understanding this," David said slowly, "is figuring out what those two mechanics meant by 'fields of ivory.'"

He turned toward the center of the room and said, "Chi, if you're here, meet me at Chou's tomb. I need to know what 'fields of ivory' means."

He then turned back to the brothers and said, "Be right back," and left the room.

When he arrived at Chou's tomb, Chi was waiting for him. She was opening and closing her mouth as if she was starting to speak, but remained silent. Finally she said, "It means 'fields of ivory.'"

She huffed and continued, "It's an idiom, like when you said something about a T-shirt. I don't think it translates into English even in the mirror. I don't know how to make you understand what it means."

"OK," David said. "It's an idiom. But what does it mean? What is someone describing when they say it?"

Chi took a deep breath. "An ivory field is where a great battle took place– a great massacre. One side kills all of their opponents, so there is no one left to bury them. Their bones lie in the sun and become a field of ivory."

"A bone yard," David yelled out. "They are taking the plane to a bone yard."

Chi was now the one to look hopelessly confused.

"In English," David explained, "a cemetery is sometimes called a bone yard. The places where they take old planes is called a bone yard. The planes are all set out in the sun and slowly stripped of parts until they are finally crushed and melted down for the metal."

He grabbed Chi by the hands and jumped up and down with joy. "I have to report back," he yelled. He pulled Chi into a tight hug and said joyfully, "The First Lady is aboard that plane... and now we know where it's going."

He paused slightly and added, "I think."

"Text me,' Chi said as the tomb faded away and his bedroom reappeared.

Grabbing his robe and running into the living room, he yelled out, "Agent Nash... Agent Nash, is there a bone yard in Roswell?"

"A what?" came the startled response.

"An airplane bone yard?" David said rapidly. "Is there an airplane bone yard in Roswell, New Mexico?"

"Yeah, there is," Detective Robert said, standing up from where he had been seated on the couch. "Used to be about nothing, but now a lot of commercial airlines scrap out their planes there or store them for resale."

When both Mark and David turned to look at him, he pointed at David and said, "He's not the only one who watches The History Chanel."

He then turned to his brother and asked, "Why are they going there?"

Mark looked down at the floor as he spoke. "They are hiding in plain sight again. If the cargo airlines are really phasing out the 747s, there are probably hundreds of them at Roswell. A lot of them are probably from China Air Cargo. It would take forever to search through them all... even if I could get the authority to do so."

"You know what that means?" Robert said with a smile.

After both Mark and David had turned to look at him, he held his arms above his head and shouted, "Road Trip!"

Mark turned to look at David. He shook his head from side to side and gave a short laugh. "My big brother has never really grown up... but he's right. I have to go to Roswell and physically find the First Lady."

His face became strangely firm and set as he pointed at David and said, "They have officially written you off. No matter what you say, they won't believe it. I have to see her with my own eyes before I report her location."

"No," David said. His face also looked set and determined. "*WE* have to go to Roswell. You need me to guide you, and you need your big brother to guard your back."

Robert looked intently at his brother while pointing his finger at David. "He's right... on both counts. We won't find jack shit without him, and if you go charging in there alone, somebody's liable to put a bullet in your back."

He then looked over at David and asked, "How will you be able to do this? Do we have to take that mirror off your wall and carry it with us?"

David laughed slightly and said, "I would say, 'You aren't going to believe this,' but after the past two days, I think you are ready to believe anything."

He started walking into the kitchen and said softly, "Follow me."

A few moments later they were standing in David's garage. There was a small convertible, an off-road motorcycle, and an oversized van with windows on the side and a strange-looking box on the top.

"That's a Class B camper," David explained. "It's got a bed, a kitchen, and– pointing at the box on the roof– an RV air conditioner." He opened the side door, which was about the size and shape of a regular house door except that it was rounded at the corners. "And even more importantly," he said pointing inside, "it has a black mirror."

"Son of a..." Robert said as he looked into the van.

"I use it when I have cases in other states," David said.

He then turned and faced the brothers. "Des Moines to El Paso is about 18 hours of driving. Roswell is about three and one-half hours short of that. We are just under two hours from Des Moines, so my best guess is we have over sixteen hours of actual driving ahead of us. Even pushing it, the trip will probably take twenty hours."

"You'd better let your little friend know what's going on," Robert said, pointing back at the house.

"I can talk to her on the way," David replied. "At least, I think I can." He took a deep breath and set his lips before he said, "I don't know that I can't."

"How soon can you be ready to go?" Mark asked, looking back and forth between his brother and David.

"I'm ready," said Robert. "I'm officially on vacation... or working with the Secret Service on a special op... or maybe I don't have a job anymore. In any case, I'm ready to go whenever you are."

"All I have to do is to pull a few things out of my car," Mark said. He then looked over at David.

"I have a go bag in my closet with four days' worth of clothes and five thousand dollars in cash." David replied. "The water tanks are good on the van and there is food in the cupboards."

"Prepared for anything, aren't you?" Robert said with a laugh.

"Inspector Harris isn't the only one who wants to talk to me downtown when I call in the location of a body," he replied. "Some are even bigger jerks than he is."

Robert laughed loudly.

Agent Mark said, "Go get dressed and grab your bags. We roll in ten minutes."

***

79

It was actually eight minutes later when the van pulled out of David's garage. The last thing David checked on his laptop before taking it out to the van was the flight time from Shanghai to Roswell. Depending on winds and the chosen speed, it was somewhere between sixteen and twenty-two hours.

The van had a curtain which hung just behind the driver's and passenger's seats. David pulled it closed, saying, "I need a little privacy for this to work." He laughed softly and added, "Besides, we don't want to cause any crashes or have someone call 911 because they saw something weird."

"Nothing weird going on here," Robert said. "Just two cops who may be out of their jobs and a nut job who walks in mirrors driving twelve hundred miles to the middle of wackoville to find a kidnaped woman that the rest of the world thinks is in China." He shrugged his shoulders and added, "All sounds reasonable to me."

"Uncouth," Agent Nash said, "but direct and to the point."

"I'm going to have Chi come here so she can see what this place is." He stopped as if he were debating whether or not to continued. "... and also so she can come back to this van in case something happens to me."

"What good would that do?" Mark asked.

"I don't know," David replied with a sigh. "But if she knows we have failed, maybe she can get someone on her side to listen before everything goes south."

"That's worked so well on this end," Robert said derisively. "Good luck on that."

"Try to not make any sudden maneuvers," David said before closing the curtain. "I'm going to be standing up back here, and I'm really not sure how well my body responds when I'm not there."

"Not weird at all," Robert answered. "Not weird at all."

David sat on the couch which folded out into a bed and sent the text, "Return to Home Page." He then dropped his robe and stood in front of the mirror. The swaying of the van made it much more difficult to concentrate, but after a few minutes, he felt the familiar tug of the mirror.

Chi was pacing waiting for him at Chou's tomb when he arrived.

"What is wrong?" she asked nervously.

"Everything," David replied angrily. When Chi backed away from him, he said, "I'm sorry. I'm not angry at you." He paused and took several deep breaths. "I'm angry at our government... or at least at the stupid people in high places in our government."

Chi put her hand on his shoulder. "If it helps at all," she said softly, "yours is not the only government with stupid people in high places."

"But those stupid people... on both sides," he answered, "might just destroy the world."

Both he and Chi stood looking down at the floor of the tomb in silence. Finally Chi asked softly, "What do we need to do?"

David gave a hollow laugh and said, "For now, I need you to come to where I am. We– Agent Nash and Detective Nash and I– are driving to Roswell, New Mexico, in hopes that we can free the First Lady once the plane arrives there. The head of the Secret Service pulled all the agents back to the regional office when he found out how they were getting their information about where the President's wife is."

He looked down again at the floor and said softly, "If we fail... or if something happens to me... you need to be able to get to the van to see what happened." He took her hands in his own and turned her so that they were looking into each other's eyes. "If I fail, you may be the only hope left for the world."

"Then *WE* cannot fail," she replied firmly. "There is nothing either of us can do right now, so you probably need to go back and sleep. I will come to where you are and study your van so I can return to it if I need to."

David nodded his head in agreement and said, "We have about eighteen hours of driving before we get to Roswell. We will be on major highways, so texts should go through... unless they shut down the phone system out of fear of terrorism."

Chi answered, "OK," and shimmered into nothingness.

"Home," David said softly and once again he was standing in the back of the van.

Chapter Eleven
"Road Trip"

It soon became obvious that the trip was actually going to take much longer than eighteen hours. Massive columns of troops and National Guard units were pouring down the interstates so civilian traffic was shunted to the surface streets and regular highways. Many of those were clogged with traffic as frantic people attempted to get back to their homes or loved ones before war began.

Mark and Robert did most of the driving. David insisted that he should do his share, but Robert explained in his very plain style, "God help us, but our only hope of finding the First Lady is a nut job who takes off his clothes and stares into a black mirror. That's you, and going into that mirror takes a lot out of you. You've got to be ready to do whatever mumbo-jumbo you do for as long as it takes when we get there. Once we have her located, little brother and I will take over, but we need you at the top of your game until then. So, I want your ass in that bed resting up for the big game. There ain't gonna be no second half to recover. We've already had our double overtime and are playing sudden death."

He sputtered slightly and said, "Maybe that last one wasn't the best analogy."

"Maybe it was," Mark said as he wove through traffic. "This could be sudden death... for any of us."

All three remained quiet for quite a while following that. The silence was broken by a text arrival chirp from David's phone. Before David could reach it, it chirped once again. The first text said, "cargo." The second text said, "Return to Home Page."

"Chi wants me at the tomb," David said and pulled

the curtain closed.

As soon as he arrived, Chi said heatedly. "Where is the President's woman?"

"What?" David sputtered back.

"We are assuming she is on that plane, but *WHERE?*"

"I don't know," David answered. "But she has to be on that plane. It's the only thing that makes sense."

"We need to look in the cargo containers," Chi said firmly. She then took David's hands and said, "The plane."

***

Chi and David found themselves once again standing on the main cargo deck of the 747-400. Chi walked forward to where the walls began to curve inward.

"You said they must have opened this to put the cargo container aboard," she said, pointing at the nose. "Why did you say that?"

"Because this is a single container," David answered. "It's too big to have come in the side door."

"How long is it?" Chi asked.

David chuckled and said, "That's a little difficult to tell from here. Some of these full load containers go all the way to the tail. They are like miniature warehouses with goods stacked within them."

"Then we need to explore," Chi said as she pushed against the door on the front of the container and gradually flowed through it.

David followed behind her. He expected to be walking into darkness, but instead, there was dim lighting... and a second door. They were standing in a small passageway between the two doors.

"Why are there two doors?' Chi asked.

Both stood staring at the second door for several seconds before David said, "Sound control?"

"Of course!" Chi said. "Like they use in smuggling people on a boat. It looks like a cargo container, but several people can live inside of it for days... or even weeks."

"Well," David said, "let's see if the First Lady is inside."

He reached out and pushed his arm through the second door, and then followed it into a small room. The floor, walls, and ceiling appeared to be covered in a thick carpeting. As he looked around Chi was at his side running her hand over the carpeted wall.

"That's the First Lady," he said, pointing to a woman apparently asleep on one of four bunks built into the side of the room.

"I assume those are her guards," Chi added, pointing to four men sitting at a table playing some sort of card game.

"Now we know what we are dealing with," David said. "The only problem will be finding this plane once they put it in the bone yard. Who knows how many other identical planes might be stored there."

"We need the tail number," Chi said as she turned and bent over slightly so she could push her upper body through the side wall.

"NO!" screamed David, but it was too late. Chi was pulled through the wall as if she had been sucked up into a giant vacuum cleaner, which was more or less what had happened to her.

Neither Chi nor David felt wind blowing against them or heat or cold when they were walking in the mirrors, but there was some resistance to pushing through solid objects, so they were not totally impervious to the real world which surrounded them. When Chi stuck her upper body through the side of the plane, she entered the slipstream flowing around the outside of the jet. The near supersonic wind pulled her out of the plane and slammed her into the tail section.

Had that happened in normal reality, death would have been immediate and the tail section of the plane may have been badly damaged. As it was, Chi found herself unconscious and falling thousands of feet toward the earth.

David looked at the wall where a few moments before Chi had been standing. He took a deep breath and said, "Chi!"

He was suddenly standing in her room. A tapestry had been pulled back on one wall exposing what appeared to be a polished circle of brass. Chi was standing before it. As he approached her, she suddenly fell to the ground screaming.

An older woman burst into the room. She was dressed in a mixture of modern clothing and homemade Chinese peasant garb. "Chi," she yelled shrilly. "I told you to stop this nonsense." She reached down and helped Chi to her feet. "If you keep going into that mirror, you will end up like your uncle."

She helped Chi to the bed and pulled the covers up over her body. Then she said in a much softer voice, "If your grandfather were here, he could guide you, but without a guide, you will end up in the place of fire and beasts."

"I have found a guide," Chi said softly. Then she sat up and said firmly, "And it was I who saved him from the fire warriors."

The woman stepped back and looked at her in shock. "You are not alone?" she asked.

"I am not alone," Chi replied softly. "And my guide and I have been chosen to stop this war that is almost upon us."

She stood up and said firmly, "I must go back into

the mirror for a little while, Mother, then I will rest."

The woman bowed slightly and said, "I understand, my daughter. May the winds be with you."

Chi then turned toward the center of the room and said, "David, I know you are here. Please meet me once again at the tomb. Then you can report back to the warrior brothers."

Chi was wobbling on her feet when she appeared at the tomb. David took her in his arms to support her. "I never before knew what happened to my uncle," she said weakly. Taking a deep breath, she continued, "Now I know."

She looked up at David and explained. "The brass mirror in my room belonged to him. It is a match to the one my grandfather had." She stopped to take several deep breaths. "My uncle has been asleep for many years. His eyes open and close, but it is as if he is not there." She paused and then said sadly, "Now I know that he truly is not there. He died in the mirror. I don't know if it was the fire warriors or something like what nearly happened to me today, but now I know that you can die in the mirror."

She broke free of David's embrace and turned to face him. "If I die in the mirror, please tell my family what happened and where my spirit is." She looked into David's eyes and continued, "I promise to do the same for you."

"You need to rest," David said softly. "I thought I had lost you."

"I thought I was lost," she replied. "Luckily, I was falling a long, long way. I came to and was able to return home before I struck the ground. If I hadn't..."

Her voice trailed off, and then she laughed— it was more like a huff than a laugh. "I wonder how far into the earth I would have gone before I stopped?" she asked.

"Hopefully," David answered, "neither of us will

ever have to find out." He stepped back slightly and said, "Go. Rest. I'll text you when we've reached Roswell."

Chi smiled at him, shimmered, and began to disappear. She was almost gone when suddenly she stepped forward once again. "I almost forgot," she said. "... the plane."

"What about the plane?" David asked.

"They painted it again," she answered, "...or at least the tail. It was a bright color with a strange symbol on it."

"Do you remember anything else?"

"I remember that I thought I would never see my family again... or you," she said slowly. "I am so tired," she said as she once again began to shimmer. This time she faded completely out.

"Home," David said softly and once again he was standing, weaving, in the back of the moving van.

Chapter Twelve
"A Needle in a Needle Stack"

The drive to Roswell International Air Center took a total of twenty-seven hours. The first hint that searching for the plane might be more difficult than expected came when they approached the entrance to the airport. A portable guard shack of some sort sat in the middle of the road. Sandbagged guard positions had been stacked up on the two corners.

Robert was driving. He turned toward his brother and whispered, "How in the hell do we explain what we're up to?"

Mark replied, "*WE* don't. I do. Both of you keep absolutely quiet."

The guard was wearing an Army National Guard uniform with an MP armband. He had that false politeness that indicated he was not new to controlling access to important areas. He leaned over toward the open driver's window and said, "I'm sorry Sir, the airport is temporarily closed to civilian traffic. Entry is to authorized personnel only."

"I think I'm authorized," Mark said as he held up his credentials.

He then returned the guard's smile and asked, "Am I permitted to get out of the vehicle to discuss this with you?"

The guard continued his smile, but he raised his arm and made a circling gesture with his hand. There was a loud click and one of the machine guns which had been pointed skyward lowered and swiveled to point directly at the van.

"Just don't move too quickly," the guard said with practiced politeness. "Things are a little tense around here."

"Things are tense everywhere right now," Mark replied as he stepped out of the van. Holding his badge and ID in front of himself and keeping his other arm well away from his body he approached the guard, stopping when he was about six feet away.

"I am Agent Mark Nash," he said clearly. "I am with the Secret Service. The people in the van are Detective Robert Nash, my brother, and David Malone, a civilian technician with special skills."

The guard stepped forward and took the ID folder from Mark's hand.

"I was visiting my brother in Iowa when the shit hit the fan," Mark continued. "I commandeered Detective Nash because I needed someone on my six I could trust. He knew of David's skills from his work on the police department."

"Why are you here?" the guard asked. His voice was less polite, but much more natural.

"One of the satellites," Mark answered, pointing up at the sky, "is picking up an unauthorized transmission from one of the planes parked in the bone yard. They want it checked out."

"Why you?" the guard asked. His voice was now getting slightly forceful.

"Because I screwed up and am on limited duty," Mark replied. He tried to make his voice sound disgusted as he said loudly, "This is a bullshit detail, but somebody has to do it and I'm on the director's shit list. He wouldn't even authorize air travel, we just drove twenty-seven hours from nowhere, Iowa, and are tired as hell. All we have to do is drive up and down through the rows of junk planes while the kid scans for a signal. If we find anything– which we won't– I will call you and your people can investigate it. After that, we can go back to corn country."

The guard laughed slightly. "When they activated

us," he said, "I figured we would be heading for combat somewhere." He pointed over at the airfield. "Instead, they have us guarding empty airplanes."

He took a deep breath and explained. "Because we are not in a target area, Roswell has been designated a safe haven for aircraft. Every US airline and half the airlines in the world are sending their planes here so they will be on the ground in case some idiot..." He paused and coughed before continuing. "... in case some idiot decides that it is worth starting World War Three because his wife is missing."

"I don't understand," Mark said.

"A missile barrage will create an electromagnetic pulse," David said from the van. "It would probably be almost world-wide, especially in the higher atmosphere. Planes would lose all electronics and drop out of the sky."

"So they brought them here to play dead until the dust settles," Mark said with a shake of his head.

He then looked at the guard and asked, "How many?"

"They've been landing here at ten to twenty an hour for the past forty-eight hours or so," the guard replied. "There must be a thousand of them out there scattered on the desert. As soon as they power down, we cover their engines and tarp them– if we can– and tow them out into the desert storage area."

"What do we have to do to get permission to scan them?" Mark asked.

In response, the guard keyed the radio mike on his shoulder and said, "I've got a Secret Service Agent out here who needs to scan the bone yard for radio transmissions."

The response could not be heard. Evidently the reply went directly to the guard's earpiece. "He already said that, Sir." the guard answered into his mic. "He's on somebody's shit list and the eyes in the sky say someone or something is transmitting from the bone yard. If he actually finds anything, he will call on us to check it out."

The guard stood staring at nothing for a few moments and then said, "Yes, Sir," into his microphone.

"You are cleared for entry," he said to Mark. He then pointed down the entry road and said, "Stay to your right on Jerry Smith until you get to Challenger. Turn left and keep going until you get past the AerSales buildings. There will be a gate off to your right. Someone will meet you there and escort you out to the bone yard."

"Thank you, sergeant," Mark replied.

Once he got back into the van, Robert said, "That was easier than I expected."

Mark just looked at him and said, "Drive."

The gate was where the guard had indicated. The sandbags were piled slightly higher behind the guard shack, and just beyond the gate sat a Humvee. It was facing away from the gate, but the twin fifties in its turret were aligned directly with the opening. They were pointed skyward as the van approached, but leveled as they turned and stopped at the guard shack.

"ID's" the guard said as they came to a stop.

Robert and Mark handed their credentials out the window. The guard looked at David perched just behind the seats. "Would a driver's license do?" David asked meekly.

The guard frowned and Robert spoke up. "He's a civilian I grabbed to run the equipment. He's helped us on several cases, so I know what he can do."

"I guess that will have to do," the guard answered, "if you two vouch for him."

Robert laughed and said, "I assure you we would not be here if it weren't for him and what he can do with the equipment."

"OK," the guard said flatly as he handed the ID's back through the window. "Follow him," he said pointing at an old-style Jeep. "He will take you out to where the planes are."

"Thank you," Mark said from the passenger seat.

"And," continued the guard, "he..." pointing to a young regular Army soldier standing next to him, "will accompany you as you run your tests."

"Awkward," Robert said softly as he opened his door. Then in a voice loud enough for the guard to hear, he said, "I'll ride in back. Mark can drive and our escort can sit in the passenger seat."

As the guard pulled himself into the passenger seat, Mark asked him, "Is the weapon necessary?"

The young man positioned the M4 carbine between his legs pointing upward. Then he replied, "I really won't know that until I need it, Sir, but if I do, I want it with me."

Robert laughed from the back. "How old are you, son?"

The soldier replied, "Nineteen, Sir."

Mark asked, "What's your name?"

"Anderson," the soldier replied. "Private first class Harold T. Anderson."

"Are you National Guard or regular Army?"

"Regular Army, Sir," he replied, "hoping to go to college when I finish my enlistment. It was the only way I could afford it."

"No offense to you, Private Anderson," Robert said as he pulled the curtain across behind the seats, "but the equipment we use is highly classified and I'm pretty sure you aren't on the list."

He then whispered to David, "Some asshole said that to me a couple years ago when I was working a case that involved an NSA guy that went nuts and shot up a bar downtown... or was it DIA?" He shook his head slightly and said, "All those alphabet soup guys are the same anyway."

The van rocked slightly as the guard motioned for them to proceed and Mark pulled forward.

"Now all we have to do," Robert said softly, "is find the plane."

"I've been thinking about that," David said. "Chi and I will go back to the plane. With it on the ground we can push through and look at the outside. Then I will come back here and tell you what to look for."

"Sounds like a plan," Robert said.

"Try not to make any sudden curves," David said loudly as he slipped off his T-shirt and sweat pants and stood in front of the mirror. He glanced at Robert who was sitting on the bed/bench and then directed his attention to the black mirror which took up most of one side of the van.

A few moment later, Chi joined him at the tomb. "We have to go back to the plane," he said rapidly. "It's on the ground, so it will be safe," he added as he saw the tension in Chi's face.

"I'll be OK," she said softly. She then took his hands and said, "The plane!"

***

Again they were standing on the main cargo deck. The ladder to the upper area was down. The main cargo door was open, but covered with a white plastic tarp. It looked thicker and stronger than the ones he could buy at the local hardware or sports store.

Chi walked slowly over to the open door and peered out the opening.

"I'm going to go up and check if anyone's there," David said hurriedly as he ran toward the ladder.

94

A few moments later, he shouted, "All clear," and then raced back to join Chi.

"There's a ladder thing leading to the ground," she said as he joined her. "And that cover goes over most of the plane."

"Damn," David said as they walked over to the cargo container.

"You ready?" he asked as they stood in front of the closed door of the container.

Chi didn't answer, but compressed her lips and nodded her head slightly as she reached forward and pressed her arm through the container wall. David waited until Chi was almost through the partition before hurrying through himself.

The First Lady was no longer on the bed.

One of the guards was sitting at the table writing on something. Another guard was standing at a small counter apparently making a sandwich.

"Where are the other two guards?" Chi asked nervously. "And the President's woman?"

"Let's see what's at the back of the container," David said as he started walking toward rear of the plane.

"How long is it?" Chi asked.

"If they brought it in on a truck," David answered, "I'm betting on about fifty feet."

He turned and faced Chi. "That would leave," he continued, "about thirty feet at the back of plane, plus more space in the tail.

Chi and David walked to the back of the container where there was another door. As Chi began to push through, she said, "This one is much thinner than the others."

"So is the wall," David said as he pushed through alongside her.

They found themselves in a second room. It was

slightly smaller than the first room, but soundproofed with the same thick carpeting. One corner of the back wall was taken up by what appeared to be a bathroom. At least there was a toilet symbol on the door.

The First Lady was in the other corner. She was sitting in what looked at first to be a circular shower enclosure. Her eyes were open, but they were staring vacantly into the room. David cautiously pushed his hand through the clear enclosure.

"This is very thick," he said. "I think it's bulletproof or something. It's got some sort of plastic coating on it. That's probably to prevent chips from flying back into the room, but it also keeps it from reflecting anything."

"Why would they put her in a protective cocoon?" Chi asked.

"There's no top," David said as he continued his exploration of the strange enclosure.

"It would stop bullets," Chi said as she ran her hand across the outside of the clear wall, "but it would be useless against a gas or an explosion."

"It looks pretty thick to me," David said. "It should hold up against most blasts."

She looked over at David and said, "It would protect her from the fire and debris," Chi said slowly, "but the explosion would create an instantaneous vacuum which would pull all of the air out of her lungs." She looked down at the floor and said, "It might even pull her lungs out of her body."

Looking over at David, she added, "Her body wouldn't be burned or mutilated, but she would be just as dead."

"That's it!" David yelled. "They are going to blow up this plane with the First Lady in it. They want to make sure that her body will be recognized. It would look like she was hiding here and something went wrong!"

He turned to face Chi. "I have to tell Mark and Robert," he said excitedly. "You stay here and I'll be right back."

***

The van was motionless when David returned. He grabbed his robe and sat down next to Robert before asking softly, "What's going on?"

"Little brother told our escort that we had to calibrate the equipment before we started," Robert replied quietly. Then, seeing the look of agitation on David's face he asked, "What's going on?"

"I think," David said, "they are going to blow up the plane... and the First Lady. She's in some sort of protective enclosure that will shield her from the fire and debris, but Chi says she will still be killed by the blast vacuum."

"Then we have to find her fast," Robert said. His voice was starting to get louder. "What's the outside of the plane look like?"

David's shoulders slumped as he said, "It's covered with a tarp of some sort. Most of the planes are, so..."

"So we have to figure out some way to finding that one plane out of the thousand or so scattered over the desert." Robert replied.

Mark's voice came through the curtain. "Is there a problem back there?"

David looked over at Robert and then said loudly, "The electronic signature looks like a bomb detonator. We have to find that plane before someone detonates it." He looked at the curtain as he added, "No telling who might be injured or killed in the explosion."

"Understood," Mark answered. "Can we track the signal yet?"

97

"Give me a minute," David replied.

"I have a plan," he whispered urgently to Robert. "It might sound a little weird, but I think it will work."

"Weirder than everything else so far?" Robert asked with a grin.

David took a deep breath and said, "Yeah, weirder than everything else so far." He paused a moment and then explained, "I am going to have Chi go up to the pilot's area and push herself up through the top of the plane." Pointing to the small counter near the back of the van, he said, "I will come back here to that counter, but stay in the mirror. Then I will push myself up through the top of the van. Mark will drive up and down the rows of planes and when I see her, I will come out of the mirror and tell you to stop."

Robert looked at him blankly for a minute as if he were thinking. "You're right," he said, "that is weirder than the rest of this shit... but it just might work. I'll tell Mark to drive slowly up and down the rows of planes and we will wait for your signal to stop."

David once again stood in front of the mirror. He was vaguely aware of Robert moving so that he could stick his head out through the curtain. He felt the movement of the van and the tug of the mirror at the same time and once again he was back on the plane.

Chi looked over at him. "The other two guards came up out of the floor outside that door," she said. "When the first one came back, I went through to see where they came from. There is a trapdoor and a ladder that leads down to another floor. Then there is a ramp that goes down to the ground."

David merely nodded at her before saying, "I will tell the brothers about that later. For now, we need to help them find the plane." He then explained the plan and walked with her back to the front of the plane. He noted with satisfaction that she showed no hesitancy as

98

they passed through the walls of the container.

They walked up to the flight deck together. "Where do you think would be best?" he asked.

In response, Chi stood on the pilot's seat and pushed herself through the roof of the plane. David copied her from the co-pilot's seat.

"This looks very strange," Chi said as she looked around.

"A plane with two heads sticking out of it is a little weird," David responded.

"No," Chi replied. "All of these planes parked together in the desert. It doesn't look natural."

David began laughing. "I guess our world is now normal," he said, "while the real world is the one that is weird."

He then turned completely around, scanning the parked planes. "Do you see the van?" he asked.

"No," answered Chi, "but it could be hidden by the planes. You will probably be able to see me a lot easier than I will be able to see you."

"OK," answered David. "I'm going to go back to the van and stick my head up through the roof. I will tell them when I see you."

He gave her a very distorted smile. "I'm really not sure what we are going to do after that." He shrugged and said, "One step at a time."

In response, Chi said, "A journey of a thousand miles..."

"I know," he replied, "begins with a single step."

He then shimmered slightly and disappeared.

***

Back inside the van, the mirror-David crouched on the counter top which held the sink. He stopped for a moment to stare at himself standing in front of the mirror. Robert was sitting on the bench seat which folded out into a bed. He was looking forward at the curtain in the front of the van.

"Nothing yet," he yelled loudly. "Keep going."

David looked around for a moment before taking a deep breath and pushing himself through the roof of the van. Standing there, his body stuck through the top of the van from just above his belly button.

He immediately began turning and twisting looking for Chi... and the right airplane. He wasn't sure how many rows of planes there actually were, but about a half-hour later, as they turned into a seventh row, he thought he could see something sticking out of a plane about one-third of the way down the row.

As they approached, he could see Chi waving. He waved back at her and said, "Home."

Nothing happened.

David repeated, "Home," and still nothing happened.

He froze in panic. He had to tell Mark to stop!

He pulled himself back into the van and jumped down to the floor. Again he repeated, "Home," and again nothing happened. What had gone wrong? Why couldn't he come out of the mirror?

He took a deep breath to calm himself. As he began to slowly inhale a second breath that far away voice spoke in his ear, "You are home."

That was it! He couldn't come out of the mirror because he was in the same room as his true self– no, his real world self.

He said the first thing which popped into his mind, "Front seat."

The soldier who was sitting looking very bored in the passenger seat suddenly began yelling, "Stop! Stop! Stop!" except, it wasn't the soldier's voice. It was David's.

A moment later, David's voice came from the back area, also screaming "Stop! Stop! Stop!"

Several things happened at the same time. Mark slammed on the brakes. David jerked the curtain open and began screaming, "We passed it! We passed it! It's four planes back on the right side with a red tail!" And a very startled soldier brought his weapon to a ready position and yelled, "What in the hell just happened!?!"

The private then looked at David crouching naked just behind Mark's seat and added, "And why in the hell are you naked?"

Robert laughed and said loudly, "Welcome to the rabbit hole, son."

Mark turned and said quickly. "You don't have the security clearances for the full explanation, but we have developed a device that allows you to project yourself behind doors, walls, and barriers no matter how thick they are. The only problem is you have to be naked for it to work."

"Right now," Robert interjected, "there is a naked Chinese chick waving at us from on top of one of these planes. Only we can't see her. David here can see her, but only while he is being projected."

He then turned to David and gave him a strange, half wink.

"I'm sorry I overlapped you for a moment," David said, looking at the now very confused soldier. "I didn't know that could happen, but I was having problems getting back out of the... projection."

Everyone was quiet for a moment, staring at each other, then Mark spoke. In a very slow and measured voice he said, "The wife of the President of the United States is being held captive on that plane. We are about to go to war over her kidnaping and the wrong people are being blamed. Someone has orchestrated a monumental hoax and the only way we can prove that is by rescuing the First Lady."

He waited for a moment for the impact of what he said to register with the soldier. "Private Anderson, this has to be done quickly and quietly for reasons that I am not free to divulge. You are not to notify your superiors unless it is the last resort– meaning Robert and I are wounded or dead. Do you understand that?"

"No," the private replied, "not really, but for the time being I will assume you have the authority to give such an order." He looked Mark directly in the eyes and said firmly, "What do you need me to do?"

"That, I'm not sure of," Mark said. Then he added, "... yet."

Turning to David, he asked, "What's the situation on the plane?"

"When I left before," David began, "the four guards were back up inside the container. The First Lady was still inside her protective cocoon. I don't think they will detonate the bombs until they are off the plane. There is a trap door at the back of the main cargo deck which leads to the lower deck with a ramp from there to the ground. If you can keep the guards busy at the front of the container, I can sneak in the back way and bring her out."

Robert nodded his head toward David and said, "That sounds like a reasonable plan."

"But how do we keep them busy?" Mark said. "There are only four of us. If we try to bust in, they might trigger the explosives or shoot the First Lady."

"Maybe I should call for reinforcements," Private Anderson suggested. "A show of force may make a difference."

"They wouldn't see a show of force," David said. "The container is sealed. There are no windows."

Robert suddenly brightened up. "They can't see us!" he exclaimed. Then turning to Private Anderson, he asked, "Do you have live rounds for that, Anderson?" pointing at the carbine.

"Yes, Sir!" the private barked back.

Mark must have realized what his brother hand in mind and almost shouted, "How fast can you fire and what is your biggest ammo clip?"

The private smiled, "This is the A version, Sir," he replied. "I can go full auto and I have five thirty-round clips in my pack, plus four more fifteens."

"OK," Mark said. "Here's the plan. Robert and I will go in the front and stay low. David will sneak in the back and stay even lower. You..." pointing to Private Anderson, " will spray the side of that plane with a thirty-shot clip stitching it from front to back right above the windows. Then you are going to change clips and put another row right through the windows."

Pointing at Robert, he said, "Big brother and I will then tell them they are surrounded and to stay on the floor or the snipers will pick off anything that stands up."

"Will they believe you?" the private asked.

"I think I can be very convincing," Mark answered.

"One problem," David said. "They keep moving around. One of them might be in the back... or worse even be down below the plane. We have to be sure that they are in the front portion of the container."

He looked at Private Anderson and then at the brothers before saying, "I will go back into the mirror and check things out. Chi needs to be out of the way, also. I don't want her hurt."

"I thought you were invisible when you were walking in the mirror," Robert said with surprise.

"We are," David answered, "but if something is moving fast enough, it might hurt her. She got sucked out of the plane when she tried to look outside while it was still flying. I think it would have killed her– at least her mind– but she was able to go home before she hit the ground."

"What kind of a machine is this?" the private asked, looking around.

"You really don't want to know," Mark said he opened the door on his side of the van. "You really don't want to know," he added as he motioned for Private Andersen to get out on his side.

Robert joined them alongside the van and then a couple minutes later, David stepped out of the side door. He was wearing the sweat pants and T-shirt he had on earlier. He had pulled on a pair of sneakers, but had not bothered to put on socks.

He smiled broadly. "All four of them are back in the front section playing cards. They should be there for a few minutes."

"That means they are sitting down," Mark said, so the two bursts will probably not hit any of them. I think we want them all alive, if possible, so this is a best case scenario."

Robert shook his head slowly and said, "I think I'll reserve my vote on that until after the First Lady is free." He then turned to David and asked, "Your girlfriend in a safe place?"

"She's in the van," David answered. He thought about saying, "She's not my girlfriend," but decided that it didn't matter. Besides, he wasn't sure that she wasn't.

The four of them walked down the wide aisle until they were standing before the plane with the red tail markings.

"OK," Mark said. "Anderson, give us thirty seconds to get into position and then punch some holes in that aircraft."

The private swallowed slightly and said, "What if we're wrong about this?"

Mark pulled out his badge and ID and held it up so the private could see it. "Private First Class Harold T. Anderson," he said loudly. "I, Field Agent Mark Nash, speaking for the Secret Service and on behalf of the President of the United States, am giving you a direct order that you are to put two thirty-shot bursts into the side of that airplane."

He put his credentials back in his pocket and smiled at the private. "That is your 'Get Out of Jail Free' card if we're wrong."

"Yes, Sir!" Anderson replied with a smile. "Thirty seconds and then I start shooting."

"Go!" Mark said as he and Robert started running for the plane.

There was a huge white tarp covering most of the plane. It was staked into the ground at several points, but there was still room to slip under it. Mark and Robert went under the tarp. David went to the rear of the plane which extended out from the back of the tarp.

He walked carefully up the ramp, walking even more carefully as he heard the sound of his own shoes on the metal of the ramp. "I have to remember that I'm visible now," he said aloud, "and that I make noise when I walk."

He moved forward until he could see the trap door above his head. He started to climb the ladder into the main cargo area but then stopped with his head just below the floor level.

He held his breath waiting for the thirty seconds to end.

Suddenly a very loud, "Plang, Plang, Plang, Plang, Plang, Plang, Plang," echoed through the open hold. There was a short pause before the sound repeated.

David quickly clambered up into the cargo deck. He grabbed at the door handle, hoping it was not locked in some fashion.

It opened with a slight squeaky groan. The second door, which opened into the container itself, opened silently.

David stepped into the room. The First Lady was standing in her Lexan enclosure looking around. She seemed more curious than frightened.

"I'm working with the Secret Service," David said in almost a whisper as he stepped up to the clear barrier which trapped the First Lady. "How does it open?" He asked as he tapped gently on the plastic.

"They used a button over there to open it to give me food," she answered, pointing over to her left at a panel on the wall.

"Got it," David replied as he scanned the panel looking for the right button.

As he tried to read the panel, David could hear Mark's voice from the front of the plane.

"We have you covered," Mark yelled. "The four of you stay on the floor. You can go back to your card game later. There's a sniper with a bead on each one of you. If your thermal image stands up, they shoot. A fifty-cal slug will go through the walls of the plane, you, and the next ten planes down the row. They are instructed to fire a three-shot group, so we are not talking about wounding you. If you stand up, you die. Slide any weapons you have away from your bodies before we come in. If we see a weapon, we start shooting."

The control panel wasn't in English and David didn't recognize any of the words. One of the buttons, however, had a smudge of dirt on it. "Here goes," he said aloud as he pressed it.

There was a slight whir and hiss as the enclosure opened. "We need to get you out of here," David said urgently. "... before your husband goes to war with China."

"Sometimes he's an idiot," she said in a slightly

106

slurred voice as David helped her out and guided her toward the rear opening.

They had just stepped off the ramp onto the desert ground when a voice behind them said, "That's far enough." The statement was accentuated with the sound of a round being chambered in a semi-automatic pistol.

"Turn around," the voice commanded. Both David and the First Lady turned around with their hands raised.

David did not recognize the man holding the gun. He hadn't been on the plane with the First Lady any of the times David was there.

"It's time for your magical luck to end, David," the man said. "We really didn't expect you and the Nash brothers to get this far."

He stepped slightly closer before saying, "But it makes no difference. The First Lady will just die a little earlier than planned. She will have died in a half-baked, unnecessary rescue attempt while she was hiding here in good old Roswell."

He laughed slightly and said, "People will believe almost any conspiracy theory that includes the name Roswell."

He raised the pistol and pointed it directly at David's head. "I'm actually sorry to have to do this. I would have loved to find out how you actually did all of this."

David cringed, waiting for the shot. *"I hope Chi isn't watching this,"* he thought.

Then the man moved his arm so that he was pointing instead at the First Lady.

Had David thought about it, he probably couldn't have done it. He didn't will his body to do it. It was as if his body acted on its own as he threw himself in front of the First Lady, grasping her tightly in his arms.

He flinched as a loud blast echoed in the small space under the plane's tail. David looked around in surprise. So did the man with the gun. There was blood on the front of the man's shirt and his arm was wavering. There was a second loud blast and the man's head snapped back.

He crumpled immediately to the ground.

David turned slowly toward the source of the noise to find Special Agent in Charge Patricia Woods with her service weapon held firmly in both hands.

"I was sent down here," she said, "to reign in a rogue agent before he could screw up more than he already had."

"It would seem," she added as she put her Glock back into its holster, "that he wasn't as rogue as everyone thought."

Private Anderson came running up with his weapon at the ready. Agent Mark was right behind him. Further back, David could see Robert holding a weapon on four men kneeling on the ground.

"We're good, Harold... Mark," David called out. "This is Special Agent Woods," he added, gesturing toward her. "And this is Helena Travis, First Lady of the United States."

Patricia turned toward the private and said, "We will need to use your comm center. I have to report that FLOTUS is safe."

"No!" David yelled out.

All four turned to face him.

"He knew my name," David said quickly pointing to the man on the ground. "And he made reference to the Nash brothers and my magical luck." He looked rapidly from Special Agent Woods to Agent Nash. "Someone high up... someone inside the government... someone inside the Secret Service is involved in this. The report might never get to the President."

"We have to let the President know that she is safe and on American soil," Special Agent Woods said

108

forcefully. "How can we do that if we can't trust the official channels?"

"Then we use unofficial channels," David yelled digging frantically into the pocket of his sweat pants.

He pulled his cell phone out of his pocket and said excitedly, "Live feed, hashtag FirstLadyFound, hashtag SpreadTheWord, hashtag StopTheWar." He then held the phone up in front of the First Lady. "Tell your husband... tell the world that you have been rescued and that it was all a plot by a third party to start a war between the U.S. and China."

"I am Helena Travis," she said softly, but then her voice grew firmer and more forceful with each word. "This is a message for my husband and for the world. I was kidnaped and flown all over the world by someone who wanted you to think it was done by China as an act of war. That is not the truth. The truth is that it was orchestrated by persons unknown whom shall be exposed, but not by the Chinese government. In fact, I suspect that some members of our own government, specifically Director of Secret Service Andrew Richards may be involved. He may be innocent, but he should be temporarily removed from office until the investigation is complete. I am currently at... well, I don't really know where I am, but I am on U.S. soil and am being guarded by American troops. I will reveal further details when I return to Washington, but for now, please spread this word that I am safe."

She gave a quick nod of her head and David switched off the live feed and lowered the cellphone. He then looked over toward the van. "Chi, if you are here, go home. Tell everyone in your village with a cell phone or a computer to find this video and forward it with a message in Chinese to stop the war. There may be people in your government involved as well."

Helena turned to Special Agent Woods and asked,

"Who is he talking to?"

"It's too difficult to explain," she answered, "and you really don't want to know. People wouldn't believe you anyway."

A soft bing brought everyone's attention to David. The text said simply, "sending."

He started to say something else but was drowned out by the loud roar of several Humvees roaring down the aisle from both ends.

"No sudden moves," Mark said softly. "Shots have been fired. Everyone is a little nervous."

Someone– obviously an officer– jumped out of the lead hummer and began walking toward the group under the tail. The twin fifties in the turret tracked with him as he walked. "What in the hell is going on here?!" he yelled out.

The First Lady stepped forward, "I am Helena Travis," she said evenly. "I was held prisoner in that aircraft. These people just rescued me. I need an immediate flight to Washington, DC, and a secure comm link to my husband, the President."

The man turned toward the Humvee from which he had exited and screamed out, "Defensive perimeter NOW!"

"Right here!" he added loudly, pointing toward the ground.

As a squad of soldiers scrambled out of that Humvee and the ones behind it, he turned to the other column and yelled even louder, "Take the men on the ground into custody."

Pointing to the bullet-riddled plane he added, "And guard that aircraft. It is a crime scene as of right now."

He pushed a button on the side of his helmet and spoke into his microphone, "Full protection detail and transportation needed at my location. FLOTUS is now under our protection. Repeat, FLOTUS is now under our protection."

"What happens now?" David said.

Special Agent Woods turned to face him. "That depends on what you want to happen," she said quietly. "You deserve a medal for your actions." Looking up at the Nash brothers and Private Anderson she smiled and said, "All of you."

"That would mean telling people how I was involved, wouldn't it?" asked David.

"I'm afraid it would," she answered.

"We can't do that," David said softly.

"Why not?!" Robert sputtered loudly.

David turned and faced him. "If our government knew what I could do," he said slowly, "they would want to use me as a weapon... or as a spy... or something. I can't do that."

"Oh," Robert answered. "I hadn't thought of that."

David turned back to Special Agent Woods. "I would rather not figure in this at all," he said firmly. "Robert and Mark... and Harold... ... and you... deserve the medals and the public honor. I will know that you know– and they know– what I did, but it has to remain a secret."

Turning to the Nash Brothers, he said, "Go with Special Agent Woods back to Washington or wherever. I'll drive the van back to Iowa."

He turned toward the van, then turned back around. "And Agent Nash," he said with a smile, "I will be submitting my bill for standard services plus expenses."

"Whatever it is," Special Agent Woods replied, "I will see that it gets paid."

"Stay in some good hotels on your way back," Robert called out.

Special Agent Woods then turned to the officer in

charge and said, "This young man and his highly classified van need to be escorted off base. No mention of him or his vehicle is to appear in any reports of this event."

"I don't understand," the officer said slowly.

"You don't need to understand," Helena Travis said firmly. "All you need to know is that this young man threw himself between me and a man who was about to shoot me."

"Yes, Ma'am," the officer barked. He then turned to Private Anderson and said loudly, "Escort this man and his vehicle to the front gate. Then return here."

"Yes, Sir," Anderson replied. He then gestured toward David and began walking back to the van.

As they drove slowly toward the front gate, the private turned and said softly, "There's no equipment back there, is there?"

"Nope," David answered, "just me." He smiled and added, "... and maybe a Chinese girl named Chi."

"When you... ... overlapped with me," Private Anderson said slowly. "I saw a lot of weird shit. There was a black mirror and dead bodies and some weird Samurai running after me with swords." He looked down slightly, "There was also this really cute naked girl."

"That's Chi," David said.

"I will keep your secret," he said firmly. Then he laughed, "No one would ever believe me anyway."

They were at the front gate. David stopped and Private Anderson stepped out of the vehicle. Before he drove off, David called out, "Harold!" When the private turned back to face him, he said, "If it's any consolation, sometimes I have trouble believing it myself."

Epilogue

David stood in front of the mirror in his bedroom. The television in the living room was on and tuned to network news. The special ceremony was about to begin. As he felt the beginnings of the tug of the mirror, he said softly, "Living room, living room, living room."

Chi was already waiting for him, sitting on the couch in front of the television.

"I wasn't sure if the language thing would work with television," he said with a smile, "so I dropped in on a social media friend of mine in Germany. He's about twenty years older than his profile picture, but I could understand the announcer on the television show he was watching."

Chi answered, "The ceremony is about to begin."

As David took his seat next to her, the television announcer said, "Ladies and Gentlemen, the President of the United States."

The image cut to a podium set up on the south lawn of the White House. It zoomed in on the Presidential Seal and then backed off to show the President striding up to the podium. He stood waiting for the applause to settle and then said, "My fellow Americans, and peoples of the world, we are gathered here this afternoon to honor the four people most directly responsible for the safe return of my wife, Helena. Three of them are receiving the Presidential Medal of Freedom this afternoon– not because they rescued the First Lady, but because they thwarted a plot to create war between the United States and the great nation of China."

He paused and looked down at the front row where Helena Travis, Patricia Woods, Mark Nash, Robert Nash, and Harold T. Anderson were seated. "I accept that I acted foolishly and allowed myself to be duped by skilled villains both in our government and elsewhere," he said firmly. "But Helena," he continued more softly, "has always been a tempering force for me and without her, I over-reacted."

"Wow," said David. "He has never apologized for anything ever before."

"He also personally apologized to our government and to my people," Chi said. "I think she made him do that, but I think he is honestly sorry for how he acted. I also think that my people forgave him because they recognized that it was a debt of honor and he truly believed that my government had taken his wife."

"Receiving the Presidential Medal of Freedom today," the President continued, "are Secret Service agents Patricia Woods and Mark Nash. Normally, the members of the Secret Service do not receive medals for doing their duty, but these two agents went beyond their duty and put their lives– and their careers– on the line to rescue the First Lady and prevent war. Assisting them was Mark's brother Robert Nash, who will also receive the Presidential Medal of Freedom."

He paused and then turned his gaze to Private Anderson. The TV image cut to the soldier's face as the President added. "Private Harold T. Anderson will be receiving a presidential appointment to West Point for his part in this rescue. Hopefully he will remain with the Army following his graduation. We could use many more good soldiers like him."

A voice off-camera called out, "Would Agent Patricia Marie Woods, Agent Mark Evan Nash, and Detective Robert Albert Nash please step forward?"

When the three were standing in front of the podium, the President stepped down to face them. An aide handed him the medals, one at a time, and he draped them over the heads first of Patricia, then Mark, then Robert. Stepping back slightly, he gave them a sharp salute. The two Secret Service agents automatically returned the salute. Robert looked slightly confused, but then took his cue from them and also, though less rigidly, returned the salute.

The camera pulled back once again to show the whole scene and the announcers began discussing the events when led up to Helena Travis' rescue.

Chi giggled slightly and asked, "Did you watch the news conference yesterday?"

David answered, "Sort of."

"The reporters," Chi continued, "kept pressing them as to how they were able to track the First Lady. They kept asking what kind of new surveillance equipment was used and when it would be revealed to the public. After ten minutes of being asked for details about the equipment and replying that it was all very classified, Agent Woods finally said, 'I will tell you the truth. Detective Robert has this magical friend who can jump aboard airplanes and tell us where they are anywhere in the world. He was riding with the First Lady most of the way around the world and kept us up to date as to her whereabouts.'"

Chi giggled again and said, "All the reporters laughed and then one of them said, 'OK, we will accept for now that it is classified equipment that cannot be revealed.'"

She turned to David and said with a smile, "You and I are classified equipment that cannot be revealed."

She then stroked David's face lightly and said, "Your day is my night, so I need to return home. I have been up all night so I could be here for this."

"Until next week at Chou's tomb," David said with a smile.

"Until next week," Chi replied. She then leaned forward slightly and gave him a quick kiss on the lips as she shimmered and disappeared.

THE END